SIX NOTCH ROAD

SIX NOTCH ROAD

Joshua Trail Trilogy

Early Santee

Copyright © 2000 by Early Santee.

ISBN #:   Softcover   0-7388-4175-7

All rights reserved. No part of this book may be reproduced or transmitted in any form or by any means, electronic or mechanical, including photocopying, recording, or by any information storage and retrieval system, without permission in writing from the copyright owner.

This is a work of fiction. Names, characters, places and incidents either are the product of the author's imagination or are used fictitiously, and any resemblance to any actual persons, living or dead, events, or locales is entirely coincidental.

This book was printed in the United States of America.

To order additional copies of this book, contact:
Xlibris Corporation
1-888-7-XLIBRIS
www.Xlibris.com
Orders@Xlibris.com

CONTENTS

CHAPTER ONE 9
   March 1, 1851. Saint David's Feast Day—
   Pottsville, Pennsylvania 9
CHAPTER TWO 20
CHAPTER THREE 35
   July 1851. Saint Louis, Missouri 35
CHAPTER FOUR 52
   Mid-summer, 1851 --- Enroute to The Port of New
   York 52
CHAPTER FIVE 67
   Off The Coast of South America 67
CHAPTER SIX 74
   September 1851 —The Oregon Trail 74
CHAPTER SEVEN 82
CHAPTER EIGHT 89
   Late September 1851 —The Oregon Trail 89
CHAPTER NINE 94
   November 1851 —San Francisco 94
CHAPTER TEN 112
CHAPTER ELEVEN 123
CHAPTER TWELVE 127
CHAPTER THIRTEEN 141
CHAPTER FOURTEEN 147
   Spring 1852 Mokelumne Hill—California Gold
   Fields 147
CHAPTER FIFTEEN 158
CHAPTER SIXTEEN 168
CHAPTER SEVENTEEN 175

CHAPTER EIGHTEEN	183
CHAPTER NINETEEN	197
CHAPTER TWENTY	200
CHAPTER TWENTY ONE	209
Late Spring, 1852	209
CHAPTER TWENTY TWO	213
CHAPTER TWENTY THREE	220
CHAPTER TWENTY FOUR	225
CHAPTER TWENTY FIVE	236
CHAPTER TWENTY SIX	246
CHAPTER TWENTY SEVEN	251
CHAPTER TWENTY EIGHT	265
CHAPTER TWENTY NINE	273
CHAPTER THIRTY	276

TO MY CHILDREN, DAVID AND GABRIELLE MY GRANDSON JOSEPH, ANN C. HARRIETT WHO ALWAYS BELIEVED LOUZ. AND THE LOYAL MEMBERS OF THE WEDNESDAY NIGHT LITERARY GUILD

CHAPTER ONE

March 1, 1851.

Saint David's Feast Day—Pottsville, Pennsylvania

The fierce, unforgiving winter wind came out of the West. It formed on the Arctic plateau and swept across the Bering strait into the Yukon territory. It blew powerful gusts down the snow-fed lakes drained by the Mackenzie river, through the Chillicothe pass and across the still hidden gold of the Klondike.

It picked up muscle and speed as it whipped across the Canadian Rockies into the great plains of the American Heartland. Laden with unusually heavy snows, it roared across the coastal plains of Lake Erie and down the long valleys of Western Pennsylvania. It howled across the frozen banks of The Delaware, The Susquehanna and chilled the deepest reaches of The Allegheny and Monogahela rivers where they formed the mighty Ohio at Pittsburgh.

With its final, most frigid breath, it headed for the coal fields of Eastern Pennslyvannia and the small coal mining village of Pottsville.

"*Myn Yn Brain*! By the cross!" Eli Llynne muttered in Celtic and repeated in Engish as he watched the wind rattle the walls of his small shack. He listened anxiously as the wind hurled slabs of "green" slate against the flimsy wood. Slate slabs he had wired together for protection and insulation. Eli knew the thin walls could not withstand their weight much longer. Eli Llynne felt the chill to his bones. His ramshackle shanty creaked and rattled in the wind and the roof threatened to collapse at any moment.

Eli was of hearty Welsh descent and he was able to tolerate the cold better than most. But there was something about this winter wind, a quality beyond mere coldness. There was a foreboding, an evil characteristic to the smell of it, that gave Eli pause to worry.

Eli's concern was not for himself but for his lovely young wife Lydia. Eli looked at her with love and deep respect as she pulled her shawl tight around her frail once sturdy body.

Eli had hoped for an early Spring.

He knew how hard cold was on her though she would never speak of it.

Lydia had never fully recovered from the scarlet fever she suffered as a child. Her family had all died of cholera and she had, even though she was ill, tended them. Eli knew, when she thought he was not watching, how she would still, at times, shake uncontrollably.

Such was her sturdy Irish heritage, if she were dying of consumption you would never hear her cough.

Eli smiled as he watched her bravely weather the cold, trying to hide her frosty breath as she poked at the dying embers in the small stove. Eli felt embarrassed by the puny fire. He felt it was his responsibility to provide well for Lydia. The measly lumps of coal turning to lifeless embers mocked him.

It was among life's most bitter ironies, that in a land rich with coal, their stove never held enough to warm the shanty more than a few feet in any direction.

The mean wind rattled the hut's walls and shot damp snowflakes through the cracked window of the small room in the back where Otello Jones lived. It was cramped quarters for Otello, but all Eli had been able to give him.

Otello squeezed his huge frame against the South wall where it was a few degrees warmer than the North wall.

"Horse" his huge mongrel dog lay at his feet looking lean and loyal. Otello stroked him with his left hand with the missing little finger lost to a rusty knife in a fight. A fight Otello had not started but had finished well. Otello scraped half of his meager meal onto a plate in front of Horse. Horse hesitated then gobbled it down.

No one knew who Otello's real parents were. The miners had found Otello wrapped in tattered blankets just inside the opening of an abandoned mine shaft. Inside the blankets with him, was a copy of a book of Shakespeare's plays. A bookmark opened the book to a pencil-lined passage from Shakespeare's play "Othello". The line read: "... not set down aught in malice then, must you speak of one that lov'd not wisely but too well."

The one miner who could read, Homer Jones, had concluded that the baby had been abandoned by a fancy lady or two-bit whore. In either case, the baby was considered an outcast from the start.

Homer had wanted nothing to do with "Otello" as he had misspelled the shakespearean "Othello".

His childless wife had other ideas.

Martha Jones had taken Otello in and treated him like her own son, even though she was shunned by others in the community and deserted by her husband. Otello had grown to manhood knowing the pain of social isolation. His mother and Eli Llynne were the only exceptions.

Martha Jones died young. Eli and Lydia took Otello in upon her passing.

Otello's racial ancestry was a mystery. Some thought it African, others Indian, others Mulatto. How he was judged depended on the depth of individual prejudice and brightness of the sun. If Otello lingered in the shadows he was as pale as alabaster. If he stayed too long in the summer sun, he was as dark as anthracite. If he balanced sunshine and shadow he was as bronze as an Aztec god.

He was allowed to pass for white on some occasions and was not cursed and despised near as much as other outcasts who were not welcome in the camp.

Otello was a loner.

Otello had only one friend, Eli Llynne. He considered Eli a straight talker and had no reason to doubt anything Eli gave his word to. Otello felt uneasy as he got up and prepared for work. His senses told him it might be a "black dog day." He told himself to be extra careful at watching his backside this day.

Eli was uneasy also. He was uneasy and tired. Not tired in a physical sense. Eli rarely tired from any physical labor. He was tired of the cold and the misery and the poverty. The numbing, grinding poverty bothered Eli to the depths of his soul.

It was Eli's driving passion to escape from it very soon. Not for himself, but for Lydia. There was so much he wanted to give her, so much he had planned to give her.

So much he was damned determined to give her.

A coal miner's life in Pottsville, Schuylkill County, Pennsylvania in 1851 was brief and full of misery.

It had not measurably improved since the first miner went down into the earth at Fort Pitt in 1760. It was still as unrelentingly cruel and hard as it had been for Eli's ancestors in his native Wales.

Eli would not have taken the job, having lost his father and two brothers in the mines, if there had been any other way to support Lydia and his invalid brother. Eli also knew it was the only job that offered him a chance to save enough money to finance a trip to the California gold fields.

Eli had worked hard and avoided vices since he was six years old. A god-fearing man of immense size but peaceable disposition, Eli had begun his work as a miner on his sixth birthday.

Eli had started as a "Trapper", opening ventilation doors in an inadequate attempt to circulate air through the mines.

Eli "graduated" to being a "Filler" or "Loader", filling "skips" with coal the older "men" of eleven and up had hewn from the wall. Finally, at the age of thirteen, he secured the job of a "Hurrier". A Hurrier would tie a heavy chain around his waist and pull it between his legs—at times pressing painfully against his groin. Then he would crawl on his hands and knees "sandwiched" in the narrow tunnels dragging a basket of coal to the surface. It was a job beyond most young men's ability. Eli had never been a young man.

Eli's ability to work long and hard came to him naturally. He was the son of the sons of miners out of Carmarthenshire. For uncounted generations, his ancestors had mined coal from the pits of North Wales to the mines of the Rhondda Valley in the South. They had mined every mineral the Welsh hills offered from slate to iron. The very iron the hated British used in the cannons that enslaved his own people.

There were many other hard working miners who admired Eli for his work ethic. For the most part, coal miners were good honest people who respected the virtue of honest labor. But there were those among them whom Eli's success provoked more envy than admiration.

Eli had an instinct for seams bearing the high grade, richer deposits of dark bituminous coal which brought him top money of twenty cents a ton. Others, such as the Joshua brothers, who did not have Eli's gift, mined the brown anthracite and lower grades of coal at twelve cents a ton and less. In addition, Eli was well liked by the foreman and was paid in cash money instead of the script paid most other miners.

Script was worth only forty to sixty cents on the dollar and despised as almost worthless by everyone. The last thing on the mine owner's mind was the welfare of the miners. But for a producer like Eli, they were willing to make an exception.

That anyone, even Eli Llynne, would get cash instead of script was a source of irritation and downright hatred even to some of Eli's friends.

Eli did not care. His goals did not permit him time to care. By his twenty-fifth birthday, in sixteen days, Eli figured he would have saved enough to pull up stakes and head for California. California where the tales were everyone was picking up gold hand over fist.

Eli had inherited $950 from his father and three brothers who had died in the mines. Taught the virtue of thrift by his father, Eli had saved pennies a day for almost twenty years. He now had almost two thousand dollars stashed away in, what he thought, was a secret place. Eli had no way of knowing Jules Joshua knew all about his secret stash and was, even now, plotting with his five brothers on how best to take it.

The only thing meaner in Pottsville than the brutal winter, were the Joshua brothers—and Jules was the meanest of them all.

Eli watched them swagger down the wind blown street as if the harsh winter wind were a mere nuisance.

Jules paused before Eli's shanty and stared hard at Eli.

Eli watched Jules' cold eyes through the frosty window and wondered if that was not how the devil himself would appear in human form. "*Dialls! Dialls!*" Eli muttered in Welsh.

"Eli? You promised no more swearing," Lydia chided.

"It ain't exactly like that," Eli replied.

"I know enough Welsh to know better. They are not decent men. But they are not "devils"."

Eli nodded agreement with his head. He held a different opinion in his heart.

Jules grinned, sardonically, then signaled his brothers to follow. They all followed, meekly and obediently. All of them except "Big John" Joshua who was not so afraid of his brother as protective of him. Big John was almost likeable.

Big John gave Eli a quick smile then moved out behind Jules' twin brother Ezekiel,"Sly" Joshua.

"The devil and his reflection in the looking glass," Eli thought to himself.

Sly was trailed by the even more shifty James Joshua. James was a quiet man who would cut you quick. James was followed by the two weaker brothers, Matthew, tall and skinny and Zachariah, a shifty-eyed man who took particular delight in inflicting pain on dumb animals.

Altogether as evil a bunch of men as bore biblical names in the history of religion.

Eli turned away from the window and took Lydia's hand. He was happy to see that it felt warm. He smiled as he looked at the color in her cheeks. Her eyes were purple-gray in some light and

Eli never tired of looking into them. Lydia, shy by nature, did not let him look into them very long.

"Don't give me that look, Eli Llynne. I'm fine. Now you get going before the sun get's up!" Lydia was always a little angry at Eli for being so over-protective.

Eli smiled as he nodded agreement. He kissed her hands softly. He took her in his arms and held her as if she were fragile.

Lydia grabbed him hard around his waist and held on tight. "I won't break from a good manly hug, you know!"

Eli gave her a gentle but firm embrace.

Lydia kissed him. She eased away and looked apologetic. "I hoped for an early spring. I had wanted to gather daffodils and leeks for Saint David's Day."

"We will gather many of them in California, soon!"

Lydia's eyes brightened. "California," she said as if she were talking about a fairy tale land.

Eli drew close to her. He reached in his pocket and pulled out something he hid in his huge hand.

"What? What have you got there?" Lydia wondered as she tickled his ribs.

"A surprise. It should wait until tonight."

"Oh, no! You will not tease me like that. I want it now or not at all."

"My! I suppose I have little choice," Eli said. He gave her a soft kiss on the forehead. He held her close for a long moment. He broke the embrace and slowly opened his hand.

Once it was open, Lydia saw the silver Celtic Crucifix. She jumped for joy as she took it from his hand.

"Oh, Eli! It's beautiful. It's simply beautiful," Lydia gave him a quick kiss and ran to her small dressing mirror.

Eli followed her and watched as she placed the crucifix around her long, graceful neck.

Their eyes met in the mirror and lingered. For a long enchanted moment, unspoken vows of immeasurable love passed between them.

Lydia turned toward him. She slide her arms about his waist and held him tight against her body. She lost herself in the strength of his embrace.

Eli kissed her hair. He let his nose linger over her sweet smell—the honest smell of good soap. She felt warm and he did not want to leave her for the frigid, dark wetness of the coal mines. "This next pay will do it for sure. We'll be out of this misery and on to California before St. Paddy's Day, I promise."

"California? It sounds like such a dream. I don't want to think about it before I see it." Lydia's bright eyes sparkled.

"I know. But you best be thinking about it because we're going for sure. And we're never going to be cold ever again!"

Eli stopped as he heard Jeremiah coughing from the other room. He looked a little sad. "And Jeremiah will breath well again."

From the darkness, Jeremiah grimaced in pain. Both physical pain and the mental pain of living with a great lie.

Jeremiah, Eli's older brother, had spent thirty years in the dirtiest seams of the lower mines. Jeremiah had the "Miner's Asthma". His body was so broken that he was bed-ridden and stayed drunk most of the day.

Jules Joshua supplied Jeremiah with the "medicinal" raw stumphole whiskey Jeremiah needed for the pain.

Jules also pumped Jeremiah for information when Jeremiah was drunk one night bragging about his forthcoming trip to California. Jules decided right then he would make the trip in Jeremiah and Eli's stead.

Jeremiah wanted to tell his brother but could not find the courage to do so. He coughed until his shaking hand reached for the whiskey. Jeremiah could not resist pulling the fiery liquid into his trembling throat.

Eli walked into the room and looked at his brother. "Go easy on that stuff, Jeremiah," Eli warned.

Jeremiah could not look Eli in the eye. His trembling hand almost dropped the whiskey bottle. "You shouldn't . . . . don't go to the mines today."

"That would be my wish as well. But not now. Soon. Real soon," Eli replied.

Jeremiah struggled to his feet. He fell against Eli. He almost cried. "Don't go, damn it!" Jeremiah could not finish before he went into a violent coughing spell. A cough that produced the black foam of Miners' Asthma around his mouth.

As Eli helped him back to the bed, Jeremiah lapsed into semi-consciousness. Eli covered him with a thin blanket and left the room. He looked at Lydia and shook his head, sadly. "We have to go soon for his sake and yours," Eli sighed as he grabbed his miner's tools and prepared to leave.

Lydia threw her long arms around his neck and smiled," . . . and for the sake of your son."

Eli looked dumfounded for a moment before he broke into a wide grin, then a nervous laugh. "You mean?"

"Yes! I will bear you a son in California."

"By, God! You will!" Eli started to lift her playfully. He stopped and lowered her gently.

She kissed him tenderly before she broke away.

She moved to her knitting box and withdrew something. She held it behind her back. For a few moments, she enjoyed the puzzled look in Eli's eyes. Then she showed it to him.

Eli looked at it and had a hard time holding back tears.

It was a linen handkerchief embroidered with The Welsh Red Dragon, the national symbol of defiance and courage. The Red Dragon was surrounded by leeks and daffodils, Welsh symbols of renewal and rebirth.

Next to Lydia, it was the most beautiful thing Eli had ever seen. He looked at her with love but was speechless. He folded it and put it in his pocket.

"Now shoo! I have things to do. You're in the way."

"Yes. Are you . . . are you okay?"

"Of course, you big ox. I'm not sick. I'm just pregnant."

"Oh? Yes. Well I'll come back tonight with extra coal for the stove."

"No! Don't take what don't belong to us. We want no trouble with the company before we leave. Please, Eli?"

"Yes. Yes, you're right. But we leave before Saint Paddy's day for sure." Eli insisted his tongue thick with excitement. Without realizing it, he dropped his tools and they clattered to the cold floor.

Lydia laughed at him.

Eli laughed with her. He paused and looked at her with profound love. This time she let him look into her eyes a little longer.

Eli had never told her that he loved her. Not in so many words. It was not in his nature to do any fancy sparking and, as big as he was, he was fearful of poetic speaking.

Lydia would have liked to have been wooed with a little more grace and charm, but she had always understood by looking in Eli's strong Welsh-blue eyes how he felt about her.

The deep feelings that passed between them, at that moment needed no words. The unspoken magic of their spiritual intimacy would have been quickly dispelled by the most profound poetry.

They shared a long embrace that was interrupted by a huge slate slab pounding the shanty wall. Eli did not welcome the reminder of the world outside. Eli pursed his lips to express his irritation in a Welsh curse.

Lydia put a finger on his lips and shook her head.

Eli kissed her finger and smiled. He took a deep breath and blew it out hard, then picked up his tools and moved to the door. He hesitated a moment to look back at Lydia.

In the darkness of the ill-lit shanty she seemed to glow. At that moment, Eli felt he was the luckiest man in the world. Once he opened the door to the bitter winter wind, that notion quickly vanished.

As Lydia watched him go, she held the Celtic Crucifix in her fingers and touched it reverently.

She lay it in the palm of her hand and looked at it. She kissed it and prayed for God's help to return her beloved home safe and well.

Through a small crack in his wall, Otello marveled at the love that passed between Eli and Lydia. He felt a little uneasy at spying but it made his surroundings feel a little less hostile and cold.

Horse jumped on Otello's back and licked at his neck. Horse was a mongrel, but mostly Saint Bernard and fully grown. Otello, at the age of twenty one, was six foot six and a sinewy two hundred twenty five pounds; but Horse almost knocked him over.

"Whoa, Horse! You ease off now. I gonna' make us a dollar or two. You don't mess up my floor and I'll bring you back a soup bone. You hear?"

Horse's eyes seemed to show understanding.

Otello patted him on the head. He pulled his thin collar up around his neck and moved out of the room.

CHAPTER TWO

On the surface of the earth, a soft new morning snow covered the ground in a peaceful blanket of unblemished white, broken only by the ugly manmade mountains of coal tailings. The first rays of the morning sun tried to break through the winter storm clouds as Eli lay prone on the "Fram" that would pull him into the deep cold darkness of the mines.

Eli spied Otello moving to his job as a Trapper. They smiled warmly at each other before Eli spoke. "Not much longer, Otello." Eli lifted himself up to address Otello.

"Good lord! I do want to hear those words, Mr. Eli." Otello bent down and almost whispered.

Eli had not originally planned to take Otello to California. Several times, Eli had tried to tell that to Otello. Each time, Otello's kind eyes had made Eli reconsider.

Once Eli had agreed, Otello had cut a small notch into a wooden post counting the sixty days until they were to leave. He had fifty five notches cut this day.

"Well I expect I'd better get at it." Eli lay back down on the fram.

"Yes, sir, Mr. Eli. I'll be pumping the air mighty fast today."

Eli paused a moment. He smiled. "Soon, my friend. Very soon."

"Oh! Yes, sir, Mr, Eli. Yes, sir," Otello said as he watched Eli move away.

Eli took one last look at the sky just as the sun broke through the clouds. The dazzling glow of the morning sun, a cloud-chaser to delight the heart, drove the last mean-spirited storm cloud away. As the clouds retreated, the sun lit their underside turning them into giant gold nuggets.

Eli imagined he had a gold pan full of them. He daydreamed that Lydia waited on the porch of a great house with his new born son in her arms. He could see the wonder in their eyes as they gazed on the gold.

Moments later, Eli was inside the mine and it was pitch black inches from the small lantern's light.

The distant pulsing sound of the "Atmospheric Steam Engine" straining to pump water from the mine, reverberated in Eli's ears as he began digging at the hard, dark rock. The inefficiency of the steam engine allowed it to pump only a small portion of the water from the mines. As a result, the floor of the mine shaft was always wet with ice-cold water that veteran miners learned to ignore if they were to meet their quotas.

The Joshua brothers held their picks still and listened for the rhythmic sound of Eli's pick hitting the wall.

Jules, unlike his twin brother Sly, liked the quality of the bottomless darkness. The evil intentions of his warped and twisted soul seemed more at home where there existed the least amount of light.

In a few moments, he would use the darkness to his advantage. His perverted bat-like radar enabled him to move, almost gracefully, in pitch blackness. Other men might stumble where Jules moved with wily grace. Soon he hoped to use this skill to sneak up on Eli and end his life as suddenly as possible.

Eli sensed something was wrong.

Eli did not hear the usual background noises. He perked up his ears. He heard the movement of loose rock and smelled the pungent ripeness of the Joshua brothers.

Because of his efficiency, Eli was assigned to break this new coal seam loose himself. The Joshua brothers were supposed to be working a distant seam.

Eli worked steady but looked and listened, cautiously. As he chopped at the dark, hard rock, the narrow wet walls poured cold water that added to his feeling of uneasiness. Eli paused and peered into the darkness. He saw some movement and knew the only people stupid enough to be here were the Joshua brothers.

"You boys aren't supposed to be in this vicinity!" Eli's deep voice boomed and echoed in the darkness. There was the sound of scurrying but no answer.

Eli knew someone was there in the darkness. "The boss man will be by the cage looking to hoist up your load real soon now. If I was you I'd light those lanterns and proceed to the right spot," Eli added, forcefully.

There was a long eerie silence, interrupted only by the steady dripping of icy water on the rock floor. Finally, the Joshua brothers, with the exception of Jules, lit their lanterns. Jules gave his brothers one last silent command then eased out of the mine shaft and back toward the surface.

"If I owed the company store as much as you boys, I wouldn't be doin' any dilly dallying 'round another man's seam." Eli could barely make out the flickering lanterns which outlined their shadowy figures. He could see enough to know they weren't where they were supposed to be. He also could feel in his bones they were up to no good.

Their blackened faces barely reflected any light and their eyes had the lifeless quality of dead men. Had Eli not been a god-fearing man he would have believed he had descended into hell.

Eli watched them huddle together in whispers. He did not imagine they were up to any good and decided he would not turn his back on them this day.

On the surface, Jules Joshua moved in the shadows toward Eli's house. He sweated profusely despite the icy wind in his face. He paused only to secure his long knife inside his tattered coat.

Eli worked and watched the movements of the other Joshua brothers in the narrow, wet seam five hundred feet below the surface. Eli was very worried as the Joshua brothers were working much closer now. So close he could see the evil in their dirt-circled eyes. He had never liked the Joshua brothers but he had never had any reason to believe they held any dangerous malice toward him—until now.

He knew, instantly, what they were about when James Joshua lifted a pick axe as high as possible in the narrow tunnel. James brought it down hard into the rock inches from Eli's head.

Two miles away Lydia worked at making the dilapidated shack look homey. She loved Eli and wanted to make him as happy as their income allowed.

She knew that she couldn't do big things for him on the pennies a day he brought home but she could do some very pretty things with very little.

Lydia hoped they would be able to leave for California soon. She felt in her soul that Eli could do as well as any of the gold miners she had heard about who made fortunes overnight.

Lydia hated mining as a way of life but she figured gold mining was a thousand times better than coal mining. She stopped her housework for a minute to go check on Jeremiah. He had stopped coughing and she wondered if he was all right. She was just inside the door of his room when Jules Joshua broke through the front door.

Eli's huge fist crashed into James' mouth jarring loose three teeth. James spit blood and mumbled curses as he dropped to his knees.

"You boys want to back off? I told you, I'm working this seam. You hiding in the darkness back there, Jules? You want to settle something with me?"

Eli demanded as he knelt on the hard wet floor of the tunnel.

"Don't you know nuthin'? I ain't Jules. Anyways, the boss man said we is working this here seam. You got any objections?" Sly Joshua moved closer to Eli.

Sly was flanked by Matthew and James. Big John stayed close behind. Jules and Zack could not be seen.

"Not likely, Sly. You best be goin' now!" Eli insisted.

Sly cracked an almost toothless grin. The three teeth that remained in his mouth were darker than the coal that smeared his pock-marked face.

"I won't be goin' nowhere. But you might be goin' to hell!" Sly snarled as he swung his pick at Eli's head.

Eli barely ducked in time. As he moved out of the way, the pick cracked into the wet coal spraying dark, wet chunks in Eli's face. Eli was wiping the coal chips from his eyes when Matthew came at him from the other side.

Matthew's pick narrowly missed Eli's head. Eli grabbed it and yanked it from Matthew's hands before he could swing again. Eli was slow to anger. When he was, finally, riled to action there was no more formidable opponent on, or in, the earth. "What is going on here? You boys have some trouble with me you come out from back there and we'll settle it between us!"

Eli stood up as high as he could in the five-foot high tunnel and peered into the darkness.

No one answered.

Instead Matthew plunged out of the darkness and swung his pick at Eli.

Eli blocked it. He grabbed Matthew by the collar and pulled him hard to the floor with one yank of his mighty arm.

"What are you doing in this house, Jules Joshua?" Lydia challenged as Jules came through the door.

"Ha! Ha! I ain't Jules. I'm Ezekiel," Jules lied. "I ain't here to hurt nobody, Lydia. I just want that money Eli and Jeremiah have been saving. Don't try lyin' 'bout it. I know for sure you got it!" Jules put his crude hand on the handle of the long knife.

"You get out of here right now, Jules . . . or Ezekiel, whichever you are. What are you doing out of the pits this time of day? The Boss man will fire you sure! You leave before I go get Eli," Lydia said nervously, as she moved back into Jeremiah's room.

"Eli? Well you just go get him. Now Jeremiah there, he can tell you full well why I'm here!"

Jeremiah tried to sit up but it caused a coughing fit that made him take a drink of whiskey.

Jules Joshua laughed at him as he pushed Lydia aside. "Ain't gonna' be no firing! We's quit. Now you just git outta' the way and let me have the money?"

"Go to hell, you devil!" Lydia snarled.

"Now that ain't ladylike, Missy," Jules smirked. "The money, please, ma'am?"

"If I had any money I'd never let the likes of you get it!"

"Oh? The likes of me?" Jules looked genuinely hurt. "Well I say it's ours anyway. Eli steals the best grade ore from the rest of us. It's past time he shared his bounty."

"No! Not this day or any day!"

"Miss Llynne you don't wanna git' kilt' over money."

"You'll not be touching anything of ours, Mister Jules Joshua!" Lydia picked up a big iron skillet. Jules grinned as he brandished his huge knife.

"You crazy, James? What's got into you, boy? And you Matthew? I was at your christening." Eli moved back until he felt the shadows of Sly, James and Big John on his neck. Eli was trapped between the three of them.

"That don't matter none. That money you done saved up is gonna' be ours. We gonna use your stake to take us all to 'Kalifornee!" Sly spewed with delight.

"Shut up, Sly! Shut your stupid mouth. Don't listen to him, Eli. This is about you and the boss man. It ain't fair that you get special treatment. We done seen it more than enough," Big John said.

As Big John moved out of the shadows, Eli looked at him in disbelief. "You part of this, John?"

John looked embarrassed. He lowered his pick. "Like I said, Eli. You get cash money and that 'jest ain't fair."

"Damn you, boy! I got to do every job myself?" Sly growled as he leaped out of the darkness and drove a pick hard into Eli's back.

Jeremiah stood up and, weakly, lunged at Jules. He missed and tumbled to the floor. He got up, slowly.

"It's all my fault!" Jeremiah threw the half-filled bottle of whiskey at Jules.

Jules ducked and it shattered against a wall.

"Run, Lydia! You leave, now. I'll take care . . . .of matters. I'll . . . .I'll," Jeremiah wobbled.

Jules shoved him down on the bed and picked up a pillow. Jules held the pillow up and grinned, sardonically, as he lowered it over Jeremiah's face.

Jeremiah tried to fight it off but he was too weak. His breath was pushed back into his face as he coughed and coughed, then shuddered and coughed no more.

Jules was pleased with himself until he turned to see Horse. Horse, his teeth bared and mouth foaming, leaped for Jules' throat. Horse knocked Jules hard against the wall and bit hard into Jules' right shoulder.

Jules was in so much pain he could barely close his fingers around his knife. Horse released his bite and started to take another from Jules' throat. In that brief moment, Jules closed his hand on his knife and thrust it into Horse's gallant heart.

Horse died instantly.

Jules sighed hard in relief and looked at his torn clothes and bleeding shoulder. "That damn animal done bit me clean through! Now what 'iffen he got the foaming disease? Now what about that?" Jules felt sorry for himself.

He did not have long to enjoy his self-pity.

"Damn you, Jules Joshua!" Lydia came at him with the skillet held high and her fingernails bared.

Jules knocked the skillet from her right hand.

Lydia reeled backwards before she was able to right herself. She lunged at Jules and dug her fingernails into his right eye. The sharpness of the fingernails put his eye out and he fell to the floor in agony. Lydia started to run. Jules grabbed her dress. It ripped as she fell to her knees.

Lydia struggled to her feet.

Jules rubbed his eye and looked at the blood on his hand. "Damn you, Lydia Llynne! I'm almost blind here!" Jules moaned as he glared at her.

Lydia backed away and up against the hot iron stove.

Jules gripped the long knife as he snarled at her and spit blood.

Otello was dripping with sweat in the sub-zero cold as he pumped the ventilating waffles pushing air into the mine. He paused and sniffed the air. He felt in his bones something very evil was happening nearby. He wanted to leave his post and go check on Eli. He knew he could not. He growled under his breath as he pumped even harder.

The force of Sly's blow knocked Eli to the floor of the tunnel and, for a moment, he could not see.

Eli was in great pain as he reached back and wriggled the pick axe free from in between his shoulder blades. Once the pick was free, hot blood flowed freely down Eli's back.

James raised another pick axe to finish Eli off but Eli moved just in time to dig his pick into James' leg.

"Aaarrrhhggg!" James yelled as Eli tried to wrest his pick axe free from James' leg.

Big John raised his pick axe. He hesitated.

Sly glared at him.

"I'm awful sorry, Mr. Llynne," Big John apologized just before he drove the pick hard into Eli's back. Eli fell to the floor hard and did not move.

Jules lunged at Lydia. Lydia moved and Jules' hand fell on the hot stove. "Aaarrrggghh! Damn! Damn!" He yelled in pain as he dropped the knife.

Lydia picked up the big iron skillet.

Jules grabbed her hand and wrestled it away from her. He raised it to crush Lydia's head.

Lydia was not intimidated. She picked up the knife and held it ready to stab Jules if he made the slightest move.

Jules grinned. He lowered the skillet.

"I ain't got time to kill you now. You just stand aside and maybe I won't be killin' you 'atall." Jules held a handkerchief over his eye as he staggered past her to the kitchen cupboard. Shoving with his shoulder, he moved it aside. Once the cupboard was out of the way, Jules ripped loose a board and picked up the large family bible wrapped in oil cloth. He opened it to the middle where it was hollowed out and withdrew the stack of neatly banded bills.

"It ain't fittin' to use the bible to hide money, Lydia. It's sinning." Jules paused as blood trickled from his eye. "You crazy bitch! I think you put my eye out!" He snarled as he stuffed the money in his pocket and threw the bible to the floor.

Eli was in great pain. It was hard to move but he knew if he didn't move he would soon be dead. Using all his remaining strength, he struggled to his feet.

Big John raised his axe to strike again.

Eli drove his head into Big John's stomach and sent him crashing against the wall. Big John dropped to his knees, then got up and moved away into the darkness.

Eli picked up an axe and swung it at James. James backed into the shadows with Sly and the others.

"You come back, Sly Joshua! You be a man, you hear?" Eli roared into the darkness. "All of you. Come on out and let's get this settled!" Eli's voice echoed unanswered. In the silence, his mind turned to Lydia.

"Lydia? Lydia." Eli thought as he staggered into the darkness of the tunnel feeling his way as he went. The pain was deep in his back and blood was filling his boots. He knew the Joshua brothers were close behind in the darkness.

Eli wasn't worried about his life but he was scared to death about what might be happening to Lydia. Eli was only a few yards ahead of the Joshua brothers when he stumbled into a turn in the tunnel that went three different directions. His only hope was to lose them in the darkness and worry about getting to the surface later. His knees wanted to buckle beneath his weight and each breath burned like fire.

"I know you're down that tunnel, Eli. That's okay. I'm just going to kick this here brace and it's all going to fall down on your head. Then we is gonna' go to 'Kalifornee' with your money," Sly chuckled as he worked the brace with an iron bar until it moved and the support timbers creaked.

"You gone crazy, Sly Joshua? You do something like this and if I don't get you, the company sheriff will. You owe the company more than anybody. They ain't letting you go nowhere," Eli paused and watched the ceiling tremble.

Sly looked at the loose, wet coal falling from small cracks in the ceiling and he backed away in the opposite direction as he shouted at Eli. "Well he `shore done agreed to look the other way for some cash money. They're pulling three bodies a week out of these mines and yours ain't likely to make any difference. Don't nobody in this here camp give a damn about nobody else. You know that, Eli. There's six more out there waiting to take your place and ain't no company sheriff coming looking for nobody in `Kalifornee. All they's looking for out there is gold. Thanks for the stake, Eli!"

Sly uttered a wicked laugh that reverberated down the tunnels.

Eli waited until the echoes ceased. "You boys sure got some bad information from somewhere."

"I don't think so, Eli. But, anyways, we'll know for sure soon enough!" Sly cackled.

An icy chill ran the length of Eli's spine. "I'd better not catch none of you boys near to my place . . . or anywhere near to Lydia! You hear me?" Eli tried to yell as he felt himself grow weaker.

"All you're gonna' catch is a big load of mountain, Eli? Guess what? You gonna' make your quota today!" Sly chortled as he and Big John worked at levering the short braces.

It took all of Big John's strength to get one to crack. They watched as the ceiling shivered then began to crumble. They broke into a measured run as the coal and rock began to rain on the tunnel floor.

"I hope I did put your eye out, Jules Joshua. Now give me that money back! That's hard earned money and it ain't yours to take!" Lydia threatened with the knife.

Jules laughed at her as he began to count it. Lydia raised the knife high over her head and started to plunge it into Jules' chest. Jules caught her hand. He grabbed the knife and shoved her to the floor.

Lydia looked up at him with contempt. She grabbed the iron skillet and rushed him.

Jules backed away laughing at her. As he did, he slipped and fell hard on his backside. Lydia dropped to her knees and swung the skillet at his head. Jules rolled away and the skillet hit the floor hard.

Lydia raised it up poised to strike again.

Jules looked at her and his laughter turned to anger. He thrust the knife at her.

Lydia tried to move out of the way. She could not. The long knife blade cut into her heart. Lydia staggered a moment before she dropped to her hands and knees, then fell over on the floor dead.

Jules looked pale for a moment. "Lydia? Lydia, you don't be dead now. I don't want to kill no woman," Jules choked. He was interrupted by Zachariah coming through the door. "Zack" took one look at Lydia and almost fainted.

Jules grimaced and grabbed Zack by the collar.

"It don't make no never mind. Ezekiel done taken care of Eli by now. It's what had to be done. Now nobody can link us up with nothing. We gonna' be long on the trail to California before anybody knows anything anyhow."

Zack nodded terrified agreement.

"You got them horses like I told you?" Jules questioned, nervously.

Zack looked scared to death as he backed away. "I . . . . they is with the trader. He's waitin' on the money. They is all loaded up . . . but, Jules this ain't right. You done 'kilt a woman. You didn't say nuthin' 'bout that." Zack backed away.

Jules grabbed him hard. "You weak little weasel! I got the money. So I 'kilt a woman and there's a man I 'kilt in the other room and if you don't do what you're told I'll kill one more! Now where is those horses?"

Zack pointed a shaky finger toward the street. Jules stuffed the money in his shirt and moved, quickly, to the front door of the shanty. He paused for a moment to look down the ice-strewn streets to see if anyone was looking. There was nothing on the streets but dirty tents and leeward leaning shanties.

Zack and Jules pulled their collars up against the cold wind and snow as they made their way out of Eli's house toward their rendezvous with the horse trader.

Somehow, most of the ceiling held. Eli had expected a deluge of coal and rock to bury him forever. The heavy ceiling creaked into an ominous bend, but did not break. Eli could barely hear the footsteps of the Joshua brothers retreating to the cage that would take them to the surface. The loss of blood was making him dizzy and he was disoriented and weak as he began a painful crawl after them.

Otello could fight the feeling of dread no longer. He had felt the rumble of the earth beneath him. His senses told him his friend was in bad trouble. He knew the ventilation piping was down and his efforts were now wasted. He gritted his teeth and looked around for the "Boss Man". He saw no one. He ceased pumping. He moved to a remote slag heap. He dug in the refuse for a few moments until he found the hunter's knife he had hidden there.

He moved to help Eli.

It had taken longer than Jules had figured to secure the horses because Jules had tried to cheat the horse trader. As a result, they were an hour late getting to the place where Jules was to meet up with the others.

They began to get worried when Sly, Big John, Matthew and James were a half-hour overdue.

Finally, Big John emerged from the mine shaft exit followed by Matthew. James stumbled out moments.

Sly followed, close behind.

Once they were on the surface, Sly breathed a sigh of relief as he took the reins of his horse.

"Is he dead?" Jules asked with a look of concern.

"I expect he's got half a mountain on him. That's 'bout as dead as a man can be," Sly replied as he mounted his horse.

"Looks like you done good, Jules. You found the money and got the horses?" Matthew shivered as he tried to stroke his horse's mane. The horse shied away.

"Yep. You see 'em don't you?" Zack tried to touch his horse. His horse also backed away.

"This here is a dumb horse. Make him stand still, Jules!" Zack struggled to get his horse to obey.

The horse whinnied his dislike of Zack.

Jules grabbed the reins of Zack's stallion and yanked them. The horses' eyes bulged with hate as it stomped and pawed to a standstill.

Jules grimaced. "They is dumb animals but don't you be dumber. Now you get control of that animal. We's leaving now!"

"Hot damn! We gonna' go to 'Kalifornee'!" Sly exclaimed with joy. "Which way is it, Jules?"

Jules looked at Sly with disdain. He grimaced and turned his horse down the snow covered mining road that led out of camp. "You just follow old Jules Joshua's trail. Stick close by me. I know the way." Jules concluded as he kicked his horse into a gallop.

The others watched a long moment before they followed after him.

Eli did not know how he managed to get to the surface. His will to live and his fear for his beloved Lydia had driven him upward through the coal-black darkness. The pain in his back was almost unbearable. His legs balked at his attempt to walk. His breath was becoming increasingly labored.

The storm clouds had returned. It was raining a slow freezing rain mixed with snow and it was night outside as Eli emerged from the mine. Eli swayed in the bitter wind and tried to focus his eyes on the icy street. He shivered, violently, as he took deep breaths of the crisp, cold air at the mine shaft opening.

Eli staggered through the streets of tents and shanties toward his own shack. Some children laughed thinking he was drunk. They did not see the blood soaking his shirt or spilling over the top of his boots. They laughed harder when he fell into an icy slag heap unconscious.

Otello saw the broken rock and rubble on the floor of the mine. His eyes fell on the trail of blood that led to the surface. He growled under his breath and broke into a run. He was outside in moments. He did not have to ask the name of the body slumped over in the bright red ice-flows of the street before him.

Otello leaned down and lifted Eli in his arms. He wobbled slightly until he was able to balance himself. His eyes misted with anger and fear for his friend as he made his way quickly to Eli's shack.

Otello opened the door and the shanty looked deserted. Immediately, he felt sick. The smell of death was heavy in the air.

Gently, Otello lay Eli on a small pile of old rags. He looked around then moved, slowly, away.

Otello eased into Jeremiah's room. Jeremiah's arm hung off the bed. Otello picked it up. The coldness of the hand told him his senses had been right.

The weak moonlight coming through the small window barely illuminated Jeremiah's face, adding to its ghostly pallor. Otello covered it with a blanket.

The only other room in the three room shack was the kitchen. Otello knew she had to be there.

He paused a moment then moved toward the kitchen looking for some sign that it was all a lie.

The torn bible, empty of money, lay open at his feet as he approached the kitchen door. He hesitated only a second then moved through the door. He was not surprised to see the prostrate figure of Lydia lying in a pool of blood.

Otello said a silent prayer as he found a cloth to cover her face.

Otello's ears picked up the sound of Eli groaning in the next room. His shoulders slumped from the weight of a great sadness as he moved to attend his friend.

Eli greeted Otello with half open eyes.

"Lydia? . . . my Lydia?" Eli could barely whisper.

Otello tried to keep his face still.

Otello knelt beside his friend and touched him in a cursory

examination. "Good God almighty, Mr. Eli. I expect you broke 'bout everywhere a man can be broke."

"My Lydia?" Eli's weak eyes pleaded.

Otello was not a good liar. He tried to be this one time "Ahhhh, she's just in the other room. You rest easy now."

Eli's eyes clouded over with disbelief, but he was too weak to protest. He slipped into unconsciousness whispering Lydia's name until his lips moved no more.

Otello lifted Eli's head in his arms. He rocked Eli like a mother rocking a child. Then he eased him down.

Otello perked his ears. He wondered why he did not hear Horse barking. Otello's gut wrenched in horror as he ran back into his small room.

What he saw made him vomit.

In the palest rays of the evil moon, Horse lay motionless in a pool of dark red ice.

"Oh, God! Good, God! Jesus, God Almighty!" Otello dropped to his knees and cried out to the heavens.

The heavens did not reply.

CHAPTER THREE

July 1851.

Saint Louis, Missouri

The Joshua brothers were in hog heaven. They had made it to St. Louis, Missouri without incident and they were now within a few months of the gold fields of California. Jules figured they had enough of a lead on anybody who might be following them to rest up in St. Louis for a few days. There were wagon trains forming just up the river in Independence every day. Jules figured to join one as soon as he had some fun in the big City.

Saint Louis was a fascinating town to Jules and his brothers. It was exciting and wide-open with all kinds of people crowded into streets talking about going to the gold country.

The paved streets were lined with elegant houses and high brickwork and fancy gaslights and all kinds of new fangled do dads.

The slang for Saint Louis was "Mound City" and it was readily apparent why it got this handle. All about them, the hills were full of wagons laden with dry goods and fancy carriages filled with fancy ladies and clean-shaven men.

Some of the overloaded wagons barely made it up the steep hills. "Mounds" that rose up only a few yards from the wooded banks of the free rolling Mississippi River. The mile-wide Mississippi jammed with riverboats full of good whiskey and wild women.

The river was clogged with barges and steamboats with their whistles competing for loudness, length and steam letting ability.

But it was the handsome way the ladies dressed and the good whiskey that Jules and his brothers were here to enjoy.

The saloons of Saint Louis were far more elegant than anything Jules or his brothers had ever seen. In the Salty Dog Saloon, hard by the Mississippi river, Jules and his brothers thought they had found paradise. The whiskey wasn't raw but smooth and deserved sipping more than guzzling. The free food was better than they had ever eaten and the women were flesh and blood but looked as pretty as fashion girls from catalog ads.

In the center of the room was a poker table. Close by, a handsome gambler held court surrounded by beautiful women the likes of which Jules had only known in dreams. Jules had never seen a man dressed in such finery. This Dandy was dressed in clothes almost as pretty as the clothes the women wore.

Jules thought The Dandy looked silly. He could not understand how women could like a man who wore more lace than they did. But then Jules had never taken much time to understand women. He either liked them to use for his immediate purposes or never bothered with them. Jules did not know this man but he felt a certain jealousy toward him.

Jules had always resented men that seemed to go through life without getting their hands dirty. A coal miner did a honest days work. A man's work. A miner could scrub for hours after a shift and never rid himself of all the grime he had gathered. This Dandy had hands as clean and manicured as a twenty dollar whore.

Jules smirked as he stared at The Dandy then looked at his brothers. "Hey, you boys think that there is a man or a woman?"

Jules' brothers chuckled and shrugged.

"I expect he's a little of both," Sly grinned.

"He's a Dandy alright. Thinks he's a real hot shot. I say he's about as low a man as there is,"Sara, a semi-lovely dance hall girl interrupted.

Jules looked Sara over. He liked what he saw.

"Is that a fact?" Jules asked.

Sara's eyes almost teared. She bit her lip. Her expression vied for Jules' sympathy.

Normally she would have been wasting her time. Jules was not a man given to sympathetic notions. Yet the trail to Saint Louis had been long, Jules had drank too much and she smelled real good.

"You got some trouble with this man?" Jules asked.

"Not no more. What he done to me, is done."

Jules smirked. He moved close to her and pressed her between himself and the bar. He liked the way she did not try to move aside. Her fine body against his aroused feelings he had not enjoyed for some time.

"Well I say let's go upstairs and talk about it." Jules grinned and dared to run his hand the length of the silk stocking on her right thigh. When she did not resist, he pressed his body harder against hers.

Sara ran her long fingernails through his hair. She drew her sweet lips close to his. "Yes. Just let me see him lose this once."

"What?"

"I expect he's past due to lose and I want to be here to see it."

Jules scoffed as he backed off just a little. "Well I don't have no time to be wastin' on no card games. You comin' upstairs or not?" Jules insisted.

Sara pouted a moment. She kissed Jules softly on the neck. She gave him a quick love bite. "Just a few minutes. Let me watch just a few hands. Please?"

"God Almighty, woman! Can't you see my mood?"

"Please. I want to give you my full attention."

Jules backed off. He started to walk away.

Sara grabbed his hand and pulled at him. "Please?"

Jules looked disgusted. He looked at The Dandy. The Dandy looked back and seemed to find Jules and his brothers amusing.

"What the hell is he smilin' about?" Jules asked.

"He's a real snob. I believe he thinks people . . . people like you . . . and your brothers are riff-raff."

"What?"

"He used to beat me, a lot. He's a real evil man."

"Yea. Well he better watch who he's looking down that powdered nose at," Jules snarled. He pulled down a drink and pounded the bar for another.

"You can get yourself in that game if you want. Max ain't as good a card player as he looks," Sara goaded Jules.

"Any man who wears a woman's clothes ain't much of a man in my estimation."

"Why don't you go show him how good you are?"

"What?"

"I've heard him say many times that if you aren't a gambling man you ain't nothing!" Sara ran her smooth fingers up and down the back of Jules' neck.

Jules reeled from the pleasure.

"Well I done plenty of gambling and I done plenty well at it! Ain't I boys?" Jules asked his brothers.

They looked at him like he was crazy.

"You ain't no card player, Jules," Matthew said.

"Well maybe you don't know everything there is to know about what I do and don't do!"

"Matthew is right, Jules. Ain't none of us done that much," Big John added.

"Well maybe it's my business anyways," Jules replied.

"That may be so, except if you intending on using our money," Big John said.

Jules thought it over. He smiled and nodded agreement. "I expect you're right 'bout that, Big John." Jules put his arm around Big John's shoulder. "Let's us just sip some more of this good whiskey and see what we see."

Big John looked doubtful as Jules poured three fingers of whiskey into a glass for each of them. They both downed it and easy laughter soon followed.

The longer they drank the further away from his brothers Jules eased down the bar. Soon he was only a few feet from the poker table.

Sara made sure she got between Jules and his brothers' line of sight. "You want me to get you in the game?" Sara asked.

"Just hold on, Woman. I ain't said that yet!" Jules replied.

Jules had played poker before, but only in dark places where he could cheat and stack the deck. There was far too much light in this place for that.

Yet, in his heady arrogance, he believed he knew the game well enough to play with anyone. Particularly fancy pants men who looked like they took a bath every day.

Jules downed a quick whiskey and adjusted the eye patch over his injured right eye left by Lydia's fingernails. The wound had healed real ugly and Jules was determined the world outside would never see it.

To his dismay, Jules could never adjust the patch to where it, fully, covered the ugly wound. As ugly as Jules was, he thought of himself as handsome. In his mind the only thing marring his "beauty" was the scar Lydia had left on his face. He cursed her daily for that.

Sara reached up to touch his face. He grabbed her hand and almost broke it with his fierce grip.

"Nobody touches my face! Understand, woman?" Jules pushed her aside.

Sara backed away contritely, barely concealing her anger. She adjusted her dress and moved back up beside Jules. "I didn't mean nothing by it."

Jules turned his back on her.

Sara stroked his shoulders.

It took only a few strokes of her gentle hands to relieve the tension. "I'll buy this round of drinks. Okay, Jules?" Sara said.

Jules turned back and faced her. He smiled and nodded agreement.

Sara bought one round, then coached Jules into buying several more rounds of the over-priced drinks. All the while, she fed his ego as they watched the high stakes poker game. "I can understand your reluctance to get into that game. Max is the best card player in these parts. He's a professional," she said as she looked into Jules evil good eye with phony admiration.

"It don't make no never mind what he is. I can play that game as good as anybody."

"You ain't no professional poker player, Jules," Sly said as he stepped up beside them.

Jules glared at Sly for a long angry moment.

"Shut up! Did I ask you for your two bits? It's a simple enough game. I'm goin' to beat that fancy pants and then we'll be seeing what's, what!"

"Jules, maybe that ain't such a good idea." Big John stepped up and glared hard.

Jules glared back harder.

Big John stepped back.

"What you doing, Jules? You don't know nothin' 'bout playin' cards in these kind of places!" Matthew, who was usually quiet, spoke up.

Jules was more stubborn than he was anything. No more cunning man ever lived except when his will to do something was obstructed. If pride, truly," . . . goeth before a fall", Jules' false pride caused him to take many long hard tumbles—and he was about to take one of the longest falls of his life.

"Yes I do. I been watching. It ain't no different than back home except they has newer cards. Now you and the others just go up stairs with some women and leave this to me," Jules chortled.

"Well, I don't like it none, nohow. You got most of the money on you and it's gonna to cost most of that to buy into the wagon train at Independence," Sly challenged.

"Damnit, Ezekiel . . . Sly Joshua! You go on upstairs like I told you now! Here's some money. Buy you one of those painted women. It might be a long dry spell before we find a place like this again," Jules said as he shoved some money in Sly's hand.

Sly grumped. He took the money and moved off to join Zack and James who were fondling three of the ugliest whores in the saloon.

Big John and Matthew both hesitated. They, obviously, did not like it. But they had been into the whiskey even longer than Jules. Their judgement was almost as clouded as the dark amber of the Kentucky sipping whiskey served in the saloon.

Jules prided himself on always being in command.

Jules never wavered or showed the slightest doubt or weakness, except when Big John or Matthew looked upset. Jules did not want to get on Big John or Matthew's bad side. He figured, in some respects, they were almost as smart as he. He gave them his best contrite look and seemed apologetic as he spoke. "I'm just gonna' watch for awhile. Okay? Why don't you go with those nice ladies over there and have some fun. You deserve it, John, Matthew," Jules smiled.

"You want me to keep the money?" Matthew offered.

"No! You know I don't like bein' talked to like a child, Matthew."

"It ain't that way," Big John added.

Jules sighed hard. He nodded agreement.

"I understand your concerns. But you gotta' trust me. I done right by you so far, ain't I?"

Big John and Matthew thought it over. They nodded reluctant agreement.

They did not see Sara motion for two of her best looking girl friends to join them. "Boys, this is Fifi and Camille. They are just here from France and don't know English very well. You will have to speak slow to them. I assure you they will make every effort to understand whatever you say," Sara introduced.

Matthew and Big John tried to ignore the ladies.

They were worried about what Jules was up to. They could not. Their noses had never smelled such sweetness, their eyes had never beheld such beauty and their hands had never touched such finery.

Their thought processes were caught in a vapor lock formed by too much whiskey and perfume.

"I gotta' say those are mighty fine lookin' women. You agree, John?' Jules asked.

Big John looked at the ladies. He looked at Matthew. Matthew was already leaving with Fifi. Camille put her long arms around his neck. Big John grimaced before he nodded agreement.

"I'm goin' upstairs with this nice lady for just awhile, Jules. You just take it easy 'cause I'm comin' down to check on you real soon!" Big John tried to insist as he wobbled into the ladies arms.

The petite lady was barely able to holdup Big John's huge frame.

Big John steadied himself. He grabbed a bottle of whiskey. He took Camille by the arm and pulled her along up the staircase.

Jules smiled and chuckled as he watched them go.

"Them brothers of your'n, they shore do take an interest in your affairs," Sara cooed.

"Well they can say what they want but it's me that says what counts!"

"You gonna beat Max for me?" Sara sighed hard.

"I never said that!"

"He once called me a whore! A two-bit whore!"

"Well I expect that is between you and him."

Sara stroked Jules' hair. She pulled her body close to his and cooed in his ear. "If you will play him and beat him . . . humiliate him in front of everybody. I will give you pleasures you have only dreamed of!"

Sara kissed Jules gently on the cheek.

Jules pushed her away. "If I do it. I do it for my own reasons in my own time. You understand?"

Sara looked hurt. She started to turn away.

Jules grabbed her arm and spun her around. He kissed her hard and mean on the lips. He broke the kiss and sat her down in a chair. He laughed.

Jules turned to see if his brothers were out of sight. Then he walked, cockily, across the crowded waterfront saloon floor to the poker table. The table was peopled by the well dressed gambler, Max, who sat with three steamboat sailors.

"Can I join this game, boys?" Jules asked.

The men at the table ignored him.

Jules took offense. "Ain't you heard what I 'jest said?" Jules growled angrily.

The sailors looked at Jules and recoiled.

Max smirked. "Anybody who has the wherewithal is welcome. Just hand over the buy in," Max replied without looking Jules in the eye.

"Buy in? That's easy enough. How much?" Jules pulled a wad of bills from his pocket. He waived it in front of everyone.

"Why, only fifty dollars. Five card stud. Table stakes," Max tried not to smirk.

"Yep. Whatever. Here's my fifty." Jules counted out the money as if it didn't mean anything.

"Sure. Sit down. I'm Maxwell Mellon," Max offered his hand.

"I'm Jules Joshua." Jules shook Max's hand and knew right then he had Max beat. Any man with such soft hands had to be a sissy boy and Jules beat up on sissy boys every chance he got.

The others mumbled their names as Jules sat down. "Five card stud, gentlemen. Table stakes. High card deals." Max turned over an ace that gave Jules the deal.

Jules took the deck and tried not to smile.

Jules figured if they trusted him to deal he had them. He only wished it were a little darker. He fumbled the cards trying to shuffle them. He cursed under his breath as he, finally, managed to get a down and up card to each of the players. There was quiet as they waited for him to call the bet.

"Oh! The high card bets," Jules cleared his throat. They looked at him, quietly, again.

Jules looked down at his cards and his face turned red as he saw he had a King high. "I bet two dollars," Jules said as he threw his money on the table.

There was a slight chuckle from one of the sailors.

"Your two and twenty five dollars." A steamboat sailor upped the bet. The table "called" the bet.

"I call too," Jules took his turn. He hesitated to the chagrin of the others, then dealt the next round of cards.

"You play this game a lot?" Max quizzed holding back a smirk.

"I played it enough," Jules snapped. "Pair of threes bets!" Jules looked at the pair of threes in front of Max.

"Right you are?" Max acknowledged. Jules looked back at Sara and she smiled encouragement.

"Threes bets fifty dollars," Max threw his money into the pot.

Everyone "called" the bet.

Jules looked at his King high and the size of the bet. He started to fold but saw the look of contempt in Max's eye.

"Your fifty and fifty more," Jules growled.

The table called his bet.

Jules dealt the final round. He almost dropped the deck when a pair of Kings came up in his hand.

"Yep, I played this game a lot. Maybe a lot more than you," Jules said, arrogantly, as he threw a hundred dollars into the pot. Jules hoped no one could see the sweat pouring off his body and trickling down his back and into his boots.

Max looked at his pair of threes with a ten back and shrugged. "Your fifty and five hundred more."

Everybody but Jules folded.

Jules almost fell out of his chair. He glared at Max angrily. "But we ain't playing for them kind of stakes."

"Table stakes, Mr. Big Time Gambler. For your edification that means you can bet the amount in the pot. There is over six hundred in this pot. Four hundred and fifty to you, sir," Max needled.

Jules looked at Max's pair of threes and his pair of Kings, Jack-backed. He figured Max to be bluffing, but it would take most of the rest of his ill-gotten gains to prove it.

Jules started to fold. But now a crowd had gathered and Sara was watching him with doubt in her eyes.

Jules wanted dearly to make Max look like a fool in front of her and everyone. "Your five hundred and two hundred more," Jules said with a tight throat.

Max grinned as he counted out a neat stack of hundred dollar bills. He calmly and coolly placed them in the pot. "Let's see, that's two hundred to me and . . . oh, let's say. Hhhhmmmm! Let's say five hundred more," Max shoved the money into the center of the table. He smirked as he eased back in his chair. He stared at Jules with the most unrevealing poker face Jules had ever seen.

Jules was furious. If he bet the five hundred more and lost they wouldn't be able to buy into the wagon train. It was so risky that his knees were shaking under the table. But he wouldn't have backed down if it meant he'd die on the spot.

His gnarly hands were trembling and dripping with sweat as he counted out the remainder of the stolen money. One twenty dollar bill had big spots of dried blood on it.

No one but Jules noticed. "I call your five hundred," Jules wiped sweat from his forehead.

"Three threes," Max turned over a third trey.

Jules leaped out of his chair. "You cheated. I don't know how you done it but you cheated! You think I'm a dumb country boy, but I ain't. You cheated and it ain't right!" Jules started to reach for his long knife. He stopped when he felt the cold steel of a gun barrel against his head.

"Just settle down, Mister. Max don't cheat. Besides you dealt. Now, ease on out of here and there won't be no trouble." The heavy-set man with a badge on his shirt instructed. He cocked the hammer of the 1836 colt his finger resting on the extended trigger.

"Well I know he cheated somehow. I just know it!"

"Move!" The man shoved Jules away from the table.

Jules moved to the side then turned, abruptly. He shoved the sheriff in the face as he grabbed the gun. The gun went off and blew a hole in the ceiling. Half the saloon cleared as Jules had the man's revolver and swung to point it at Max.

Max, already, had his Allen and Thurber Pepperbox revolver out.

Max fired a round that took hunks of wood out of a post by Jules' head. Jules moved toward the staircase that led upstairs. He fired three rounds as he did. All the bullets missed their mark.

"Big John! Ezekiel! James! Matthew! Zack! Damnit! Come on down. I need help!" Jules yelled as the men in the bar formed a semicircle that seemed to be coming for him.

Max fired another round that hit the banister and threw splinters into Jules' face. Jules fired one more round which tore through the lace of Max's fancy shirt and killed him dead.

Jules enjoyed the moment of triumph and the feeling of power as everyone cowered before him—until he saw Sara run to Max's side.

"Why you two-timing whore!" Jules cocked the gun, arrogantly. He looked at Sara and the crowd with contempt. He fired a round that just missed her head. The gun clicked empty. He spit at her, then he bounded up the stairs and began rattling the doorknobs. Jules swung one door open to find Big John in flagrante delicto. He shut the door halfway. "Damn it, Big John! Come on. There's trouble here. We got to go now!"

"Now? I can't go now, Jules," Big John said.

"Damnit, I said come on now!" Jules swung the door open and aimed the empty gun at the girl.

The frightened girl slid out from beneath Big John and ran into the corner of the room. She pulled a Walker colt from a drawer and aimed it at Jules.

"Hold on, Lady. It's just my brother!" Big John paused to admire the gun. He approached her, slowly, and held out his hand.

She, reluctantly, gave the gun to him.

Big John admired the shiny gun, then put it down to dress. He put on his clothes grumbling at every button. He picked up the Walker colt and, awkwardly, put it in his belt. He took a moment to touch the girl's hair, gently.

She gave him a half-smile in return.

Big John followed Jules out of the room just as five men reached the head of the stairs.

Jules turned and yelled at Big John. "Get James and the others. Hurry! You go get them, then you come down this here back way. We gotta leave right now!" Jules instructed as he threw the Sheriff's empty gun away and pulled his long knife from his belt.

Big John put his huge hand firmly on Jules' shoulder. "What's the damn hurry, Jules? You done caused some trouble down there?" Big John cursed.

"Not exactly. I'll explain all that later. `Jest let's get goin'. Now!" Jules instructed.

Big John did not buy it at first. Then ten rounds from several revolvers whizzed by his head. Big John released Jules and backed, slowly, down the hallway. He kicked open the doors to the rooms holding his brothers and routed then from their lover's embraces.

Ten well-armed men filled the hallway with gunfire. Bullets tore into wood and glass and sent splinters into Jules' face, blinding his good eye.

Big John grabbed Jules by the shoulder and pulled him into a deep nook in the hallway.

Bullets made near misses as he crouched and peered into the gunsmoke. Hard as he strained his eyes, Big John saw nothing but muzzle flashes and smoke.

Jules wiped the blood from his good eye and looked hard at Big John.

"You the only one what has a gun. Use it, John!"

Big John, reluctantly, pulled the brand new Walker Colt from his belt.

"I ain't never shot no gun, Jules," Big John said.

Big John's Lady friend poked her head out of the room. A bullet struck her in the heart, killing her, instantly. She fell into Big John's huge arms. He held her, tenderly. He, slowly, lowered her to the floor as bullets whizzed about his head.

Big John was slow to anger but he was furious now. He raised his gun and walked into the gunfire dropping two men with three rounds. The gun clicked empty. Big John picked up the dead men's guns and began firing, as naturally as if he had done it forever.

The guns felt as if they had always belonged in his hands and there was no feeling of remorse to see them fell a man.

Two more men caught hot .44's in their chest and were sent reeling to their deaths. The others scattered. In a matter of moments Big John stood alone in the gunsmoke.

Jules looked at Big John with a mixture of wonder and fear. "We'd better go now," Jules suggested.

James and Sly moved out of their rooms followed by Matthew and Zack. They stared at the dead men and looked puzzled as they saw the smoking guns in Big John's hands.

A broken kerosene lamp soaked the blood red carpet and ignited. The fire spread, rapidly, filling the hallways with smoke.

Big John coughed hard as he moved through the thick smoke.

Jules and his brothers held onto each others shirts. They followed Big John through the smoky hallway in a single file procession like some perverted circus elephant train.

Big John led them to a back window. He kicked it out. They paused, only briefly, to enjoy the smokeless air that rushed in, then, quickly, made their way down the wooden back stairs.

Without hesitation, they mounted their horses and did not look back. In the confusion caused by the fire, they rode fast and hard out of town. They ran the horses until the horses were lathered and spent. They were twenty miles outside of St. Louis when Jules, finally, pulled them over to a stop under a grove of oaks. Sly was still buckling his pants as Jules addressed them. "They done stole most our money. I tried to get it back, but they just held me up. They was too many," Jules intoned in a sorrowful manner.

"You mean we ain't buying into no wagon train. You mean we ain't goin to 'Kalifornee?" Sly almost cried.

"I ain't said that. I said I was robbed. Now, there's ways of getting into wagon trains and there's plenty of them to choose from. Don't go gettin' all riled now. I'm in charge here and I'll get us there!" Jules insisted.

The others looked doubtful, a little scared and very disappointed.

"Besides there ain't no other way. Big John must of killed four men at least back there. 'Iffen we go back they'll hang us for 'shore," Jules sighed.

Big John looked angry. "You 'shore that's the way it happened. Them men was mighty mad at you, Jules. If you lost that money playin' cards then I'm not standin' by you no more!"

"Well if you stole two thousand dollars from a man and that man wanted it back you'd be mad enough to kill him too!" Jules challenged Big John.

"It sounds mighty convenient, Jules. Damnit, Jules they got all . . . all our money!" Matthew was mad.

"Yea. 'Jest like the way I said. You don't believe it you go back there and ask them. Go! Damnit, go!"

"Well I just have to think on it, Jules. That seemed like a peaceable town," Big John said.

"I say let's go on to 'Kalifornee'," Sly offered.

"And jest how you expectin' to do that, stupid?" James snarled. Zack and Matthew nodded agreement.

"You got no call to say I'm "stupid", James!" Sly spit. He looked at Jules. "I didn't get us in this mess, nohow."

"Shut-up, Sly! The rest of you too!" Big John toyed with the fancy shooting irons he had taken from the dead men. He looked, angrily at Jules.

"I think you done, done somethin' that's got us in a whole heap of trouble. I don't know exactly what but I'm thinking of goin' back and finding out."

"John, I told you. They done robbed us. I swear that's God's own truth."

Big John looked doubtful.

"Then let's go back and tell the law," Sly said.

"You are stupid, Sly!" Zack smirked.

Sly and Zack almost jumped each other.

Big John moved between them. "Maybe there is respectable law in that town. Maybe Sly is right, Jules."

"The law?" Jules laughed. He stopped, quickly as he saw the

angry look on Big John's face. "But, John. You done kilt' the sheriff and three of his deputies."

Big John looked doubtful.

"There ain't no goin' back, John. That's the way it is and that's the way it will be," Jules said.

Big John was not convinced. He gripped the handle of his gun. He and Jules had a staring contest.

Jules won.

Big John eased his hand off his gun.

Jules sighed.

"We gotta' find some more horses. These done near 'bout dead." Sly insisted.

"Yep. That's what's up first. Then we gonna' find that small wagon train that we saw in Illinois last week. It was mostly farmers. Them wagons was mostly oxen. We can catch up easy and find us a place with those clodbusters," Jules said soothingly.

"Yeah. They can't be far ahead," Sly said.

Jules looked at Big John with admiration.

"You with me, John?"

Big John looked hard at Jules before he turned his head away in doubt and anger.

"That was 'shore some kind of fancy shootin' for a man that don't know nuthin' 'bout shootin," Jules said.

"Yea, John! That was shore some fancy shootin'," Sly added.

The others smiled in agreement.

Big John looked embarrassed but his anger dissipated for the moment. "We'd better get goin'. They sure to be sending the law after us."

Jules looked back down the empty road.

"Maybe not. That law was in with some crooked gamblers. Maybe the other law ain't so quick to help them," Jules replied.

"You mean the law is on our side?" Sly bubbled.

"No, you idiot! Let's ride!" James huffed.

"You ain't got no business callin' me that, James!"

"Will you two stop it? We got enough trouble without family squabbling!" Big John insisted. "Now let's get goin'!"

They all thought it over for a long moment.

"Which way we goin', Jules?" Sly wondered aloud.

Jules looked at the bright gold of the setting sun. He smiled. "West. We ride West," Jules said, triumphantly, as he kicked at the tired horse. The horse whinnied, weakly, then moved out in a measured trot down the long, winding Missouri road.

Sly, James and Zack rode behind Jules.

Big John and Matthew paused a moment and cursed Jules. They looked at the setting sun. They looked back down the road leading back to Saint Louis. They sighed hard and reluctantly followed Jules Westward.

CHAPTER FOUR

Mid-summer, 1851

—Enroute to The Port of New York

It had taken six months for the wound in Eli's back to completely close and heal over. Without the aid of proper medical care, Eli had suffered fever and delirium and narrowly escaped deadly blood poisoning. The scar from the wound ran half the length of his back and the scar tissue made it difficult to move his right arm freely.

The drunken Doctor The Company finally sent to attend Eli said he was lucky not to have suffered permanent paralysis. Eli had looked him in the eye and told him there was no chance of that ever happening. Not while he had to have two strong hands and arms to pursue those responsible for the death of his wife. The Doctor had looked at him like he was crazy, as did almost anyone Eli told that he was going after the Joshua brothers—except Otello.

Otello wanted them, maybe worse, than Eli.

Neither Eli nor Otello understood how anyone could suffer such pain and loss and not want to make it right before God and man. Yet many of their friends advised against it. The talk was that California was a distant place of vast territory where men could hide from their past successfully. They all thought that the chances of the Joshua brothers finding their way there were slim. Everyone agreed that, all things considered, finding the Joshua brothers would be near to impossible.

Everyone but Eli and Otello.

Eli and Otello agreed that it was not something to think about. It was something to be done, and to be done with zeal, dispatch and unwavering devotion.

This bright September day as Eli and Otello bounced in the stagecoach on the road to the port of New York, Eli felt the pain but did not flinch. He forced himself, with the limited mobility in his right arm, to comb his thick dark hair. The stiffness in his arm was a mere nuisance.

Physical pain never bothered Eli.

When it did, he could force it down and out of his system until business at hand was finished.

It was mental anguish that gnawed at him like an abscessed tooth.

Mental pain, deep inside—a bottomless permanent paralysis of the heart that ate at his soul. A persistent, nagging spiritual ache that hurt constantly. An elusive pain where he could not get his big hands on it and bust it with his fist to make it go away, that tortured him.

It was the haunting belief that he should have been there when Lydia needed him, and was not, that, as strong as he was, made him pause almost to fainting when it was upon him.

Eli looked at Otello sitting across from him. He was thankful for Otello's help but ashamed he had needed it.

Eli would always think fondly of the good, decent hard-working miners he had known. Eli had been too ill to attend the simple funeral the good-hearted, secret Miner's Brotherhood had given his beloved wife. As well as, the even more simple one for Jeremiah. Poor in cash money, the best people of the mining community always tried to do the right thing. Eli would never wax sentimental about his life in the mines.

The only thing worth remembering in that place of misery was now dead but it was a good thing to recall an honest hand extended to help in a troubled time.

The first day the feeling returned to his legs, Eli had wobbled his way to Lydia's grave. In his fever he had hoped it was all a bad dream. In the bright sunlight of a new Spring, he knew it was not a dream and he had cried his tears of grief, inside where the world could not watch and judge, and make sport. Holding Lydia's Celtic Crucifix in his hand, he had dismissed those tears as a sign of weakness and vowed to never cry again—inside or out.

The Joshua brothers, for all their imagined cunning, had not found all the money. Eli was too smart a Welshman to put all his loaves in one basket. With the $250.00 that was not taken, Eli had hatched his plan to pursue the Joshua brothers to the ends of the earth.

Eli and Otello had stood by Lydia's grave and the smaller one for "Horse". They had looked deep into each other's eyes—each other's souls. That day a silent but forever binding oath passed between them.

They would do what had to be done and God help any man who got in their way.

The first day he could tolerate the bone-jarring ride of a stagecoach, Eli, with Otello at his side, had left Pottsville Pennslyvannia and not looked back. Eli knew the $250.00 was not enough to join a wagon train to California. Since overland was out of the question, Eli and Otello had made their way to the Port of New York where he hoped, by God's grace and pure luck, he might locate his father's old friend Captain "Sam" Samuels. In any case, it was his plan to go by ship to he gold fields of California as he had heard they were looking for able-bodied men to ship aboard cargo vessels heading for the gold fields.

Otello watched Eli with interest as the coach drivers managed to hit every pothole in the deeply rutted road. Otello knew the jarring hurt Eli. He smiled with respect and admiration as he watched Eli endure the pain without so much as a flinch.

Otello was happy he had cast his lot with such a man. Otello's stomach knotted from the rage he felt at The Joshua brothers. His mind was clear of guilt and his thoughts focused. There was no hesitation in his purpose.

Otello would take his vengeance without remorse.

Eli Looked out of the window at the vastness of the New York countryside. He sighed as he remembered it was said, California was even bigger. For a brief moment Eli wondered at the enormity of the task before him. He had been told that New York was a town of almost a million people. Eli could not imagine that many people all in one place. Eli figured such tales were just braggarts' lies and that no such place existed on the face of the earth. Eli took comfort in the knowledge that there were reported to be many less people in California.

"The port of New York!" The stagecoach driver yelled out before Eli realized they were entering the outskirts of the city.

"My Lord, it's even bigger than the braggarts bragged," Otello said as he looked out of the stagecoach window at the teeming city of New York and the harbor full of sailing vessels and steamships.

In the distance ahead of the stagecoach, Eli could see the Hudson river spilling into New York Bay and a port where there seemed to be an endless waterfront teeming with people. "Good God, Almighty! Where on earth did all those people come from?"

"You think there be this many in 'kalifornee?" Otello wondered aloud.

"God knows I hope not," Eli replied.

Otello nodded agreement.

Eli pulled the yellowed piece of paper his father had given him so long ago, from his pocket. He looked at it and remembered, fondly, his father reading it to him as he told tales of leaving Wales by ship and sailing the stormy Atlantic. Eli's father had left the terrible conditions of the copper mines of Wales for the dream of a better life in America, only to end up dead of a fire in the mines at an early age. Eli couldn't read but he remembered the letter as his father had recited it:

"Captain Samuel James Samuels

The Barque Valiant

Port of New York

On receipt of this letter, you will know that one of mine is in need of your help.

In the spirit of our good friendship, and the eternal brotherhood of Welshmen, please render what assistance you can.   Signed, Eli Aberystwyth Llynne Sr."

Eli looked at the words and wished he could read them. He promised himself that as soon as this business with the Joshua brothers was over, he would hire a teacher to teach him to read.

Otello watched Eli study the letter. Otello looked at his small satchel that contained the book of Shakespeare's plays including his namesake, "Othello" He vowed that someday he would learn to read. He would learn to read and after he had finished his business with The Joshua Brothers, he would find his father and mother.

The Port of New York was a very scary and yet very exciting place. Eli had never dreamed that there could be any place that could hold so many people, speaking so many different languages, dressed in such fine clothes.

His first thought was that it was too many people to be in one place and he would not be abiding here too long.

To Eli's unsophisticated eyes, The Port of New York was a great city full of young energies but the hustle and bustle of such crowds were disturbing to Eli's sense of quiet order.

Eli looked at the letter once more. Once more he regretted he could not read it. He placed the letter back in his pocket and looked out of the stagecoach window with apprehension and wonder.

If Eli or Otello had be able to read, this September of 1851, they could have read the first edition of The New York Times describing the defeat of the Washington baseball team by the New York Knickerbockers at Red House Grounds. Or the invention of the sewing machine by Isaac Singer. Or the declaration of independence by Cuba.

But neither Eli or Otello could read and it was not time for reading. It was past time for finding Captain Samuels and heading for the gold fields of California.

Eli's heart sank as he looked out over the harbor. The cold reality of the futility of his task loomed in a dark forest of unbroken sailing masts that seemed to blot out the sun and obscure the distant horizon.

The harbor was jam-packed with hundreds of ships of every description. A man could almost walk across them like giant lily pads. Flags of all kinds flew from their masts and foreign-looking sailors were aboard.

"Mister Eli?" Otello mused aloud.

"I see 'em, Otello. I see 'em," Eli sighed. "Don't you worry none. Captain Samuel's ship will be here. We'll find it soon enough," Eli forced himself to be optimistic. Eli decided that it was simply a matter of hard work and trusting his senses. His senses had always led him to the highest grade coal seams and they would led him to Captain Samuels. The Barque "Valiant" was out there somewhere and he would find it.

Otello looked for any hint of doubt in Eli's eyes. He was glad he did not see it.

It was a beautiful clear late summer day and there was a pleasant breeze coming off the harbor. Eli breathed in the air and relished its sweetness. Due to the generosity of a few sympathetic miners, Eli had an extra pair of pants, a change of socks, the embroidered handkerchief, the Celtic Crucifix Lydia had loved dearly and a lot of hope when he left Pennsylvania.

Eli also had the remainder of the money Jules had not taken. He and Otello had vowed to live as frugally as possible. They would not spend a dime except in obtaining sure and certain information of the whereabouts of the Joshua brothers.

For knowledge of their whereabouts Eli and Otello would gladly sell their souls.

Being basically peaceable men, they had no idea, exactly what they would do upon finding the Joshua brothers. They reckoned they would find them first and figure the rest out later. They had determined it to be a day at a time thing for how ever long it took. Both Eli and Otello were patient men who deal with each day's mischief as it was dealt them.

As they stood on the dock in New York Harbor and looked at

the sheer numbers of the ships and people, they both wondered where to start looking.

If Eli were in a mine shaft he would start by touching the wall and letting his senses tune in to the vibrations of the earth. Eli got along well with the earth. Eli respected the earth and though he had taken much from it and had never failed to be grateful for what the earth had provided.

Eli walked slowly along the dock and touched the sides of ships.

Otello watched without worry. He trusted Eli's instincts. The only man he thought had better ones than himself.

Eli let his hand linger on the rough wood surface and tried to tune his senses to this new search. He paid no heed to the strange looks that people gave him. He trusted his feelings to lead him in the right direction.

After hours of searching, Eli could feel no harmony with the ships. He did not despair but figured it would just take longer than he thought.

"We could rest up and take a fresh start on the morning, Mister Eli," Otello offered.

Eli shook his head "No!". He sat on a piling and wondered what to do. He withdrew Lydia's Celtic Crucifix wrapped in the embroidered handkerchief and fondled it. He replaced it and looked over the masts of the ships wondering which one, if any, might belong to Captain Samuels.

"Looking for work?" A hoarse voice boomed.

"No, Sir. I'm looking to find the Barque Valiant and Captain Samuels," Eli addressed the man in the nice dark suit with shiny buttons and a white hat.

"Hmmpphh! Well, you'll not be finding him or the Valiant. They went down off the Cape ten years ago. Every man jack!" The man looked sad for a brief moment.

"No. That can't be. I have this letter and it just can't be!" Eli pulled the letter from his frayed coat pocket and waved it like a magic wand.

"Please?" The man offered his hand and looked at the crumpled

letter.
"Eli looked at Otello.
"Otello shrugged.
"Eli handed the letter to the stranger.
"The stranger opened and read it with obvious relish. He looked deep into Eli's eyes as if he knew him. He re-read the note several times. He paused and looked out across the harbor as he lit a pipe and took several puffs. "Captain Samuels was a good man. I sailed with him. He will be sorely missed in these parts. You look like a strapping lad. Tell me, have you ever sailed before?"
"No sir, and it don't look like I'm gonna' either."
"You don't know me, do you, laddie?"
"I'm not a "laddie". I'm full grown," Eli snapped.
"I can readily see that. My apologies. I'm Captain Isaiah Hopkins."
Eli and Otello exchanged dubious glances.
"Really! No flim flam. I sailed with Captain Samuels as a young lad . . . and I knew Eli Llynne. We both escaped the copper mines of Wales together. He sailed with us six months before he decided he was a landlubber. Pennslyvannia? Wasn't it?"
"Yes, sir. He didn't like the water so much as the land. He said he left the ships because he spent too much time on the rail. Whatever that means."
"You're his boy for sure. You favor him, mightily. He is a good man. Is he with you?"
"No, sir."
"I see. The mines?"
"Yes, sir."
Captain Hopkins paused and shook his head. "He should of stayed at sea. If you're half the man he was, you'll do fine," Captain Hopkins said as he stroked his long beard.
"Do what?"
"Sailing . . . aboard a ship. My ship. It's not the Valiant but she's a damn good one!"
Eli looked at Otello. Otello looked doubtful.

"We don't neither one of us know much 'bout sailing. But we could use passage."

"I'm all booked up with passengers, but I can use another deck hand," Captain Hopkins paused and looked Otello over. "He's with you?"

"Yes! Yes, sir. He is," Eli said, quickly.

"I see," Captain Hopkins thought it over. "Not your kin?" he wondered aloud,

"Same as, sir." Eli replied firmly.

"I see," Captain Hopkins was hesitant.

"You go on, Mister Eli. I'll get there some other way," Otello offered.

"Hush up, Otello! There'll be none of that kind of talk," Eli snapped.

Otello half-smiled.

Captain Hopkins looked them both over and thought about it. "Otello, eh? Not english? That's a certainty. A right sturdy-looking fellow."

"He carries more than his load," Eli offered.

"You don't have to be standing up for me, Mister Eli," Otello gave Captain Hopkins a steady gaze. "You show me what needs lifting and I'll be lifting it!"

"I see," Captain Hopkins pondered it once more.

"You pay us one man's wages and give us both passage and you'll get the work of four men," Eli said.

The Captain's eyes could not hide his thrifty soul. "Now that's a business proposition no man could turn down," he chuckled. "What you boys don't know about sailing, I suppose I can teach you. It's not about thinking anyways. It's, mostly, about hard work. If you're Eli's boy you aren't afraid of hard work."

"I know hard work. I can carry my own weight. Except I'm a little stiff in my right arm . . . but it don't hold me back none!"

"A mining accident?"

"Yes, Cap'n."

"I see. Well, that's fine by me. What do you say . . . what's your handle?"

"Eli. Like my father and his. And this is Otello."

"Eli? You're his namesake?"

"Yes, Cap'n. I have his name but I don't pretend to be his equal!"

"Well we'll see what sort of stuff both of you have. I'm a fair man but I don't put up with slackers."

"If there's work on a ship a willin' hand can do, I'll do it. We need to go to California in the worst way."

Otello nodded agreement.

"Yes. That you must. You come up here from Pottsville in this madness hoping to find one ship among a thousand and one man among a million?" Captain Hopkins wondered aloud.

"I trusted to my senses . . . and they seem to be doin' `jest fine." Eli looked pleased.

"I can't be denying that. You must want to get there real bad. I'll tell you, I haven't seen anything like this gold fever in all my days," Captain Hopkins said as he lit his pipe.

"It ain't gold fever. It's personal business," Otello almost growled.

Eli gave Otello a hard look.

Otello nodded understanding.

Captain Hopkins looked deep into Eli's eyes for a moment before replying. "Personal business. You ain't running from the law, are you, Mr. Llynne?"

"No sir. I'm a hard working decent God fearing man . . . as is my friend here. If you'll take us on your boat you'll see."

"Yep. Well, everybody runs to something for some reason. Yes, I have a "boat" and I'd be glad to sign on Eli Llynne's son."

Captain Hopkins paused and took a long look at the Otello " . . . and his friend. Come along. I'll show you my "boat"," Captain Hopkins said with a smile.

Eli and Otello did not hesitate. They followed the Captain as he led them along the crowded wharf until they stood before the biggest ship Eli had ever seen.

"That sure is some boat alright, Captain!" Eli was obviously impressed.

"This "boat" is the clipper "Silver Cloud". She weighs in at 1,783 tons. We haul coal, tools and mining equipment. We're the fastest ship in this harbor. She can go around the horn in less than ninety days with favorable winds. Now how's that for a "boat", Mr. Llynne?" Captain Hopkins asked as he enjoyed the look of amazement in Eli's and Otello's eyes.

"It's a real fine one, Cap'n. I would be proud to sail on this one," Otello added.

"Then you shall!" Captain Hopkins led them onto the spotless deck of the towering ship. "Johnson, sign this man on. Give Eli here work on the rigging. Put him in with Scotty," Captain Hopkins ordered a scruffy looking sailor who was sitting behind a small desk on the dock.

A line of anxious men stood in front of the desk and Eli felt embarrassed to cut in.

Captain Hopkins moved the men in the line back with one wave of his hand.

Eli turned to thank the Captain but he had already moved out snapping orders to scurrying sailors.

Johnson seemed irritated by the interruption. He looked Eli over, quickly. He took a long look at Otello.

Eli saw the negative look in Johnson's eye. "I'm Eli Llynne and this is . . . is my brother, Otello."

"Not likely," Johnson smirked.

"You want me to go get the Cap'n to vouch for us?" Eli asked firmly.

Johnson squirmed in his seat as he thought it over. "You do what you like, but, first, both of you make a mark here," Johnson handed Eli a pen and pointed to a piece of parchment.

Eli hesitated a moment, then made his "X" on the parchment.

Otello took the pen and made a similar mark.

"You go aft by the mizzen mast down below in the deckhouse. You'll both bunk in on the port side!" Johnson ordered.

Eli started to ask what the hell he was talking about. He decided he'd take his chances at getting lost rather than looking stupid. Otello nodded agreement.

They, slowly, walked down the deck that moved to and fro with the timid waves of the harbor current. Even that slight movement made Eli and Otello feel uneasy and their legs wobbled slightly.

They both hoped no one was looking.

Eli looked around, quickly, and was relieved to see that no one was looking directly at him. He took a deep breath and blew it out hard as he wondered where "aft" was. He looked out at the endless sea running to the horizon and remembered he couldn't swim a lick. He knew then why his father had decided to become a "landlubber." "Ain't `nuthin gonna happen to this big ship that would cause me to have to swim. I'll just do my best and we'll be in California before I know it." Eli assured himself as he whispered under his breath.

"Amen to that, Mister Eli!" Otello agreed.

"First time out, Laddies?" A cherubic man asked as he chuckled at them both.

"I'm not a laddie. Address me with respect or don't be talking to me!" Eli snapped.

"Don't be snapping at me. I wasn't belittling your greenhorn ways. I saw something of me younger days in the way you rocked in the quiet sea," The tall, friendly looking man said as he held up his hands.

"I'm sorry. There's a lot on my neck these days," Eli shrugged.

"I'm Douglas MacDougal, they call me Scotty," he offered his hand.

Eli shook it and smiled back. "I'm Eli Llynne. Pleased to make your acquaintance. This is my . . . friend Otello Jones."

Scotty hesitated a moment before he shook Otello's hand. "I heard you told Johnson you was related," Scotty needled.

"He was pressing me a mite too much," Eli replied.

Scotty half-smiled and shook Otello's hand. "Well on this ship what the boys is really strong about, is slackers. There'll be no trouble if he's a good hand," Scotty said calmly.

"There'll be no cause for anyone worrying 'bout that," Otello replied firmly.

Scotty shrugged with some indifference.

"Hey, you! Over here!" A huge bearded man yelled at Eli.

"Me?" Eli replied.

"Better go. That's the Frenchman. He's First Mate," Scotty said and moved aside.

Eli moved, slowly, across the deck toward the big man.

Otello followed at a short distance.

"You? You the two laggards the Captain has given me in the place of able bodied seamen?" The Frenchman grumbled.

Eli stood a head taller and fifty pounds of muscle heavier than "Frenchie". "I don't expect you know me well enough to be callin' me names!" He glared down at Frenchie.

Frenchie scoffed. "I don't care to know you at all." He pointed to an open passageway. "You both go down there and stow your . . . where is your gear?"

"This is all I have." Eli held up the small bag.

". . . and I." Otello held up a smaller bag.

The Frenchman wiped his brow. He looked at them both with disdain.

"The Captain he sends me all these slackers. '*Les Miserables*'. You have never sailed, no?"

Eli did not back down. "You will not call me a slacker. I am an unashamed workman that does well at whatever I put to my hand to."

"*Sacre' Bleu*! You are a cousin of *Le Capitan*' or a friend of a friend? I do not care! I do not know how this captain keeps his license. You will quarter in the port side hold. Please try not to sink us," he sighed.

"I do not come here as a beggar. In the mines, I was the quota-maker!" Eli insisted.

The Frenchman eyed Eli with contempt. "The months

ahead will decide what kind of men we all are. The Cape will wean out any slackers very quickly. Now get below with the rest! We sail soon." The Frenchman huffed, then turned and walked away.

Eli watched him go and trembled with anger.

Scotty moved up behind him. "You'd like to bust his head?"

"It ain't nothing I can't handle, thank you."

"Aye! I believe that well enough. Just be careful with the timing. A short fuse can get you in more trouble than you need."

Eli wondered at himself. He used to be so slow to anger. Now he seethed inside at even the smallest perceived insult. "Please just show me what to do. Tell me where to go and I'll be mighty grateful to you."

Scotty looked at Eli with concern and curiosity.

Scotty studied Otello's face. He saw the same deep etched pain on both of them. Scotty had never met such young men with such an, obviously heavy weight on their shoulders. He wondered and worried. "There will be a season for the busting of heads. This is not that season. Be careful, my friends. The men on this vessel are as hard and unpredictable as the seas they sail. You will not be seeing as scurvy a lot anywhere."

Eli started to challenge Scotty's notion. He knew the worst man on this ship could not be as bad as the kindest Joshua brother. Eli thought he would make a needed friend instead. "Thank you, Scotty. We'll be watching our backsides."

"Good! Good, Laddies. Now come I'll show you what this strange beast is like on the inside," Scotty said as he moved inside a dark passageway.

Eli and Otello waited only an instant, then followed.

Once in the narrow passageways of the ship's innards, Eli froze in his tracks. A terrible feeling of claustrophobia he had never felt before almost overwhelmed him. His legs wobbled and he felt faint.

"Eli? Are you alright?" Otello looked worried.

Eli staggered a little before he replied.

"I think my father called it "sea legs". I do not have them yet. I'm okay." Eli insisted.

"Yes. They'll be coming. You'll do fine," Scotty said.

Eli was not so sure. He fought the dizziness with all his strength. Since the early days of his youth, he had crawled about narrow, dark places with ease. Never, in all that time, did he feel as cramped and confined as he did now. He had survived cave-ins and methane gas explosions and, never once, had he felt as frightened as he felt now.

The huge exposed timbers of the ship's interior reminded him of the wooden beams supporting mine shafts. Each time they creaked, Eli's skin crawled.

The narrow passageway was almost identical to a mine shaft and the lanterns glow that lit their path was just like that of a miner's hat.

Eli did not like the feeling of near panic. Panic and the fear it generated were foreign to his being. He was determined not to let it get the best of him.

Otello turned and looked at him with concern. "You want to go back topside?"

"No!" Eli's eyes insisted

Otello returned a steady gaze of concern.

Scotty stopped and looked deep into Eli's eyes.

"I was only nine when I first came down here. As a wee lad there was a lot more room to move in. They build 'em to haul things, not people. We can go back topside for a wee bit."

"No! If it is to be done it should be done now!" Eli insisted. "Thank you, Scotty. How much further is it?"

"Not too much further. I realize it's tight in this part of the ship so you just let Scotty know if he's going too fast. Okay?"

"Okay. It's okay." Eli sighed hard and tried to assure himself as Scotty led him down the dark passageway into the even darker decks below.

CHAPTER FIVE

Off The Coast of South America

The Silver Cloud was a majestic ship. A sky tall windjammer that could stir the heart of any sea-going man. A fully ship-rigged, three masted, Boston built "California Clipper", she was 210 feet from stem to stern and had the extreme sharp bow of the fastest clippers of the day. Captain Hopkins often boasted, but had never proven, that she had made twenty knots per hour on one trip around the horn. Whether or not she had ever made twenty knots, the Silver Cloud was fully capable of sustained speeds of fifteen to seventeen knots per hour. Running before a favorable wind, perhaps, she made the good Captain an honest man.

She carried a crew of forty men when fully manned. Such was the lure of the gold fields, that this day she was running with a crew of 21 men, the absolute margin of safety for foul weather sailing.

A fact Captain Hopkins had failed to mention to Eli and Otello upon recruitment.

Captain Hopkins had also failed to mention that, he felt in his bones, this would be the ship's last voyage.

The Silver Cloud had been built for speed and in so doing cargo space had been sacrificed. Instead of a broad beam like steamships, she was slender and well trimmed and beautiful. Steamships, to the Captain's mind, where broad-assed whores and unfit to weigh anchor beside the Silver Cloud.

With steamships undercutting the rates he could charge for freight and sailors abandoning ship at the first sighting of California,

Captain Hopkins did not expect to be returning to New York and on to his home in Boston.

They were a month at sea before both Eli and Otello got over the desire to heave their guts every time the horizon moved.

The Frenchman took great delight in their misery. Scotty took a liking to them and became a good friend.

Eli was glad to have such a friend. Particularly, in his moments of melancholy enhanced by Jamaican Rum.

Golden Jamaican Rum, the pleasures of which Scotty had hastened to introduce to him.

Eli had been given a strong Welsh religious upbringing and the thought of strong drink was not ever uppermost in his mind.

Eli had seen it used by miners, like Jeremiah, to kill the pain of "Miner's Asthma", but he had also seen it lead to sinful and riotous living.

"Me ancestors would be haunting me regularly if they knew I be drinking anything but the finest scotch whiskey. They not be allowing any of it aboard this vessel, this rum be all there is," Scotty smiled.

"Rum you say?" Eli looked uninterested.

"Rum?" Otello repeated.

"Aye. Rum it be, Laddies. So here's to your health and a safe voyage," Scotty said as they shared a pint of rum the sixth week at sea.

Eli frowned as he looked at the burnt-brown liquid. "Never did hold much for strong drink, but this has a pleasantness about it. A mite on the sweet side."

"Aye, that it does. For a foreign drink it's just about drinkable," Scotty laughed.

Eli smiled then laughed.

Otello coughed and put his cup down almost full. Otello had a fondness for hard liquor but it had no respect for him. He thought it best to keep his distance from it.

Scotty studied their faces as he sipped from his cup. Scotty was no busybody but he had to know what ailed these men. "It's none of my business but you Laddies appear to carry a heavy weight around. If it be anything you want to talk about, when you're taking your ration of rum be the time," Scotty probed.

Eli and Otello exchanged glances. They thought it over. They decided to pass.

"I think maybe we just look to be the tired men that we are," Eli said

"I believe everyone aboard this ship is running from someone or something. There's no shame in it, be it lawful, or in some cases, unlawful."

"Lawful?" Otello almost laughed.

"We are not ones to put stock in the law, Scotty," Eli sighed.

"Be that as it may. I'm not one to pry, but you're young laddies with bright futures 'afore 'ya. If you're running from the law, you be in the right place. This vessel is damn near nigh a prison ship. We be so short next trip we'll be gang pressing . . .,"

Scotty stopped himself.

Eli did not pick up on Scotty's verbal mistake.

Scotty did not realize Eli had no way of knowing what "gang pressing" meant.

"We come this way on personal business, Scotty. We run from no man. Thanks for asking anyways," Eli said.

"I'm sorry, Laddie. I seen the ugly scar on your back. They done that in them mines?"

Eli winced, slightly, as he nodded "Yes."

"You were a young boy down in those pits?" Scotty pressed.

"Just past my sixth birthday. It was a birthday present," Eli paused and swilled some rum. "Some birthday present, eh?"

"Aye! They love the wee ones in those tight seams. Aye, I remember it well."

"How is it you came to sea, Scotty?" Otello wondered.

Scotty thought it over a long moment. "It was easy. It was the sea or the mines of the Firth of Forth. My father was a collier. The lowest of the low. A slave by an act of parliament. I owe my life to him. Such freedom as I have he gave me by not "arling" me to the company at birth."

"Arling? Yes I heard talk of it from the Scotsmen in Pottsville," Eli sympathized.

"Aye. A sort of pledge that I would be the company's slave for the duration of me life in exchange for a few shillings. I tell you, Eli, there is no circumstance that could compel me to go down into the mines, evermore. Not man or beast or God!"

Eli and Otello nodded agreement.

Scotty took a long drink and looked mighty angry. "My brother died there at the age of eight and my sister at the age of eleven. My father lasted until he was twenty seven."

"Maybe the gold mines is different?" Eli said.

"Nope. Mines is mines is mines. Wet seams or dry, narrow shaft or open—it don't matter, they're all below the earth and God never intended man to go down in that hell until after he dies," Scotty said.

Eli started to reply, but the ship lurched, sharply, to one side and threw him off balance.

Scotty's eyes narrowed and he looked worried. "It's the beginning. The first squall off the point. We'll be headed into the straits full in a few hours." Scotty looked at the creaking timbers of the ship.

"Maybe there's one thing worse than a mine."

"What might that be, Scotty?"

Scotty paused and watched the ship rock in the high wind. "Aye, maybe it be a small ship in the full of a storm at the Horn is worse. Aye, we'll soon see, Laddie. We'll soon see," Scotty swallowed hard. "I'd best be getting to me post. Your watch is after mine, and Otello's after that. You can have another pull or two if you're a mind to," Scotty said. He put down his mug and made the sign of the cross as he left.

"I think I've had enough," Eli said.

Scotty was out of the room and did not reply.

Eli and Otello stayed behind for a moment and watched the lantern begin to sway back and forth in an ever increasing arc. His nostrils picked up the smell of wet, raw coal coming from the cargo bay. The smell that had once been so familiar was now foreign and nauseating.

"You smell it too?" Otello asked.

"They be carrying a load of low grade anthracite."

Otello agreed with his eyes.

Eli started to put down his cup. Instead he took two long pulls and emptied it completely. He took deep breaths as he watched the ship begin to rock and the creaking of the timbers become louder and louder.

No mine shaft had ever closed in on him like it seemed the ship's bowels were about to. Fighting the onrush of fear, Eli decided to start his watch early.

"I'll be heading up topside. You stay here if you're a mind to," Eli said.

Otello looked at the creaking timbers. His eyes hinted at the fear inside. "I just as soon be topside with you."

Eli did not reply. At a measured pace, he made his way up to the angry sea slapping the decks above.

Eli was happy to be on the outside no matter how angry the wind. It was strange, but for a man who couldn't swim, Eli did not fear the sea. Indeed, the rolling sea held a certain fascination. If you did not fear them, the huge waves were imposing works of God. They came with an invigorating wind of untainted, fresh air that soothed, for a time, all the damage the thick, acrid coal dust had ever done to his lungs.

Eli did not fear anything the world outside could throw at him. But he knew something deep inside was wrong and he no longer could tolerate enclosed spaces. He stayed topside as much as possible. As he, slowly, got his sea legs and became adjusted to the ship's routine, Eli thought that he made a passable sailor. The pride Eli took in everything he did would not let him do otherwise.

Frenchie did not agree and seemed to pick Eli out for the scrounge details more often than any other sailor. Captain Hopkins always seemed to be looking over Eli's shoulder and watching.

However, he never interfered with any action his first mate, Frenchie, took no matter how unjust it seemed.

As the weeks had passed, Eli had come to understand that Captain Hopkins loved the majestic ship and his love was only surpassed by Frenchies'.

Eli did not quite understand how men could love a ship above their fellowman, or like a wife. He only knew that Frenchie and Captain Hopkins talked about their ship like he used to talk about Lydia.

Eli could never love a ship or anything like he had loved her.

"Look at how she holds the wind and runs before the sea. Have you ever seen anything like this ship Eli?" Captain Hopkins asked as he stepped up behind Eli.

Otello backed away and busied himself with checking the foul weather gear.

"No. No, sir. It's a fine one alright."

"Only a few more weeks and we'll be in San Francisco. Tell me, Eli will you be sailing back with us?"

"I don't think so Captain. I'll most probably be there awhile."

"I see. Well I could use you. Most certainly, I'll lose most of this crew to gold fever. Captain Mitchell lost his crew and had to sell his ship for lack of replacements. I'll pay double wages if you want to sail back with us, Eli. Frenchie says you have the makings of a good sailor," Captain Hopkins looked pleased.

Eli was dumfounded. He looked at Captain Hopkins, doubtfully. "Frenchie said that? About me?"

"Surprised? Frenchie judges a man hard but fairly. I will hold a spot for you until we sail back. Maybe your personal business will not be taking as long as you imagine?"

"I have no way of knowing. I will have to stay however long it takes. But I have been proud to sail with you. I would be proud to do it again."

"We shall see. Nothing changes so fast as a man's fortunes in the gold country these days. There has never been, in my experience, anything going on like what is going on in California these days."

"I long to see it for myself," Eli replied.

"Ah, the lust for gold is such a destructive thing to many who retrieve little or nothing for their efforts. But it is something to see, alright."

"The fever has not affected you, Captain?"

Captain Hopkins looked insulted. He looked out at the majesty of the high waves slapping at the side of his sturdy ship. He looked deep into Eli's eyes. "I have seen men kill men over a half-ounce of gold dust. Men have abandoned wives and children. Men have turned into half-crazed animals. For what?" He held his gold watch in his hand. "For a shiny metal and the price it brings. No, the sea is my only passion, Eli. That is passion enough."

Eli stared at the sea quietly a moment. "I'm sorry Cap'n. I didn't mean nothin'. Except I done seen well enough what evil men will do for money."

"Don't let the fever get you, Eli. You seem to be a good man. I don't know what your personal business is, but don't let that gold madness seep into your soul. It will destroy you."

"I ain't goin' there looking for gold, Cap'n. But I know them what are. If it destroys them. That's all to the good."

"I see. Well, good luck in your quest, my friend. Whatever it is," Captain Hopkins smiled and walked off. Eli stood up tall in the high wind. He took a deep breath and blew it out hard.

"Let's get a move on, sailor. Don't be standing there taking up space." Frenchie's voice broke into Eli's reverie.

"Aye, sir!" Eli snapped as he moved smartly down the deck. "Aye, you big old phoney," Eli mumbled to himself. His smile almost dispelled the dark mood created by the storm clouds moving in over Cabo Dungeness and the entrance to the strait of Magellan.

CHAPTER SIX

September 1851

—The Oregon Trail

In the manner of a wolfpack after a wounded stag, the Joshua brothers stalked the wagon train for weeks. They followed at a safe distance watching and waiting, probing and backing off. They licked their lean, hungry chops until they decided the wagon train was weak enough to prey upon.

They waited until the wagon train had moved past the sun-bleached limestone of towering Chimney rock on the high flat plains of Nebraska. They held back until it had passed the lessor presence of Jailhouse and Courthouse rocks, and moved beyond the massive promontory of Scott's Bluff.

Most of all, they waited until it had passed the protection of the army at Fort Laramie. They lay back until the wagon train was into the wilds between Fort Laramie and the North Fork of the Platte River.

They had received quite a scare when a herd of buffalo, which seemed to be coming right at the wagon train, parted just before reaching it and thundered off over the horizon. Once their fear of the buffalo was past, they used it as a food source and had survived on dried meat until they tired of it. They longed for some of the beefsteak the cowmen in the wagon train cooked up each night. The hunger inducing smell of the smoke from the charring meat causing them to salivate like ravenous timber wolves.

"I ain't seen nuthin' but, mostly, sodbusters, children and

women folk. There is nine armed men. They sure don't look like too much. I want me a big beefsteak," Sly said as the Joshua brothers sat upon their horses on a high hill overlooking the wagon train encampment.

It was twilight and the ancient spires of the limestone rock monuments that filled the valley, were outlined like giant tombstones in the shadows cast by the lingering sunset. The campfires of the wagon train cast an eerie glow as Sly sniffed at the wind.

"Lordie, mercy! That ain't beefsteak, Sly. That's beans and pork for sure!" Zack salivated.

Jules and the others smelled the aroma, as well.

"I agree. This hardtack and buffalo jerky done wore my teeth out," Matthew said.

"We gonna' go down there and eat now, Jules?" Sly asked anxiously.

"I don't think it's a good time yet. Let's wait until they get fed good and get real tired," James said.

Big John agreed with James.

Jules thought it over as he watched the activity of the encampment. Jules was as cautions as the leader of a wolfpack. He was also as hungry for hot food as the others. "Well I shore don't expect they's `jest gonna' invite us to dinner? `Jest like that? When we ain't even dressed in Sunday going-to-meeting clothes?" "I expect not, Jules. But John, he's got two guns!" Sly spurted before Jules stopped him.

"We ain't riding in there shootin', you `ijit! There's too many. We's gonna' start off polite and see where it gits' us. Now, we ride in nice and easy and I do all the talking. John, you hide them guns."

Big John shook his head in defiance.

Jules frowned at him then shrugged. He dusted himself off. He spit into his hand and slicked down his matted hair.

The others, except Big John and Matthew, followed Jules' lead.

Jule's tired, over-ridden, horse shivered beneath his weight as Jules kneed the unfortunate animal into motion. The others followed, in single file as they, quietly, descended the hill into the long valley.

The wagon train was made up of two dozen wagons composed of decent, hardworking, god-fearing Ohio folk. They were not "sodbusters" as Sly thought, but English and German "Cowmen". Theirs was not the quest for gold but for good cattle country far from the "overcrowded" environs of the Ohio Valley. They were not cattlemen by training but by nature and temperament. They resented all the fences they had left behind them. They had not yet taken on the hard edges that they would develop upon the advent of barbed wire.

The lure of "open range" was as compelling to them as the lure of gold was to the "Forty Niners."

Eric Gabrielson, the wagonmaster, affectionately called "The Swede", watched with apprehension as he saw the six riders make their way down the hillside. His instincts told him there was trouble in those saddles.

From the beginning, Eric had worried about the skimpy make-up of this wagon train.

Eric had been given no money to hire outriders and his only experience with a gun was deer hunting. He did not like the look of the Joshua brothers from the moment they rode into camp. He was busy with the maintenance of two broken wagons and did not greet them at first. He watched as they rode in like they were invited. He shook his head as they pushed in at a cooking campfire. A campfire where his wife Martha gave then a plate as if they had earned their keep.

Eric stopped working on the wagons. He stood up to his full six feet five inches and moved, purposefully, to meet the Joshua brothers.

They were busy eating his beans when Eric approached. Eric looked at Martha with censure. "What's going on here, Martha?" Eric grumped as he stepped up and looked The Joshua brothers over. Their unkempt appearance made him itch.

"Oh, Eric. These are the Joshua brothers. They want to join the wagon train. You were late so I asked them to share our supper," Martha tried to smile.

"Doggoneit, Woman! You know this train is overcrowded already," Eric paused. "It ain't that we're not hospitable. It's just that . . . like I said, we lost a provision wagon at the last river crossing."

Jules and his brothers stuffed their mouths as if Eric was not addressing them.

"You're welcome to that plate but, like I say, we're short on provisions ourselves."

"We didn't eat much. This is just my fourth helping," Sly chuckled through his missing teeth.

The Joshua brothers laughed.

All except Jules. "We've been riding mighty hard and we're kinda lost. But if you don't want to share a little christian charity with us, I understand." Jules threw his plate to the ground.

Martha, quickly, picked it up and put it aside. She got a clean plate, heaped it with beans and pork, and handed it to him. Not since Judas gave Jesus a kiss was cordiality so wrongly placed.

"That's right kind of you Ma'am. I'll remember you in my prayers this very night," Jules chortled.

"Thank you but that won't be . . ."

"Where you fella's from?" Eric interrupted.

"Penns . . . ," Sly started to speak. He was interrupted by Jules.

"We're from all over. We drifted up . . . up . . . from Texas. Just looking for a good place to settle. We thought we might try Oregon."

"I see. Well, I'd really like to help you out, but there's just no way to accommodate you. I'm sorry. We can give you enough food for only a few days."

"No. If it's all the same we'll finish these beans and be on our way," Jules grinned. He tipped his hat to Martha. "Thank you kindly, ma'am," Jules said as he gave her his plate and moved to his horse.

The others followed.

Eric looked at the Joshua brothers horses. He was appalled. The white foam of excessive riding oozed from their mouths. Their eyes were red with weariness. Eric had the cattleman's love and respect for horses. He could not believe what he saw. "Wait. Wait just a minute!" Eric moved between Jules and his horse. "You won't be riding this animal nowhere for awhile!"

"What's it to you, mister?" Zack, who's horse was in the worst shape, challenged.

Eric glared at Zack. "I've never seen animals in this bad of shape. I don't care where you're from or where you're going or why. There's no call for treating an animal this way." Eric waved a young boy over. "David, I want you to get some help. Take these horses and water them good. Then feed them and brush them down. No one is to ride them until I say so."

David looked at the horses. He looked at the Joshua brothers. He moved to get help.

"You expect to take a man's horse 'jest like that?" Jules put his hand on his long knife.

Big John pulled his coat aside.

Eric looked at the two Walker Colts in Big John's belt. "How far did you expect to get on those poor animals. Can't you see they're rode near too death?"

"It's none of your damned business!" Sly snarled.

Jules held up his hand. "No, maybe it is his business. It's okay. Don't it say in the bible an eye for an eye. A tooth for a tooth?"

"That's what it says alright," Sly agreed.

"Then if he takes six horses. We take six horses and God's justice is done," Jules said.

"That's not going to happen. We don't have six horses to spare. You can just sit tight until those animals are fed and well rested. That's all," Eric said. He backed off looking for his rifle.

Jules walked up to Eric and glared in Eric's face.

"My brothers and I truly appreciate your hospitality. Your wife has tried mightily but the beans were a mite salty. Now, we're going to take six horses or join this here train. That's all there is to it."

"You don't just ride in here and give any orders, mister. I'm the wagonmaster here. You can bed down tonight while those animals rest, but you'll be gone in the morning."

"We'll be goin' when we want to be goin'. If you have something to say 'bout that, say it to Big John here. He's done got three notches on his gun and there's room for lots more." Jules threatened as Big John stood taller than the Wagonmaster.

Eric saw the crudely cut notches in Big John's gun. He wanted to laugh but thought better of it.

"Martha, you go inside the wagon and see to your sewing!" Eric stepped around Big John.

Martha started to object. "You boys are welcome to what's left in the pot. Everyone else has eaten."

"Now, Martha! Please."

Martha hesitated, then moved toward the wagon.

Eric waited until she had left before he addressed the Joshua brothers. "I don't know just who the hell you fellows think you are, but there's people here that will have something to say about you taking any horses or joining this here train. Now, there is no need for any trouble. Trouble won't do any of us any good. So you eat, rest and prepare to leave in the morning."

"No! I don't see it that way 'atall," Jules said.

"Mister, you're trying my patience," Eric replied.

Jules looked angry then gave Eric a wry smile. "I expect we did get off to a bad start. But we're both men of responsibility."

"I don't think so . . ."

"You have the people in this here wagon train. I have my brothers. We can speak, man to man, about being the leaders and what all comes with it."

"I, really, don't think so . . ."

"Well think again, mister! You ain't tryin' one bit to be reasonable. Are you?"

"You've heard my terms. They remain the only offer I will propose."

"Oh? Well here's what I 'prepose! Big John here has brand new colts. Ezekiel's got a breach loader rifle. We's all good at using guns. You need the help going over the mountains and we need you to show us the way West. It's a fair bargain as can be made," Jules drew close to Eric and blew his foul hot breath at Eric's face.

"Then you got the wrong train for sure. We're headed up to the open range in Montana." Eric seemed relieved as he turned his face away.

Jules looked doubtful.

Jules looked at the other Joshua brothers. They looked blank. "I don't believe you, mister. No body is goin' to Montana when they can be goin' to California." Jules paused and took one of the Colts from Big John's belt. He played with it a long moment.

"California? I thought you said Oregon." Eric looked suspicious.

"It don't make no never mind. Wherever this wagon is goin' so is we." Jules spat through his teeth.

Eric started to pick up a rifle he had leaned against a wagon wheel.

Big John put his huge hand on a Colt's handle.

"Like you said, mister. There ain't no need for trouble," Jules said coldly.

Eric took a deep breath and sighed, then he shuddered, angrily. "You ride along if you've a mind to, but I wouldn't rile these people too much. They look a little ragged but them looks are deceiving. Yes, sir, you ride along but don't rile nobody too much."

Jules grinned. "Now that's the christian thing to do, ain't it?"

The reference to religion by the likes of Jules Joshua was too much for Eric to stomach.

"Like I said. We're going to Montana. If you want, I'll point the way to California for you in the morning. I'll see if Martha can put together a few days rations. That's my best offer," Eric sighed hard.

Jules kicked at the dust and stirred the spoon in the pot of beans. "Well why don't we 'jest sleep on it and see what we feel like tomorrow?"

"Yes. You can spread your bedrolls in the clearing behind the last wagon. The wake up bell will be rung an hour before first light. Goodnight . . . gentlemen."

Eric gave them one last look then turned and walked away. Jules and his brothers watched him go.

"We stayin', Jules?" Zack wondered.

"Yes. We'll spread our bed roles right here by this fire."

"But we ain't goin' to Montana?" Sly looked puzzled.

Jules gave Sly a hard look. He turned his back on him and ate a spoonful of beans. He looked at the others. He frowned, looked westward and smiled. "No we ain't goin' to Montana!" Jules paused. He spat. "And neither is this here wagon train."

CHAPTER SEVEN

Eli was coughing and it made him fearful. He had watched Jeremiah dying from "miners asthma" and he had hoped it would never affect him. But he was coughing hard now and he would rather have a bullet in the head than to waste away with such a disease.

Otello had watched his friend with interest and concern. Otello saw Eli as a fearless man who's quiet strength was admirable. Otello modeled his behavior after Eli's. In all the time he had known Eli, Otello had never seen Eli afraid—except when he had a coughing spell. Otello was helpless to do anything for Eli except stand in the shadows and be there if needed.

The deck was rolling in heavy seas off the coast of "Tierra Del Fuego", the sailors dreaded passage through the Cape of Good Hope that lay ahead. As he coughed, Eli wobbled until he felt a firm hand on his shoulder.

"Laddie? Laddie, what's the matter now? This is not a time to be bothered with the consumption," Scotty offered.

Eli coughed, silently, for a moment. "Thank you, Scotty. It's nothing. Just a touch of hay fever," Eli said.

Otello stood in the shadows and smiled.

"Are you okay?" Scotty wondered.

"Yes! Of course!"

Scotty chuckled, then looked serious. "It's the miner's cough, Eli. There's no denying it. You stay topside much as you can. This ocean air is a damn sight healthier than down there in the deep part of this ship," Scotty said.

Eli started to deny Scotty's truth. He thought better of it. "It ain't nuthin' I can't handle! . . . you mind not telling the Cap'n?"

"Tell him what?" Scotty shrugged. "It's okay, Laddie. Captain Hopkins sees only what a man produces. We have seen you work on the rigging when your stomach was sick. You would be one helluva sailor if you wanted to stay with us but you will be leaving us in San Francisco," Scotty paused and looked at the dark, foreboding sky "... if we make it to San Francisco."

"More of that "Deadman's Cape" stuff, Scotty? Still trying to scare a greenhorn, right?" Eli looked doubtful.

Scotty's eyes took on the serious look of a man who had been severely frightened. "I wouldn't be tellin' it but that it be true. The ocean has been good to me and I have reason to love it. But not in this place," Scotty sighed.

Eli still looked disbelieving.

"Look at the sea around us. It's simmering now. Soon it will begin to boil faster than a tea kettle. When it begins to boil, everyman Jack better get his soul right with his maker," Scotty intoned ominously.

Eli half-smiled.

Scotty looked upset. "You don't believe me? You don't think this ocean is a killer?"

"Maybe so. But I tell you, Scotty, nothing on this earth will kill me before I take care of my personal business. Not God, or man. Not the devil himself or even a boiling sea."

Scotty looked deep into Eli's angry eyes. He nodded understanding. "Your eyes, they tell of a lust for vengeance."

"Vengeance? No ... Justice."

"Justice comes out of the law, Eli."

"The law? Ha! The Company Sheriff? He was most probably in on the killin'."

"They ... someone killed someone dear to you?"

"Dear to me? Yes. I think I done said enough. No need to get you involved in personal business," Eli said. He winced and backed off.

Otello moved out of the shadows. His face was contorted with anger. "They had no right to kill no dumb animal."

"Did I miss something?" Scotty wondered.

"Otello, this ain't nobody's never mind. Okay?" Eli snapped.

"No, Eli. I don't agree. I say we take any help we can, anywhere we can. Maybe Scotty heard something in his travels?"

"Aye, that be the truth! Lot's more than I wanted to hear," Scotty chuckled.

Eli and Otello exchanged hard looks. Neither would back down, but each mellowed just enough to avoid harm to their friendship.

"Mister Eli can say or not say what he wants. The truth is we're after some bad men what done a terrible thing to both of us!" Otello gritted his teeth.

Eli stepped in between Otello and Scotty. He nodded agreement. "You ever been married, Scotty?"

"Good Lord, no! I get conniption fits just being close to a woman. This matter involved your wife?"

Eli's sad eyes answered.

"And who is it you would be killing to take this vengeance? This justice?" Scotty asked.

"They be the Joshua brothers. The godless Joshua brothers! They killed my bride," Eli paused as his throat grew tight. "Just killed her dead. Killed her and my brother and took off running to California like those rats in the hold down below. Except those rats don't kill their kind!" Eli spit into the wind.

"They killed my dog," Otello grimaced.

"I'm sorry, Eli. That's as bad a thing as I've ever heard tell of. They killed a dog?"

Otello's eyes answered.

"Aye, that's a helluva' thing alright. I'll be glad to help in any way," Scotty said.

"You don't need to bother yourself none, Scotty. It's just Otello and me what needs to get this done," Eli looked at Otello with concern. "Mostly me."

"That's a mighty heavy load even for a man as big as you, Eli," Scotty said.

"No, sir! It ain't nuthin' I can't handle. I will find all six of 'em. I will kill 'em every one!" Eli held fast to a lanyard in the ever increasing wind.

Scotty studied the unwavering look in Eli's eyes. He looked at Otello. Otello's eyes were just as hard.

"That's a right mean anger you boys have inside. A man has to be careful with such anger. Sometimes it can destroy a man's soul."

"That might be true but it don't change what I have to do."

"Eli, it's none of my business. It's a bad thing they did. That's true enough. You are two men . . . . . two good men. I give you due respect, but California is a big place. These men, they could be anywhere. The gold has been found on a thousand hills. How could you find six men in such a huge place?" Scotty wondered as Eli looked away for a moment.

"Scotty, I like you. You have been a good friend. I tell you, Scotty they will go where the gold is easy to take. They will not go down in mines. They will go to places where it can be stolen easily. They can be smelled they stink so bad. You will find them at dry diggin's. They never liked a wet seam. I'll find them where the digging is easiest. That's where!"

Eli looked at Scotty with cold determined eyes. Scotty had never seen such a malevolent look in his life. "Oh!" Scotty shrugged as the force of the wind threw him up against the forecastle.

Another stronger gust forced Eli and Otello flat against the main mast.

"Aye. Maybe you will find these lads, but first, we have to get around this beast and safely into the Pacific. First we beat this devil then we can look for yours," Scotty said as he helped Eli to his feet.

Eli reached back and helped Otello up.

"My, God! I've never seen water go that high or move that fast," Eli exclaimed just before a wave hit the deck and knocked Otello rolling down the deck. Eli was about to go help Otello when another wave knocked his feet out from under him. Eli tumbled, uncontrollably down the deck, until a big hand grabbed him and pulled him aside.

"Get the double O canvas up there on the top sail mates! Hurry! Get all the other canvas down. Get to it now!" Frenchie thundered as he ran about the deck encouraging the men.

Eli watched the big Frenchman with some respect, as Frenchie seemed to defy the wind.

"You stay on the deck. You help with the sail when it's down. I don't want you on the ratlines," Frenchie instructed Eli, forcibly.

"This will be a real `pampero'. When that dark cloud up ahead hits, all hell will break loose. Stay close by the rope on the companionway," Scotty added after the Frenchman had moved on down the deck.

"Nothing to report on the lookout. The lights are clear!" The lookout on the forecastle yelled.

Captain Hopkins nodded acknowledgement as he moved back to check the canvas, now square-rigged to protect Frenchie who took the wheel. Frenchie held the wheel tight as salt-water pounded his body hard.

"Stand in tight, Frenchie this will be a big blow. More than the others I fear!" Captain Hopkins yelled into the wind.

"I'll keep her south-southwest, Captain. Don't worry none about that," Frenchie yelled back.

Captain Hopkins was about to move down the deck when a huge wave hit the Silver Cloud broadside. It rocked her into a steep list that sent him sliding hard against a bulkhead. Fifty feet above, a boom broke loose and pulled a lanyard along the deck so fast Captain Hopkins could not get out of the way.

The lanyard was pulled upward by the falling boom and the high wind whipped it about the Captain's neck like a noose. As the boom crashed into the deck, the Captain was hoisted upward in the noose two feet off the deck as if by some ghostly hangman hiding in the rigging.

Frenchie watched with horror as his Captain swung to and fro in the wind. He, quickly, tied down the wheel and was about to move to the Captain's aid.

Before he could act, a thunderous wave tore his square canvas cover loose and washed Frenchie into a bulkhead knocking him unconscious.

There was dark ice and cold, wet snow in the wind now. Small icebergs floated by the ship. A huge black cloud was directly overhead and it brought with it all that Scotty had promised.

The wind blew a gale out of the Northwest that held the ship still for a moment. Then the wind shifted, suddenly Southwest. Then, quickly, due West again. The shorthanded crew could not get the sails down in time and the wind filled the sails with anger. The full sails jerked the ship back against herself so violently that the main mast snapped off and crashed onto the deck. It killed three crewmen instantly.

A huge wave hit the port side moments later and washed Scotty and two crewmen into the deck well.

Eli was washed down the deck and hit his head hard on a spar. He was dizzy, but not unconscious, as his eyes fell on the Captain dangling from the rigging. The Captain's eyes were bulging and his tongue was already swollen. The grim reaper had a bony hand on the Captain's shoulder and would escort him to eternity in a matter of moments.

The ship was at the bottom of a great swell, as Eli wobbled to his feet and climbed up on a bulkhead. He made his way beside Frenchie, lying at the Captain's feet.

Frantically, Eli fumbled for the big knife Frenchie always carried as the ship rose to the crest of the swell. Huge, ice-laden waves poured over the deck and their fury was only matched by their coldness.

Eli's fingers were numb from the cold. His heavy oilskins were almost frozen and paralysis was creeping into his right arm. He shivered as he managed to free Frenchies' knife from the sheath.

Captain Hopkins was coughing blood as he jerked to and fro in the high wind. He struggled with all his strength trying to free the rope from his neck.

The ship paused at the top of a wave crest, then fell fast. Eli found it almost impossible to keep his feet. He, also found it almost impossible to lift the knife in his right hand. The cold and the scar tissue from the old wound locked his arm up and he cursed as he tried to make it free itself—it would not move.

Eli took one more look at the Captain and moved the knife to his left hand. The ship was tossed about so violently now that Eli despaired he could reach the Captain, much less cut the rope with his left hand.

The look of terror in the Captain's eyes as he gasped for breath, prompted Eli to make one last effort.

Eli braced himself on the top of a slippery bulkhead. He clinched the wet knife handle hard. He waited until the ship began a downward fall. The fall took Eli's feet out from under him just as he swung the big blade at the rope around the Captain's neck.

Eli never saw the result of his efforts because he was thrown to the deck and rendered unconscious.

The Captain hung in the air for an instant after the rope was cut. Then he fell, hard, to the deck. He lay motionless a long moment before, with his last ounce of strength, he ripped the rope from his neck.

Captain Hopkins got to his knees and took large, wonderful, gasps of air deep into his lungs. He crawled over and looked at Eli laying supine on the deck. "God . . . bless . . . you. God bless you!" Captain Hopkins bent over and kissed Eli on the forehead.

Eli did not move.

"Eli? Wake up, Eli? Help! Get me some help over here. Let's get this man below. Now!" Captain Hopkins rasped into the unyielding wind.

CHAPTER EIGHT

Late September 1851

—The Oregon Trail

Eric Gabrielson and nine other men crept, slowly, across the meadow towards the grove of trees where the Joshua brothers lay sleeping. The big harvest moon was too bright for Eric's liking but he was determined to do what had to be done this night.

The Joshua brothers had made him a laughing stock. They had mocked him and his people, daily. They had pushed their way into his train and he was going to push them right back out.

The night was cold and there was a hint of snow in the air. Eric wore a heavy coat but he was uncomfortably warm. A man of some fierce pride, he could not stop his palms from sweating or make all the fear flee from his gut. He gritted his teeth as he approached to within fifty yards of the six blanket rolls lying on the ground in the middle of the grove.

Eric fondled his double barreled Needham shotgun. He snapped it open and checked his load. The nine men behind him, similarly armed, checked their loads and moved up closer beside Eric. A cold wind blew across the prairie and Eric turned his collar to the wind.

"Pa, you plan to do any shooting if they resist?" David, Eric's son asked nervously.

"We'll do what we have to do to get them gone."

"But Pa, I ain't never shot nothin'. Not even a deer or nothin'!" David chortled.

"I'm not asking you to shoot anybody. I'm asking you to make them believe you would shoot. That'll be enough. You just hold your mouth firm and look them in the eye. My guess is the likes of them is, mostly, cowards anyways," Eric said.

An older man drew up beside Eric. "They's a rowdy bunch, Eric. You think they'll be coming back after we done run 'em off?"

"No. Ssssssh! Just be ready and stand behind me. I'll do the talking." Eric took a deep breath and blew it out hard. He paused as they were now on top of the six scattered blanket rolls. "Jules Joshua, it's Eric, the wagonmaster. Wake up!" Eric poked at the first bundle with the tip of his shotgun barrel.

There was no answer and no movement from the bundle. Eric poked it harder. He began to feel uneasy when the barrel touched nothing but wool. He almost dropped his gun when he heard the click of a revolver from behind his back.

"You looking for me, Eric?" Jules Joshua stepped out into the moonlight holding one of Big John's revolvers. He cocked the gun and aimed at Eric's gut.

The other Joshua brothers stepped out from behind him. Big John brandished a revolver. Sly held a breech loading rifle he had stolen from a drunk on the trail.

Three of the men with Eric dropped their guns and ran.

Eric turned and swallowed hard as he replied. "You're going to have to leave this train. There ain't room for you. You and your brothers have been molesting and disturbing the womenfolk. Besides you didn't pay your rightful share like the rest. I want you gone, Jules Joshua. I want you gone tonight," Eric said.

"Well that's fine, Eric. That's 'jest fine. But supposing' I don't want to go tonight?" Jules grinned. Big John moved up beside Jules. The Walker Colt he held in his hand weighed five pounds but Big John handled it like it was a feather.

"I don't want no bad trouble, Jules. I just want you to pack up and leave quiet," Eric said.

"I ain't leaving quiet or any other way, wagonmaster. Not tonight or any night," Jules glared.

Eric, nervously, leveled his shotgun at Jules' stomach and gripped the handle tightly. "That's right, Jules. I am the wagonmaster and I'm telling you one more time, I want you gone!" Eric blew hard.

Jules turned his head and spit into the wind. He turned back and chuckled under his breath for a moment before he replied. "You'd better get back to the wagons with the womenfolk, Mr. Wagonmaster, while I still have a mind to let you go back." Jules insisted as he toyed with the hammer of his revolver.

"I'm not going back until you're gone, Jules Joshua. We came here to see you gone and that's what we're going to do."

"We?" Jules chuckled.

Eric was puzzled for a brief moment. He looked around and found he was alone, except for his son David. He turned back just in time to see the muzzle of Jules' gun flash and hear the report. He did not see the slug crash into his heart and throw him to the ground dead.

David looked at his dead father, then looked at Jules. "You done `kilt my, Pa! Well damn you!" David raised his gun to fire. He pulled the trigger and nothing happened.

In his haste he had forgotten to load it.

Jules was frightened until he heard the rifle click empty. When he was satisfied he was safe, Jules smiled wryly. "Damn me? Is that what you said?"

"You `kilt my Pa! You had no call to do that." David, backed away nervously. He looked down at his father's shotgun lying on the ground.

"Go ahead. Pick it up. It ain't in me to shoot an unarmed man," Jules chortled.

"He's just a boy, Jules," Matthew interrupted.

"Not if he picks up that gun he ain't!" Jules smirked at David.

"No. I ain't no boy!" David snapped his voice trembling with fear.

Jules looked around at his brothers. They were not totally pleased, but remained silent. "Well, Mister. Let's see you show us how a "Man" would handle this affair," Jules said.

David looked at Jules in disbelief as he moved, slowly, to pick up the gun.

Jules followed David's head with the barrel of his colt.

David knelt beside his father a moment then reached his hand out for the shotgun.

"How do you know that one is loaded?" Jules toyed with the young boy.

The Joshua brothers nervously laughed at Jules' cruel joke. All except Big John.

David thought it over for an instant. He looked at his dead father and anger overcame his fear. He grabbed the shotgun and started to fire.

Jules waited until David had the shotgun half-way aimed before he fired four rounds into David's chest. David rocked to and fro for a minute before he dropped the shotgun and fell over his father's body.

Jules looked almost sad for a brief moment.

Sly walked through the acrid gunsmoke over to Eric's body. He picked up Eric's shotgun and looked at David who was still twitching in death throes. He pressed the barrel of the shotgun hard against David's back and discharged both barrels. "Guess what, Jules. This one was loaded!" Sly danced a perverted jig.

Jules balled his fist and punched Sly full in the face.

Sly fell to the ground hard.

He looked up at Jules and spit blood. "What'd you do that for?"

"I ain't for killin' no younguns'. You saw I was sorely provoked. That there boy was just a little too big for his britches. You my witnesses," Jules said almost apologetically.

Big John frowned then nodded agreement. The others did likewise. Big John grabbed Sly by the shoulder and helped him up. "What about the others, Jules?" Big John wondered. "Them folks ain't gonna believe it was self defense."

"I don't give a damn what they think. Burying the wagonmaster will make them all true believers in minding their own business.

We won't have no further trouble. This wagon train is now the Joshua train and we'll be taking it down the Joshua Trail to California," Jules said.

"Ain't it the Oregon Trail, Jules?" Sly wondered aloud.

"Not no more it ain't," Jules grinned as he put his revolver away and moved toward the encampment to claim his prize.

CHAPTER NINE

November 1851

—San Francisco

When James W. Marshall, accidently discovered gold in the tailrace of Sutter's Mill in 1848, he was simply trying to dig a little deeper ditch. Neither he, nor his mentor John Sutter, had any idea of what his discovery foretold.

Even in an era without telegraph, wireless, pony express or any form of quick communication the news of the discovery spread fast. It spread so fast that by the winter of 1851 there were over a hundred thousand prospectors in the California gold country from countries all around the world.

Many of those who came were honest, decent folk who wanted to work hard make a good strike and return home to enrich those they had left behind. They had no way to know there were many—far too many—who came to take, in the quickest way possible, by fair means or foul, all others had earned by hard labor.

California in 1851 was still in transition from being a Mexican possession to being a fledgling state. Where there was law, it was a mixture of Mexican law, laws of the United States and local laws. Laws that changed as fast as the emotions of mankind can change—which is damn fast when you're talking about earning twenty thousand dollars a day from even small claims.

When Eli and Otello disembarked from the Silver Cloud, there were hundreds of ships of all shapes and sizes anchored in San Francisco Bay. There were three bodies hanging from a gallows with a sign reading: "Compliments of the California Vigilante Committee."

The California Vigilante Committee was not an outlaw group of lynch crazy '49ers, but a loose confederation of men who were "vigilant" to the lawlessness of the era. They began as a reaction to the influx of New York street toughs, called "The Hounds" who came to California with no intention of mining gold when it could be easily obtained by thievery. The Hounds were not blood kin to the Joshua brothers but would have felt at home in their company. The Hounds used blackjacks more than six-shooters and had a particular bent for terrorizing and murdering Mexicans, Chinese and "darkies" for sport.

As long as their malevolence was limited to these minorities, The Hounds were more or less tolerated. It was when they blackjacked a claim-jumping white man to death that the ire of the citizenry was aroused and The California Vigilante Committee was formed to deal with it. The day the committee was formed they proceeded to roust The Hounds from their tents and hung them high. In a tribute to the committee's extraordinary sense of justice, a New York lawyer who attempted to come to the defense of The Hounds was accused of "horse trading" the law and hung also.

Eli looked at the faces of the bodies. He was relieved no one had beat him to the Joshua brothers.

"Welcome to Frisco. Keep your eyes open and your money close to you person. Here everyman is a law unto himself," Captain Hopkins said. He looked back out over the harbor. From the moment the Silver Cloud limped into port he had worried about what he was going to do with her. The harbor was crammed with ships abandoned by their crews who had fled to the hills the moment the ships dropped anchor. It was no different for the crew of the Silver Cloud. Although Captain Hopkins threatened them and tried to ply them with three months wages in advance, he could not retain his crew.

He also knew, there was no likely possibility of raising another without resorting to shanghaiing. Captain Hopkins knew ship's captains who had no problem with sailing with a crew of gang-pressed men—mostly drunks or criminals with little or no sailing experience. But that was not his way.

As majority owner, Captain Hopkins had three choices. He could sink The Silver Cloud, sell her or rent her out as a hotel. He had already had three offers to sell her but they were all below what he felt his great ship was worth even in a storm damaged condition. Finally, it was his decision to rent her out as a hotel. He decided on this option in the belief that he could wait until the damned gold fever left enough able-bodied men to make up a crew.

He prayed it would not be a long time before the gold fever died down and good men could be encouraged to put out to sea once again. That was what he hoped in his great sea-loving heart. In his mind he knew it would be a long time, if ever, before this fever left men. He had spent five grueling hours in the shipmaster's office working out an agreement to let her be used as a hotel. It was a bitter compromise. It was, also, a sad thing to do.

Captain Hopkins could hardly bear to look at the beautiful ship as he moved his gear onto the dock and stood beside Eli, Otello, Frenchie and Scotty. "Well, damn it! If I can't sail her, I'll let them make a hotel out of her! God forgive me, it's as painful a thing as I have ever done," Captain Hopkins swore to the empty timbers of his ship.

They all nodded agreement as they walked down the crowded docks of San Francisco and admired the beauty of the fog clinging to the gentle rolling hills.

"It's a right beautiful land," Eli said as he stepped on the new land for his first time.

"Look at the hills. They *are* golden," Otello admired.

"I know they're out there somewhere. Somewhere where the gold is easiest, they're out there," Eli whispered under his breath. "I can feel it."

Otello looked into Eli's eyes and understanding passed between them.

"What did you say. Eli?" Scotty probed.

"Nothin'. Just admiring the view."
"So you haven't changed your mind, Eli?" Captain Hopkins shook his head, sadly.
"Sir?"
"Eli, you have the eyes of a man who hunts men. That is why you are here?" Eli looked at Scotty. Scotty shook his head "No!" He looked at Otello. Otello shrugged.
"No one has to tell me, Eli. You saved my life. Whatever you want to do I can not condemn. I will say that vengeance is a consuming fire. It burns everyone it touches. I ask you to consider leaving it in the hands of the Lord."
"I'm sorry, Cap'n. It ain't exactly like that."
"I see. Then good luck to you. May God bless your efforts." Captain Hopkins paused. "Do you know which way you might be headed? Do you need financing?"
"No, Cap'n. The generous wages and the bonus you've paid is more than enough. You have my undying gratitude." Eli reached to shake The Captain's hand.
"I don't want your gratitude. I want to see what I can do to repay my debt to you."
Eli looked puzzled. "As I said, the wages and bonus are mighty generous."
"You don't think an old seadog like me is going up in those hills without a great deal of help, do you?" Captain Hopkins gestured toward the hills across the bay as he lit his pipe.
"You'll be going up there?" Otello wondered.
"Yes, Otello. I want to accompany you and Eli. I want to help in any way I can."
"Well, Cap'n that's hardly necessary," Eli said.
"Come on, Eli. The Chinese say that I am your servant for life!"
"Sir? What about the Silver Cloud. You couldn't just leave such a lovely ship," Eli replied.
"Oh? And who will sail her for me? Will you, Scotty? Frenchie?"

The Captain challenged as he rubbed the black and blue rope burn around his neck.

"I'll sail with you anytime, anywhere, *Mon Capitan*!" Frenchie almost saluted.

"Aye, I would too sir, but first I'd like to take me chances in those gold fields. If it's all the same to you," Scotty replied.

"Tell you what, Lads. We'll go down to the Brass Rail saloon and see Millie. The paperwork on the ship should be done and ready for signing. I'll go sign them while Millie acquaints you with her finest ladies. I'll meet you there as soon as I'm done and we'll really celebrate. Then we'll take Eli and Otello up in those hills and see what we can find," Captain Hopkins said as he put his arm around Eli's shoulder.

"Cap'n Hopkins, I can't let you do that. This is personal business . . . real personal business. Me and Otello is plenty enough. Nobody else needs to get messed up in this."

"And you can't stop me either, Mister Llynne. It's a free country and since I'm going no matter what, why don't we go together? What do you say, Otello?"

"I'm sorry Cap'n. I say what he says."

"Six men be too much even for two men as ready and able as these two are, Cap'n," Scotty smirked. "But I say they couldn't take the four of us!"

"The five of us!" Frenchie stepped up.

"Six men? You are after six men? Good, Lord! Then it's settled. We will accompany you," Captain Hopkins insisted.

Eli and Otello looked at each other and agreed with their eyes that they did not like it. They also agreed to play it out, as it was, for now.

"I would ask that you not go. But if you must, you will step aside when the time comes," Eli said.

"Aye. We'll step aside and watch with interest when that time comes. Enough said. It's time to celebrate life. To the Brass Rail with you!" The Captain ordered.

"Aye, Cap'n. Today is a glorious day for celebrating it. Right this way, Laddies. I'll buy the first round and kiss the first woman!" Scotty laughed.

"I'm not much of a drinkin' man, Scotty. But I'll hold your coat while you kiss the ladies," Eli smiled. He started to cough. He was able to hold it back, easily.

Otello smiled understanding "This is right good air for a man's body. I ain't a drinking man neither. Maybe I'll just wait here for you boys."

Eli nodded agreement as he breathed in the sweet San Francisco air. "Maybe I'd better wait with Otello."

Captain Hopkins looked at the concern in Otello's eyes and thought it over. "You will like it here, Otello. There's lot's of bad things about, but there is not too much prying into people's business. In general you'll find, out here, they take a man for what he is."

Otello was not so sure, but he was willing to take the Captain at his word. "I have enjoyed a beer on occasion, Mister Eli?"

"You understand, I do not wish to tarry long, Cap'n?" Eli insisted.

"Of course, I understand. Even knights in shining armor must feast before the crusades."

Eli nodded slow agreement.

"Now go with Scotty and I'll join you shortly," Captain Hopkins said.

"Aye, follow me, but the solid land does feel strange. I don't know how long I'll be able to take all this quiet walking," Scotty mused.

"If we go up in those hills and strike it rich, Scotty, I'll buy you a schooner." Frenchie smiled. "Maybe two," Frenchie offered as they turned down a great hill lined with tents.

"You boys headed up to the gold fields?" A grizzled old man asked as he stepped out of an alleyway Eli, with Otello, Frenchie, Scotty and the Captain trailing behind, paused from their climb up the steep San Francisco hill. Eli started to pass.

"You're sure goin' at the right time. Why just yesterday they had a strike over at Dry Diggins and just last week the biggest find of all at Auburn. Didja' hear about Whiskey Joe's find at Grass

Valley? He was looking for his cow and stubbed his toe on a nugget that weighed two pounds!"

Eli was not amused. He started to push by the old geezer.

Scotty and Frenchie stood back and watched.

"Yes, siree. You done come at a good time. Couldn't be better unless the Mexicans and Keskydees weren't crowding in . . . ," The old man paused and looked at Frenchie.

Frenchie grimaced.

"Well anyways, I'm the man what will get you outfitted with all the latest equipment. Yes, siree! You need go no further."

Frenchie was a little irritated. "Keskydee" was a derogatory term for Frenchman. "No! We have already made some arrangements to buy our gear, step aside, *Monsieur*," he said.

"It don't make no never mind. I'm cheaper and I got options on all of the best horses out of Stockton stables. If you want to sluice or pan or dig it, I got it all."

"Then how come you ain't up there in the hills with everybody else?" Eli challenged.

Otello nodded, admiringly.

The old man was stumped for just a moment. "Well, I done been up there and got mine. How do you think I can buy all this fancy equipment?" He pulled up the balking mules loaded with tinkling pots and pans and mining equipment.

"It looks good, but as Frenchie told you, we done made other arrangements," Eli insisted as two men turned the corner at the bottom of the hill.

The old man's eyes bulged as he looked at the two men. Before he could move, they opened fire—both with twin colts. The old man dropped the horses' reins and took off across the street and into an alley. Bullets went ricocheting off the ground all around him. Eli, Otello, Scotty, Frenchie and Captain Hopkins headed for cover. They watched with intense interest as the two gunmen ran by them and pursued the old man down the alley.

"*Wee*! No wonder they call it the wild west," Frenchie mused aloud as he hid under a carriage.

There were a dozen more shots.

Then quiet.

Then two shots in rapid succession followed by one more angry shot.

Then quiet once more.

Moments later, the two gunmen came out of the alley looking pleased. They walked over and grabbed the pack mule's and horse's reins.

Eli, slowly, eased out from behind the water trough where he had taken cover.

"Did you boys give Mulehead Johnson any money?" A gunman with a thick mustache offered

"You mean the old man?" Captain Hopkins asked.

"The one and the same!"

Eli nodded "No!" as he looked at the gunman's twin colts with admiration.

"He was about to sell our mules and this horse for the third time today. You're lucky. He sells them, then his bandit friends steal them back."

"Yep. But he ain't selling nothin' no more," A tall thin gunman added as he stroked a shiny new colt affectionately. He took out a knife and whittled a notch into his gun handle. The gun handle was riddled with notches.

Eli looked at it with great interest.

"You guys just in, eh? Heading out for the gold fields today?" The gunman asked.

"That's right," Captain Hopkins replied.

"Well, I can sell you these animals. They know the way and they're sturdy enough. This one horse here is a champion runner. You'll get a bill of sale. All legal and everything."

"Thanks anyway, but I don't think so," Captain Hopkins wondered.

"Well, it's your tough luck, Mister. These would go cheap and there's everything you need except guns." Captain Hopkins waved them away.

Eli looked at the mustached gunman's twin colts and stepped in front of the Captain. "I suppose a man needs a real good gun out here. Those are fine looking guns you have there. What are they?" Eli asked.

The man pulled one of the shiny revolvers from his belt. "It's a Colt, model 1851. This is one of the first made. Only weighs three pounds," The man bubbled with pride as he handed the gun to Eli for his inspection.

"What would a gun like this bring?"

"This one? A lot of money . . . two hundred, maybe more."

"That's a lot for a gun."

"It's a lot of gun."

"I'll give you one hundred for it."

"One fifty."

Eli stepped back and thought it over.

"How much for the mules, that horse, the equipment and the all the guns?" Captain Hopkins asked.

"Five thousand dollars. A helluva bargain for these parts."

Captain Hopkins looked at Eli. Eli looked back as if to say, "Don't look at me."

"I'll give you thirty two hundred and I want a bill of sale, itemized, signed and duly witnessed." Captain Hopkins said firmly.

The gunman looked at his partner. His partner shrugged. "Make it forty two hundred and you've got yourself a deal."

"Thirty seven hundred and that's my last offer."

"Okay. Thirty seven hundred dollars it is. Welcome to the gold country, mister. May you find a bonanza and may you live to enjoy it," The mustached gunman said. He grinned before he broke into a loud raucous unnerving laugh.

Captain Hopkins wondered if he had done the right thing. "So, why is it you boys aren't up in the hills?" Captain Hopkins asked as he counted out the money.

"We done had our go. Since '49. We picked up a right good sum but we decided we're city boys. We miss Boston," The tall gunman said.

"Boston lads are ya'?" Captain Hopkins
"Born and bred!"
"Well I can understand your wanting to go home." Captain Hopkins waxed melancholy a moment. "Tell me, where are the best strikes at these days?"
"That's easy. The Southern mines." The tall gunman seemed sincere.
"Southern mines?" Eli wondered aloud.
"Yep, down by Sonora. They took out almost two hundred thousand in pure gold in one day. You'd better take a big gun and lots of ammunition. There's lots of trouble with the Mexicans and Tongs down there."
The mustached gunman handed Eli the revolvers.
Eli took the guns and hefted them, gently. He gave one to Captain Hopkins. The other he gripped and smiled as he liked the way it felt in his hand.
"Yes sir, that's a good gun there," The tall gunman said as studied the strange look in Eli's eyes.
Eli ran his fingers over five notches in the handle of the gun. He looked puzzled.
The mustached gunman smiled, knowingly. "There's more than that been `kilt with that there gun, mister. After awhile cuttin' more seems like unnecessary braggin'. If it bothers you, you can have the handles redone down the street."
"These cuts . . . notches . . . they are for men you done kilt'?" Eli wondered aloud.
"Yep. Like I said, I should cut maybe two three more. Both them colts is mighty straight shootin' irons. I wouldn't sell `em to anybody. But you look like you'll be takin' good care of `em."
"Yes! I will. I truly will!" Eli insisted.
Otello watched and, quietly, agreed.
Frenchie and Scotty attended to the mules and checked the equipment tied to their backs. When they were satisfied they nodded "Okay" to the Captain.
Captain Hopkins thanked the gunman.

Both gunman tipped their hats then walked off into the first saloon down the street.

Eli stuck the gun in his waist band, then pulled it out, quickly. He felt a little embarrassed as Captain Hopkins looked at him, critically. "It's a good gun. I just wanted to hold it, Captain. Here, it's yours," Eli said as he held the gun out to the Captain. Captain Hopkins shook his head, slowly. "No, I bought it for you. And I also want you to have this horse. It does look like a mighty fine animal." Captain Hopkins handed the reins to Eli.

Eli stepped back a moment before he took the reins from Captain Hopkins. "A horse? It is a fine animal but this is too much, Cap'n."

Eli looked at Otello.

Otello shrugged.

"Thank you just the same, Cap'n, but Otello and me, we will outfit ourselves."

"No you won't. For God's sake take a gift and like it! If you don't want to incur my famous anger you will accept it with grace."

Eli looked at the chestnut mare with the silver spanish saddle. "A horse? Good lord! I don't know much about horses except one threw me when I was sixteen. Thank you, Cap'n. You sure you don't want this gun?"

"I have no plans that include the use of firearms. Besides I have my Navy Colt. Also, that one revolver . . . the one with the notches, well that isn't seemly. Keeping count on killing men? That just isn't proper!" Captain Hopkins insisted, forcibly.

"Maybe they was people that needed killing," Eli gritted his teeth. "Maybe, if I'm lucky, I can cut ne some notches beside 'em," Eli intoned seriously.

Otello nodded agreement. "I expect to find one just like it, real soon."

Captain Hopkins shook his head, sadly. "I do not portend to judge you, Gentlemen. Not this day. This day we will sample the delights of this fair city."

"Aye, Cap'n!" Scotty agreed.

"By Neptune, I say We have all earned it! A cold tankard of ale sounds good! It's on me, Gentlemen," Captain Hopkins added.

Eli stuck the gun in his waistband as the others nodded agreement with Captain Hopkins.

Otello looked at the gun, then at Eli.

Eli nodded understanding.

"I'm off to the shipping office to settle accounts. I'll meet you at the Brass Rail Saloon in half an hour. Don't drink all the whiskey and don't fondle all the ladies!" Captain Hopkins admonished as he moved off down the street.

"Well, laddies, let's hitch up these animals and start fondling and drinking," Scotty said as he pulled the mules over to a hitching rail.

"*Wee, Monsieur*, Scotty, `ze fondling most of all," Frenchie replied as he put his arm around Scotty's shoulder and they moved off.

Eli watched them for a moment. He pulled the revolver from his belt and pointed it South. He pretended to pulled the trigger six times as he mouthed the "bangs!" and smiled.

Otello enjoyed the imagined vengeance, quietly.

Scotty stopped, turned and looked back at them.

Eli looked a little embarrassed.

"Can't you forget about that for a little while and have some fun with us, Eli? Otello?"

"I'm sorry, Scotty. I've decided I can't be wastin' no time. I best be goin'."

"Aye, Laddie. But from what you be telling me about these boys, I suspect a saloon is as good a place as any to start looking."

Eli stuffed the gun into his waistband. He studied Scotty's eyes and thought about the wisdom of his words. He looked at Otello.

Otello's eyes agreed with Scotty. "We could start asking `round there as good as anywhere, Mister Eli."

"That ain't Scotty's purpose but we'll give it some time," Eli said.

Otello and Eli waited until the others had gone inside the saloon. They said nothing for a long quiet moment, then moved inside themselves.

The saloon was the most elegant thing Eli had ever seen. The walls were covered with velvet wallpaper and three crystal chandeliers hung from the ceiling. There was a one hundred foot polished mahogany bar and the brass rail and spittoons reflected each others shine. Mixing among the rowdy clientele, were a dozen of the prettiest girls Eli had ever laid eyes on.

Eli would never had believed there was another woman as pretty as Lydia until now.

Eli watched as Frenchie and Scotty greeted the painted ladies like old friends. It was hard for Eli to get used to the fast way people did things out here. He felt real uneasy when the prettiest lady he had ever seen came over and put her arm around his neck.

"Hi, handsome. Want to buy me a drink?" She purred.

Eli swallowed hard. He looked to Otello or Scotty for help.

Otello smiled. He turned away and sipped his beer, quietly.

Scotty was already across the room with another lady.

The Frenchman was not to be seen.

"Why, yes, ma'am," Eli nodded.

She moved closer. "Give me a beer Sam and this gentleman . . . .say what's your name, handsome?"

"It's Eli. I'll just have a little rum please."

"Rum? No. A beer and a shot for Eli here, Sam. You're not at sea anymore, sailor,"

She said as she played with Eli's ear lobe.

"You know about me being a sailor?"

"Nobody drinks rum but you sailors. Here in San Francisco we have the finest of everything including real sipping whiskey. Try it. You'll like it!" She insisted as she pulled herself even closer.

Otello eased down the bar and watched from a safe distance.

As she moved her warm body closer and closer, Eli remembered what a good feeling it was to have the intoxicating warmth of a woman next to him. It was a mixed feeling because he had been raised a religious man and Lydia was the only woman he had dared to desire in his life.

Eli truly believed it was a sin to lust after a woman you weren't married to, but he couldn't help the feelings he had for this lovely and sexy lady.

He almost peed his pants when she ran her hand up and down the inside of his pants leg and gave his private parts a quick massage.

"You want to go upstairs with me?" She cooed.

"No thank you, ma'am." Eli backed off a little.

"Oh? Well I felt somethin' that tells me otherwise."

"You gave me a start alright. I ain't exactly used to that."

"I see," she said as she fiddled with her blouse exposing more cleavage.

"I expect there's better men here to suit your purposes."

Sue looked around the bar. She shook her head. "I don't see any better men. Do you, Sam?"

The bartender nodded agreement.

"Be that as it may, ma'am. But I gotta' tell you I'm a widow man."

Sue fought back laughter. For a brief moment, she looked at him with genuine sympathy.

"In that case, I intend to give you my widow man's discount," she said. She pushed close to him and let her arms ease around his huge girth.

Eli could not deny he liked the feeling. He gulped down the whiskey and called for a double. "I don't even know your name, ma'am."

"I'm Dianne, or Julie or Sarah. Who do you want me to be?"

"Nobody," Eli sighed hard. He looked her over and liked what he saw. He sniffed her perfume and liked the smell of it.

Eli let his hand feel her silk dress and liked the touch of it. "Just whoever you are is alright."

"Okay. Call me Sue. Now can we go upstairs?"

"I reckon. I don't see why not. It's more quiet up there?" Eli shrugged as he downed the double like it was spring water.

"Give Sam twenty dollars and me thirty, then we can go upstairs."

Eli balked.

Sue gave him another quick massage and he forked over the money.

Sam took the money and Sue pulled Eli along upstairs.

Eli held back long enough to grab a bottle of whiskey to take along.

The woman's soft hand felt good. Eli felt a little more at ease as they made their way to the room.

Eli's religious objections were almost drowned in ten ounces of good tasting whiskey he guzzled on the way up the stairs. Yet he felt awkward being around such a pretty girl without benefit of clergy.

Once inside the room, the girl began to unzip her bodice.

Eli turned his eyes away.

Sue laughed. "What's the matter, have I got a disease or something?"

"No, ma'am."

"Well quit looking at me like that."

Eli averted his eyes and looked embarrassed. "I wasn't looking at you, ma'am."

"Oh? You paid fifty dollars to come up here and not look at me?"

"Yes, ma'am. Well, no, ma'am."

"Quit calling me "ma'am"."

"I'm sorry, ma'am."

"Hey are you some kind of virgin or hick or something?"

"No! . . . ma'am. I . . . I was married for almost two years. I had a good woman."

"Hey. I'm not being bought for hurting things?" She paused.

"No. I'm sorry I came up here. Maybe it was a stupid thing to do. I reckon I should be up in the hills! I'll be goin' now!"

"Another bright-eyed gold prospector? Well take some advice

from someone who's seen it all. You'll have better luck merchandising in this town than trying to strike it rich at those diggings in the hills."

Eli was about to leave. Her words peaked his interest. He stopped. "You done it, ma'am?"

"Done it? Yes. I had my time."

"Is there much dry diggin's up there? Is there a place where finding the gold is easy?"

"There's all kinds. Mostly them damned water guns and placer mining. But up around Drytown there's dry diggings. If you want . . . if you go there I have a friend Mac Culligan. He owns the Eagle Bar in Drytown. You look him up. He'll tell you what's going on. But like I say, there's easier gold to be had right here."

"Thank you, ma'am. I'll do that. Thank you. Bye, now!"

"Bye now? Ha! Don't that beat all? You a defrocked psalm singer or religious nut or something?"

"No, ma'am. I'm just a Welshman brought up on Mister William Morgan's bible."

Sue thought it over. She looked Eli up and down. "You really don't want to be here do you?"

"Parts of me do and parts of me don't."

"Well do you reckon the parts of you that do, can boss the parts of you that don't?" She stepped out of the bodice and revealed her voluptuous body to Eli's lonely, hungry eyes.

Eli tried to look away but could not. "I don't mean no insult, ma'am, but you're a right healthy woman."

"Healthy? I believe that is for livestock. Try something more endearing."

"Yes, ma'am. You're . . . you're about as handsome a lady as I ever seen."

Sue shook her head in amazement. She leaped up on the bed. "Well don't just stand there. Take off your clothes and let's get to it. We only got ten minutes and five are almost gone!" Sue insisted as she eased down on the bed and lay on her back. She struck an almost irresistible pose.

Eli wanted to go. He wanted to stay. He had not realized how much he had missed the smell, the presence, the wonder of a woman—until now. He paused to drain about half of the bottle of whiskey.

The whiskey had the intended affect and his moral conscience was now numb. Eli fumbled with his shirt. He finally got it off. He, slowly, walked over to the bed. He touched his belt buckle. He stopped.

"My, you have a muscular body," Sue said with genuine admiration. She stroked the length of Eli's chest with her fingernails. She kissed it softly.

Eli shivered with pleasure.

"Thank, you. So do you," Eli replied as breathed in the aroma of her sweet smelling hair.

"I have a muscular body?"

Eli laughed. He unbuckled his trousers. As they fell to his knees, the embroidered handkerchief with Lydia's Celtic Cross fell to the floor.

They both looked at them for a long, awkward moment.

Eli picked them up and swore long and loud. "Oh, my God! What am I doing? Oh, God forgive me! I'm sorry, ma'am, I have no right to be here!" Eli cried out in anger as he dressed, quickly.

Sue looked at him in disbelief.

"Are you some kind of mental case or what?" She backed off.

"No, ma'am. I'm sorry, ma'am. I have to be goin' now!"

Eli picked up the whiskey bottle. He looked at it with disgust. He threw the whiskey bottle against the door shattering it to bits. He, tenderly, folded the crucifix in the embroidered handkerchief and put it in his pocket. "Goodbye, ma'am." Eli tipped his hat as he stormed out of the room.

"Goodbye! Good riddance!" Sue swore.

Eli ran down the stairs, through the saloon and into the crowded streets of San Francisco.

Once he was on the now foggy streets, Eli walked, aimlessly, for hours.

Finally, he returned to where he had left the horse Captain

Hopkins had given him.

Eli paused and thought it over only a moment. Eli still had bad memories of being thrown by a horse, but he mounted the chestnut mare with a fair amount of grace. With quiet determination he pulled the reins until the horse's head turned East.

He stopped and thought about Otello. He almost dismounted to go find him. He decided against it. He believed too much had gotten in his way already. He was determined, from now on, nothing would slow him down.

Eli nudged the horse into a measured trot. He ignored the dense fog closing in all around him. With some inner sense, he rode to the ferry that would take him across the bay and on to Drytown. Drytown and the dry diggings where he hoped to find the Joshua brothers.

CHAPTER TEN

There was the noble Redman. The Native American who walked with the Great Spirit, respected the works of nature and was devoted to communion with all of creation. The proud warrior who stood in fear of no man and whose bravery in battle was without question. An exalted nation of people who lived with a great sadness, but held their heads high. And then, there was the "Digger" Indians of the Nevada Desert.

These "Indians" were so barbaric that most tribes avoided them entirely or sold them into slavery to the Spanish. Even the Spanish slavers thought twice before agreeing to take more than a few "Diggers". They were without question among the meanest of human beings, and perhaps the most desperate. They literally dug their homes in the earth and ate whatever came along in whatever form it happened to be. They were outcasts in every camp but their own.

For weeks now, a loosely organized band of Diggers had been following Jules Joshua's almost equally unorganized wagon train across the Nevada Desert.

The Diggers had been satisfied with picking off stray animals, eating many of them while they were still warm. They had grown in number and in boldness as they watched the fumbling way Jules tried to lead the train. It was clear, even to the Diggers, that this wagon train was not well armed or well lead and might be easy pickings.

Trucca, the leader of the war-painted Diggers, smiled, wryly, as he watched Jules position the wagons with their backs to the flooded Humboldt River. Trucca wondered what kind of stupid white man this could be. He knew it wasn't a trap because there were not enough gunmen in the train to challenge him.

Trucca figured it would only take half of the two hundred ponies in the war party to take this prize. He waited until the sun was at the back of the war party. He held his hand high. He paused and waited for all their eyes to focus on him. He brought his hand down, slowly. Immediately, one hundred of his best braves, in full dress and war paint, whooped their way down the hill toward the wagons.

The Indians were only a thousand yards away when Sly, sitting in the new saddle on the new horse he had stolen, saw them coming.

"Oh, my God! Oh, my God!" Sly yanked the reins and nudged his horse into a gallop. "Indians! Indians! Indians!" Sly yelled as he galloped by the wagons and pulled up in front of Jules Joshua.

Jules looked across the desert toward the war party and choked on a piece of steak he was eating.

"Well damnit! Don't just sit there! Aren't the wagons supposed to be in a circle or somethin' like that? You 'git to it!" Jules swore at Abe, his liaison with the cattlemen.

"I don't know. Ain't none of us been in this before except Eric. He would of known what to do," Abe said as he looked at Jules with contempt.

"Well, he ain't here, is he? Now get these wagons pulled around so's we can get behind them," Jules yelled as Big John and the other brothers joined him.

Abe glared at Jules. He started to say something else. He thought better of it and moved away.

"You seen them, Jules? They's real Indians and they's coming for us!" Zack chortled as he pulled his horse close beside Jules' horse.

Jules looked at Zack and shook his head with disdain. "Well now, ain't that a revelation? That damn trapper at Fort Laramie told us we'd have no trouble with Indians. Damnation! Big John, help get as many wagons between us and them as you can," Jules snapped as he pulled his horse away from the train. "I'll be looking for a shallow crossing while you hold 'em off. Understand?"

"Damnation, Jules! We ain't no indian fighters!" Big John sighed hard.

"I say we just ride on an leave these here people to their own devices," Sly said.

"You seen that merchandise wagon with all them dry goods. We ain't leaving nuthin'. Now I got you all good guns and I 'spect you'll be usin' 'em! I'm counting on you, John." Jules snarled as he kneed his horse into a gallop

"John? You talk to him. We have to go. Them there is real indians and they's awfully mad!" Sly's voice trembled with fear.

"Shut-up, Ezekiel. You heard him. Git to it!" Big John said as he pulled his Colts from his belt. He turned and shouted at the farmers to organize the wagons into a defensive posture.

Sly looked at the oncoming war party and decided to find a safe place to hide.

Ever since the French first traded matchlock rifles to the indians at Lake Champlain in 1609, enterprising men have made fortunes trading guns to the indians. Mostly inferior guns that were more dangerous to the indians than to those at whom they were shooting. For this reason, Trucca trusted the bow and arrow and the few good quality colt revolving rifles he had obtained.

The Diggers were good marksmen with the bow and arrow and could fire, at a gallop, accurately from a distance of sixty yards.

The first arrows fell on the wagons as the circle was half formed. Seven wagons were pulled in between the river and the oncoming Indians. The first arrow, fired by Trucca himself, pierced Abe's throat and he was unable to emit a scream before he fell to the dust. A volley of twenty arrows rained down on a group of women and children and plunged into the backs of mother's, who bravely, protected their children. The few braves who had colt revolving rifles or Springfield muzzle loaders, fired them with less accuracy than the bowmen. Their bullets were not a factor in the fight.

The few poor bowman among the Diggers, instead of taking careful aim, made a point of firing volleys of arrows hoping for the lucky shot.

One lucky shot hit a young Missouri lad in the eye. The boy fell to the ground dead before he had fired a single round in anger.

His mother, brandishing a needham shotgun, blew the indian in half then tended to her boy.

The few Indians who had old Christian Sharp's pistols, waited until they were closer in before they fired their unreliable guns. The first one to fire killed himself when the gun blew up in his face.

Big John Joshua fired the first shots for his side. With an uncommonly steady hand, he aimed his colt revolvers at the lead Indian's head and squeezed off three shots.

The big guns jumped in his hand and at first he thought he had missed the Indian completely. Then the Indian rocked back and forth on his pony until he, finally, tumbled off onto the desert floor.

"Hot damn! Did you see that shootin'?" Big John yelled for joy until a bullet whizzed past his ear. He, quickly, pulled his horse around behind a wagon. He fired two more rounds as he went.

Big John took a good position and emptied his guns, taking only one indian with five shots.

Zack watched big John and gathered the courage to fire also. From his waistband, Zack pulled the brand new colt Jules had "liberated" from a Cowman. Without taking aim, Zack fired all six rounds from his revolver.

Only one round hit an indian pony, spilling the rider into the dust. At that moment, it occurred to Zack that horses were easier targets than people. He reloaded and started to shoot more horses. He stopped as an arrow grazed his head and another just missed his body. Suddenly, his hand trembled from fear. He could not bring himself to fire. A bullet sprayed wood chips in his face. He dropped to his knees and crawled under a wagon. He tried to hide in the shadows. He was not surprised to see James already hiding there.

"You get back out there, Zack! This is my place. Jules ain't gonna' like it 'iffen he finds you here."

"He ain't gonna' like it no better 'iffen he finds you here, neither!"

"Well damnit! I ain't had no practice shootin' no guns like Jules and Big John!" James flinched as bullets whacked at the boards of the wagon above them.

"Me neither! Here," Zack held the new colt out to James. "You take this new gun. You the oldest, James. Pa always said you was to look out for me!"

"Well that's fine if we was talkin' 'bout being beat on by some bully. But that don't mean nothin here. You keep that gun and you use it to save yourself. Right now, it's everyman lookin' after his own backside!"

"You cowards. Get out from under my wagon!" Martha Gabrielson snarled as she leveled Eric's double barreled shotgun at them.

Zack and James looked at her in disbelief. Then they grinned.

"Now Miss Gabrielson you jest go easy with that there gun. That there gun's got a hair-trigger."

"Yes. Yes it does. You should know. One of you used it on my husband and my boy. I oughta shoot you both where you lay. I would but we need all the guns we can muster now. So get out here and start helping. Now!"

Zack looked at his colt and then at James. He looked at the business end of Martha's shotgun "Okay. Okay. We's comin' out. Just point that thing away," Zack said as he eased toward her.

Martha didn't buy it. She held the gun on them both until they were out from under the wagon. "I'll be watching you both. Now get down there where the fighting is and get to helping!"

"Yes, ma'am," James swallowed hard as he looked at the ferocity of the fighting only a few yards away.

Zack looked at the fighting and then at Martha.

"Yes, ma'am. We'll be goin', " Zack said as he pretended to leave. He started to move away. A volley of arrows fell all around them. Martha ducked a near miss and Zack used the opening to bring his colt up in her face.

The difference between good and evil manifests itself in many ways. When it comes to a split second that means the taking of a life to save your own, a decent person like Martha Gabrielson, because, innately, she is against killing anyone, hesitates. Zack, a truly evil person, who in some ways enjoyed killing, had no moral restraints—and he did not.

As a result Martha soon lay dead with two bullets from Zack's colt in her heart.

"Damn, Zack! You done shot a woman!" James looked genuinely surprised.

"Well you saw it. She was gonna' shoot me!"

"What you boys doin' here. 'Git on down with us where there's fighting," Big John interrupted them. He paused and looked at Martha's body. "Indians?" He asked.

"Yea, it was Indians for sure!" Zack lied quickly.

"That's right, Big John. That's what it was alright," James echoed.

"Well jest come with me. Where's Sly? Anybody seen Sly?"

"No!" Zack and James agreed.

"Well jest come on! You git down there. I'm gonna' find Sly. We might have to make a run for it. These cowmen don't know nuthin' 'bout fightin' no indians," Big John snapped as he rode off.

Sly was huddled as close behind a big wagon as he could get, cowered down in his saddle like a frightened child.

"Damn it, Sly! What you doin hiding out here? You get that gun out and you get to shootin', you hear?" Big John screamed as he rode up.

Sly was more afraid of Big John than the Indians and he nodded "Yes". He pulled out his gun and fired wildly at the Indians. One of his errant shots felled an elderly woman, who dropped without uttering a sound.

The Indians hit the wagons that were strung out first. In a matter of minutes the men and women in their slow oxen pulled farm wagons, wielding axes and pitchforks, were overcome by the superior numbers of Indians. The Indians didn't waste bullets, as they overpowered the settlers with knives and hatchets.

As soon as they had slaughtered the people in the ten wagons left behind, the Diggers regrouped out of rifle range of the remaining semi-circled wagons.

They argued among themselves for several long minutes. Trucca joined them and quieted them with one wave of his hand. Trucca was pleased with the results of the first raid. He looked at his warriors and smiled. He paused, them motioned for another attack.

Jules came riding back into camp just as the Indians broke out of the pow wow and began to charge the semi-circled wagons.

"It's a little more shallow down there 'round the bend where it widens. We can get that St. Louis merchant's wagon over down there. Swing it out now! Let's go!" Jules shouted to his brothers.

Sly and Big John came riding up to join them.

Sly had an arrow in his saddle. He looked frightened to death.

"We got to get out of here. There is a million indians back there. They done killed all those people back there in them wagons. Women and children and everybody!"

"Shut up, Sly! We are getting out of here, but we're taking that merchandise wagon," Jules insisted.

"What about the others? There's womenfolk still alive, Jules," Big John posed.

Jules looked at the genuine concern in Big John's eyes. He though it over a long moment. "Soon as we do this, we'll come back and help the womenfolk out. Just help me with this first. Okay?" Jules smiled benignly.

Big John glared at Jules. He spit then nodded reluctant agreement. He paused, then followed Jules toward the merchant's wagon.

The Missouri merchant who had invested all he had in a wagon full of silk, broadcloth and tools saw the brothers headed his way. He knew, instinctively, why they were coming.

The merchant had two double barreled shotguns and a revolver, all fully loaded. He eased down in the back of the wagon and took up a position between two heavy bolts of cloth. Sweat poured from his brow as he watched the Joshua brothers.

He cocked the hammer of one gun and waited.

The Indians were, now, only two hundred yards away, coming at a full gallop, The cowmen were giving a good account of themselves dropping an Indian with every third round. But it wasn't enough. There were more indians than bullets and in a few moments the wagons would be overcome.

In those few minutes, Jules hoped to get the merchant's wagon across the river. He knew that fine cloth would bring a lot of money in California. He wasn't going to let any savage take it away from him.

Jules was fifty feet from the wagon when the merchant blasted him with both barrels from the shotgun. The hot lead pellets tore into Jules' horse's front legs. The horse dropped out from under Jules like a falling rock. Jules hit the desert floor hard and tumbled in the dust cursing the merchant.

Big John saw Jules go down. He squeezed off four rounds that tore into the bolt of silk throwing fine shreds of cloth into the merchant's eyes.

Jules got to his feet and drew his revolver. He took advantage of the merchant's temporary blindness and moved in close enough to get a clear shot. He pulled off the final two rounds from his revolver.

The merchant was wiping shreds of cloth from his eyes. He was dead before he could see again.

Jules jumped in the driver's seat of the wagon and pulled it out of the line.

Big John, Sly and James rode behind, providing covering fire, as Jules whipped the team into a gallop along the muddy river bank. Jules was thankful the merchant had been rich enough to have the only team of horses in the train. He hoped they would be fast enough.

A band of Indians led by Trucca, broke off from the main party and gave chase.

Big John trailed twenty yards behind the others as the wagon neared the big bend in the river. His revolver was empty and he was using it like a club to beat off three indians. Suddenly, he felt a sharp pain in his shoulder that made his arm go limp. He looked back to find an indian on the back of his horse and a seven-inch knife in his shoulder.

The Indian withdrew the knife and was poised to strike again when Sly fired a round into the Indian's mouth. The bullet blew his tongue through the top of his head. The Indian fell into the dust as Big John pressed down on the wound.

The warm blood oozed through his fingers and he slumped in his saddle.

Big John had never let anyone see him cry out in pain, but he was sorely tempted now.

The river was running fast as Jules turned the wagon into the shallow ford. The horses balked until Jules whipped them on. Jules sighed in relief when the wheels sank, only slightly, before finding rock. The wagon lurched forward as his brothers turned to fight off Trucca and his warriors.

Trucca was no fool. He knew the value of the goods in the wagon, as well. He pulled away from the others in hot pursuit.

"Hot damn, I think we're goin' to make it, John!" Sly shouted, joyfully, as the wagon began to pull out on dry land on the other side of the river.

Big John was leaning over in his saddle in agony. His shirt was soaked with blood. He didn't reply.

Sly grabbed the reins and pulled Big John's horse along behind him.

Sly, Zack, Matthew and James flanked each other between the indians and the wagon. They fired their guns in deadly volleys that tumbled seven indians into the dust in seconds.

The other indians decided to turn back to the easier prey of the other wagons—all except Trucca. Trucca, suddenly, found himself alone with the Joshua brothers. He turned and cursed his retreating braves.

"They done turned to go back with the others, John. They's leavin' us alone!" Sly yelled. "We's goin' to make it to 'Kalifornee. We's gonna' make it!"

Just then, Trucca, who was deadly with a bow, turned and fired an arrow that struck Sly in his chest and unseated him from his horse. The horse bolted to the other side of the river. Sly coughed water and blood from his lungs. Big John sat up straight. He loaded his revolver, quickly. He leveled it at Trucca.

Trucca paused, he reached into his quiver. The quiver was empty of arrows. Trucca looked disappointed only a moment. Then he sat up high on his pony. Pride spread across his face as he charged into the guns he knew would kill him.

Jules watched him with a glint of admiration in his eye. He waited until Trucca was eyeball close. He squeezed off all six rounds from his revolver.

Five of them tore into Trucca's body. Trucca sat high on his pony for moments after he was dead.

Sly was in too much pain to celebrate.

Sly wobbled and almost fell into the river.

Big John reached down and pulled Sly up on his horse.

James rode back and picked up the reins. He pulled Big John's horse along to the other side where Jules waited.

"Throw the merchant's body out. Put them both in the wagon and tie the horse along side," Jules ordered as James pulled up beside the wagon.

James helped Sly down and lay him in the wagon. Big John eased himself down and leaned, weakly, against his horse.

Jules dismounted the wagon. It took all his strength and the others straining hard before they were barely able to put Big John in the back of the wagon.

After they had thrown the merchant's body in the river, Jules took James' horse and motioned him to drive the wagon.

James leaped into the driver's seat. He grabbed the reins and whipped the horses into movement. They headed for the mountain pass.

Jules waited for a moment and watched the Indians burn and loot the farm wagons. He hoped it would be enough and they would not follow.

Jules felt very pleased with himself as he turned his horse's head west toward the distant Sierra Nevada mountains and the gold fields of California.

CHAPTER ELEVEN

Otello sat on the edge of the hotel bed and looked into Captain Hopkins', normally, kind eyes. Otello flinched as he saw the anger and disappointment in them. Anger that Eli had left them so abruptly. Disappointment that Eli had not had the decency to say goodbye.

Frenchie and Scotty were out looking for horses and other provisions that would take them in pursuit of Eli.

Otello knew in his heart that Eli did not want to be pursued. He had mixed emotions about pursuing him. Otello's need to avenge Horse was, in his mind, as great as Eli's need to avenge Lydia. Otello would have preferred to have Eli at his side, but it did not alter his plans. Whichever of them found the Joshua brothers first, would do the right thing. It mattered only that they be found and justice be exacted.

"Your friend is a strange one," Captain Hopkins mumbled as he chewed on his pipe stem.

"That be true, Cap'n."

"You believe the whore?"

"Pardon me, sir?"

"The whore he was with. What she said."

"Yes, sir. I think he'll be headed that way for sure."

"Then that is the way we'll be heading."

Otello thought it over. He got up and walked over to where he had placed his small satchel. "With all due respect, Cap'n. I think he has made his intentions clear."

Captain Hopkins bit down on his pipe stem even harder before he replied. "There is a proper way to do things and an improper way. I stand with those who do things the proper way."

Otello let the Captain's words die. He rummaged in his satchel. He looked at the book of Shakespeare's plays. He looked back at The Captain. "He don't want us following after him, Cap'n."

"You do what you want, Otello. My course is fixed."

"You don't owe him nothin', Cap'n."

The Captain's eyes turned stern and unyielding. "That's not for you or he to say," the Captain paused and looked determined.

Otello backed away a little.

"I would not allow a casual acquaintance to go up against such odds, much less a man who saved my life. You are welcome to ride with us, Otello."

Otello picked up his satchel. He started to leave. "I thank you for all you've done, Cap'n but if you don't mind I'll ride alone," Otello said. He started to move past Captain Hopkins. As he did, the book of Shakespeare's plays fell out of his satchel.

Captain Hopkins picked up the book and looked it over with interest. "Shakespeare, Otello? Otello? Othello! Ah, I see!"

"You do?" Otello wondered.

"Your parents were fond of the bard."

"Sir?"

Captain Hopkins flipped through the book until he came to the play "Othello". He pointed to the name in the book. "There, your name. It's "Othello" not "Otello". Right?"

Otello looked at the strange writing and wished he knew what it meant.

Captain Hopkins saw the look on Otello's face and was a little embarrassed. "You can't read. Can you?"

Otello hung his head in shame.

"It's nothing to be ashamed of, Otello. There's many more that can't, than can."

Otello thought it over. He lifted his head in hope. "You can read, Cap'n?"

Captain Hopkins nodded agreement.

"You can read this story to me?" Otello bubbled.

"Oh, yes. Though I must say, I do not think it one of his best works."

Otello looked puzzled.

Captain Hopkins studied Otello's features for a long moment. He had a difficult time putting Otello into any racial category. Even knowledge of his namesake did not help. Otello did not look like a dark-skinned Moor, nor did he favor any other kind the Captain had ever known. Captain Hopkins had to wonder how he came by the name. "Your father named you, "Othello"?"

"Homer was not my real Father."

"I see. Homer? He was someone who took you in?"

"No! He never had much to do with me. My mother, what adopted me, Sarah, was the one what raised me."

"I see."

Otello took a deep breath and blew it out hard. "I don't know nothin' 'bout who bore me to this world."

"I see."

"I 'spect it's all in that book somewhere. Can you read it all and help me out, Cap'n?"

Captain Hopkins thought it over. He laid the book down and turned his back on Otello. "No!" he replied firmly.

Otello picked up the book and looked at The Captain in disbelief. "Please, Cap'n. I'm dying inside to know who I am. Where I come from. Please?"

Captain Hopkins turned around and stared hard at Otello. "Oh? Really?"

"Yes, sir! Yes, sir! You help me. You tell me the price and I'll pay it."

"I see."

"No, sir! You don't see. You know all 'bout yourself. You know where your roots done been put down. You been touched by your real Momma and Poppa. You ain't been called "bastard" and can't say nothin' back 'cause you don't know if it ain't true!" Otello paused his eyes brimming with tears of anger. "You help me, Cap'n. You read this for me. Please?"

Captain Hopkins weakened just a moment before he looked

stern once more. "No," he replied coolly.

Otello recoiled in disbelief.

"Well, I say you're not nowheres' near the man I thought you was. That's mighty mean of you, Cap'n."

"No! No it isn't."

"And I'm saying it is."

"Give a man a fish and he eats once. Teach him to fish and he eats when he wants," Captain Hopkins smiled.

Otello was puzzled for a moment. Then a smile of understanding broke across his face. "You . . . you will teach me to read, Cap'n? You'll do that?"

Captain Hopkins paused to light his pipe. He studied Otello's face. He made him wait. "Perhaps," he replied.

Otello turned his back on the Captain.

"It will take some time to teach you under the best of circumstances. I would venture that by the time we help Eli find the Joshua brothers, we would have made sufficient progress," Captain Hopkins offered.

Otello turned and smiled. He reached for the Captain's hand. They shook hands as men who respect each other shake hands.

CHAPTER TWELVE

Eli was saddlesore after the first day's ride over the trail south to Sonora. The horse Captain Hopkins had purchased and given to Eli was a fine, sturdy but gentle mare. Eli had named her, "Jeremiah" in honor of his brother. Jeremiah was a chestnut mare, but the matter of gender did not affect Eli's choice of names.

Jeremiah exercised an uncanny patience with such a greenhorn rider. After only hours in the saddle, Eli felt a kinship with this horse. He wondered if his brother's spirit might be helping make it so.

As Eli stood by the hitching post in the crowded saloon of Drytown, California eating his beans standing up, he thought well of Captain Hopkins. He hoped the Captain would understand why he, now, rode alone. He vowed that when he learned to write, he would pen his first letter to Captain Hopkins thanking him for all the kindnesses extended to him.

Eli was, constantly, surprised by the numbers of people on the roads and crowded into these ramshackle towns. He couldn't believe the prices and thanked God for Captain Hopkins' monetary benevolence.

The plate of beans he was eating was $2.50 and a steak was going as high as $20.00. Beer was cheap but Eli wasn't much of a drinking man. Yet being around Scotty and the Frenchman had somewhat changed his habits on that matter.

Frenchie could down a schooner of beer quicker than any man alive and Scotty was a close second. Captain Hopkins delighted in their raucous behavior for they had earned their wages fairly and were entitled to spend them in whatever manner they chose.

Eli was more cautious about his money. The wages he had

earned working on the ship and the generous bonus Captain Hopkins had given all the men, would go fast at the prices charged in these camps. It was important to Eli that he not have to go begging or owe a man a debt he could not pay.

As Eli sipped the schooner of beer, his eyes searched the faces of the miners. He desperatly hoped to find one of the Joshua brothers among them. He tried not to stare but to look carefully and well.

He did not let the improbability of his task dim his desire. He knew there were hundreds of camps on the trail to Sonora and thousands all over the state. He sincerely believed that Providence would help him find the one camp where the Joshua brothers would be found.

He did not let his mind dwell on what he would do once he found them. He believed Providence would also help him when that time came.

Eli waited until the bartender had a breathing spell and pushed up to the bar. "Excuse me, sir. If you don't mind, I'd like to ask you a question?"

The bartender wiped his brow with his apron and shrugged "Why not?"

"I was told your name is Mac Culligan?"

"Well that's no big thing. Everybody anywhere knows that!"

"Sue in San Francisco said you could help me if I was in these parts."

"Sue? I don't know a Sue. What did she look like? Petite, pretty little thing with shiny auburn hair, dimples and emerald green Irish eyes?"

"That would be a fair description."

"Sue? Ha! That's has to be Stella. She changes names more often than I change shirts. So you know Stella?"

"Well . . . sort of?"

"Well that's good and bad. She was a friend alright, but she still owes me forty dollars. You wouldn't be willing to make that up for her would you?"

"I expect so if you could help me with some information." Eli dug forty dollars out of his pocket.

Mac took the money and looked at Eli suspiciously, at first, then shrugged and gave Eli his full attention. "There is something you want to know real bad, Mister. As long as I know it and it don't hurt my friends, I don't mind tellin' it. So here." Mac paused and poured Eli a whiskey. "Have a drink on me and ask away."

"Thank you, Mac. Have you seen six brothers come in here? One of them is a very big man over six and a half feet about my size. The others are average sized men. They stick close together and are ornery enough to stand out in most crowds," Eli said.

"And who would they be to you?"

Eli didn't answer for a moment. It was hard for him to speak the name of the Joshua brothers. "They are the Joshua brothers. They owe me some money. If you could help me locate them, I'll be glad to give you a small percentage," Eli lied without blinking an eye.

"Six brothers like that would stick out among these loners. If they were in Drytown I'd know about it. Sooner or later everyone comes to the Eagle. How much you paying?" Mac picked up a glass and began to polish it.

"Well, that depends on how long it takes me to catch them. You see, the longer they have my money, the more of it they'll be spending. If I offered ten per cent and got it all back that would be a good sum of money," Eli said over the top of his whiskey glass.

"Six brothers sticking together in these times and in this place? I'd say more likely they all took off in different directions from here to Rough and Ready. No, I'd like to take your money, Mister, but they ain't around here," Mac said as he moved away to service other customers.

"Well I thank you for considering my proposal. It will remain open until they are found." Eli started to leave. He almost dropped his teeth when he saw Captain Hopkins walking through the door.

"Any luck, Eli?" Captain Hopkins wondered. Frenchie Scotty and Otello trailed behind him.

"Cap'n? Cap'n Hopkins! How? How on earth did you find me here?"

"A lady of your recent acquaintance said you might be coming this way. You were looking for dry diggings and these are the driest in California. Besides there is only one chestnut mare in this vicinity with a spanish saddle like the one outside."

"I see."

Captain Hopkins smiled. "I was worried about you, Eli. You left without saying a proper goodbye. The lady you were with told us you were acting a little strange. Are you alright?"

"Yes, sir. Sue? . . . I mean, Stella. Yea, I guess I spooked her a little bit."

"As I said, any luck in your quest?"

"Nope. They ain't here. I don't feel it in my bones and nobody's seen 'em. The gold's too hard to come by here. There's talk that in Sonora they pick the nuggets up off the street. That's where they'll be," Eli replied as he greeted the others with a smile.

They returned a warm greeting.

"The talk is that Amador City has a good sized find. Frenchie wants to stop by Moke Hill. There's a large contingent of his countrymen there. We'll spend a couple of days there and move on to Sonora. Will your quest hold a few more days?" Captain Hopkins asked as he put his arm around Eli's shoulder.

"I don't know, Cap'n. Like I said, I reckon I should go down this trail alone. You been more than kind to me and I owe you for it. You don't need none of my trouble," Eli said as he drew a random line in the spilled beer on the oak table.

Captain Hopkins looked very angry for a moment before he gave Eli a fatherly smile. "Young man, I'm only going to tell you this once more. I wouldn't be alive if it wasn't for you. It is *I who owes you*. But more than that, I'm a free man and I go where I damn well please! It so happens, I please to go to Sonora. Enough said!" Captain Hopkins concluded as he stuck his pipe in his mouth and tried to light an empty bowl.

"Aye! And me too, Laddie. You aren't going to Sonora and strike it rich without Scotty sharing in it."

"You tell me how you want to handle it, Mister Eli and that's the way I'll do it," Otello said.

Eli looked embarrassed for a moment. He had never had such friendship and did not know exactly how to handle it. He smiled at Scotty and Otello. He noticed Frenchie was missing.

"Where did Frenchie go?" Eli changed the subject.

"Oh, I suspect he went down to the cowpens," Captain Hopkins smiled.

"Cowpens? Frenchie is a cowman?" Eli quizzed.

"No and there's no cows in those cowpens," Scotty laughed. He nodded and winked at the skimpily clad girl with her legs up on the bar.

"Oh," Eli smiled.

"Would you be for going down and paying the lassies a visit now, Eli?" Scotty got up from the table and grabbed Eli by the arm.

"No! No, I don't think I'm drunk enough to stand in one of those lines, Scotty," Eli joked.

"Out here it's the line or nothing and I get the shakes when it's nothing for too long. See you at the camp, laddies," Scotty said as he made his way out of the saloon door.

Otello watched him go and moved to the bar. He looked at Mac. "A beer if you don't mind?"

Mac gave Otello a puzzled look. "You an indian or something, boy?"

"I don't know," Otello replied honestly.

"What? Ha! You don't know? Christ, boy! Everybody knows what they is. So what the hell are you?"

"I'm a Pennsylvanian."

"You trying to be smart with me, boy? You're black ain't 'cha? That's it. You're one of them light-skinned negroes, ain't 'cha?"

"Your guess is as good as mine," Otello replied.

"One thing I can't abide is a smart 'alecky nigger. You get the hell out of my bar!" Mac picked up a sawed off Needham shotgun and pointed it at Otello.

Eli stepped in between them. "You want to put that gun down and give my friend here a drink?"

"You want some of this, Mister? There's plenty for both of you," Mac snarled.

"You got enough in that old thing to shoot all three of us?" Captain Hopkins stepped up.

"Maybe so. Don't push me no more. Just ease on out the door and we'll let this pass," Mac chortled.

"It's okay, Cap'n. I ain't thirsty no more," Otello held his anger in.

"That is no longer at issue. This gentleman's attitude appears to be in need of some adjustment," Captain Hopkins replied.

"You talk like an English sissy boy, Mister. You leave. You all leave now, or so help me God, I'll shoot you dead where you stand!"

Mac seemed ready to fire.

Eli, without realizing it, pulled his colt from his waistband. He brought it up to fire. He pulled the trigger and fired point blank at Mac. The bullet missed the mark by five feet.

Mac fired his shotgun as, everyone, except for Eli ducked for cover. Eli grabbed the shotgun barrel and yanked it from Mac's hands. He busted Mac in the face with his huge fist. Mac dropped to the floor without uttering a whimper.

Otello looked at Eli with admiration.

Captain Hopkins looked at Eli with concern. "Good God, Eli!" He looked at the smoking colt in Eli's hand. "Please put that gun away."

Eli nodded agreement. He looked at the gun. He wondered at his ability to use it. He stuck the gun in his waistband.

"I would say we've outlived our welcome here," Captain Hopkins sighed.

"Amen," Otello said.

Captain Hopkins looked at Eli with concern. Then he chuckled. "That was some exhibition of shooting."

Eli nodded agreement. "I expect there's some things 'bout shootin' I need to know, Cap'n."

"The understatement of the hour," Captain Hopkins grabbed a fifth of whiskey. He counted out fifty dollars and placed it on the bar. He motioned for them to leave. "Let's go find us a place to practice. We need lots and lots of practice," he turned to leave.

Otello and Eli looked at each other.

"Good. That'll be good, Cap'n. Yes, sir. I would really like that," Eli replied as he hefted the big revolver in his hand. He froze as someone put a strong hand on his wrist. Eli looked up to see a bearded man with strong eyes and a tin star on his chest.

"Easy now, Mister. I saw it all and there's no blame that needs to be placed, here," The Lawman said as he released his grip.

Eli backed away and eyed the badge.

"Don't let that worry you none. It's not official, unless it needs to be. I'm just plain Tom Jenkins picking up a few dollars between claims," Tom offered.

"Eli . . . Eli Llynne," Eli replied.

"If you don't mind my asking, where did you get that revolver, Mister?" Tom wondered aloud.

Captain Hopkins returned and spoke up. "It was purchased from a man in San Francisco. I have the bill of sale."

Tom thought it over along moment. "That was not my concern. It looks like Boston Jack Hornsby's gun. If it is, it's got some innocent blood on it. There's widows and their friends in these parts that might take exception to anyone carrying that piece. *Cuidado, Mi Amigo.* Careful," Tom grimaced.

Eli touched a finger to the notches cut into it. "You know the men he 'kilt?"

"There's only five notches there. He 'kilt more than that before he was run out of these parts and most other parts in the gold country. He had a bad habit of killin' miners and selling their goods to . . . pardon me . . . newcomers like yourself. No offense intended."

"Damn! I've been took!" Captain Hopkins fumed.

"It ain't that he's the only man that `kilt anybody hereabouts. God knows there's plenty of that. It's just that he was a backshooter and he `kilt an unarmed boy only nine years old. That's an evil gun, Mister. I'd think about buying me another."

Eli looked deep into Tom's troubled eyes. Captain Hopkins did also.

Both of them concluded the man made good sense.

"Thank you, Mister. I'll be heeding that advice." Eli tipped his hat to Tom.

Tom returned a half-smile.

Eli, Otello and Captain Hopkins walked out of the saloon. Once outside, Eli took the gun form his belt and looked at Captain Hopkins. He offered it to him. Captain Hopkins declined to take it. Eli threw it into a rain barrel in the darkness of an alleyway.

Captain Hopkins smiled his approval. "There's a gunsmith across the street. We'll get you a brand new navy colt. A real gun!" Captain Hopkins insisted.

"Maybe so, but you won't be buying it for me," Eli shot back.

Captain Hopkins smiled as they moved across the street into the gunsmith shop. There Eli purchased a used, but still handsome .36 caliber Navy Colt, model 1851.

Otello thought it over and bought one for himself.

"It is a mighty big piece. I suppose it does take some learning to shoot one of these," Eli mused as he followed the Captain out of the gunsmith shop and into the Captain's buggy.

"It is something a man can depend on. It is well made and shoots as true as any gun made by man." The Captain agreed as he drove them to a secluded spot off the road outside of town.

The principal reason most gun carrying men of the lawless era, when gunfighting was common place, did not shoot straight was a practical one. Cartridges cost cash money and were not to be used with abandon. Most men could afford the initial price of a gun and a box of cartridges. To buy boxes and boxes of cartridges for shooting at targets to gain proficiency in targeting, was beyond the means of most men.

It was not beyond the means of Captain Hopkins and he intended to see that Eli, and Otello, had as many bullets as it took to become better than good with a revolver.

Captain Hopkins admired Eli for saving his life, but he also admired Eli as men admire other men of strength and character. Captain Hopkins did not like the nature of Eli's quest but he knew it was useless to try to stop him. As a friend, Captain Hopkins could make sure Eli, and Otello, had the best chance possible to be successful in what they intended to do.

"We'll start with Eli, Otello. I suggest you find a safe place from which to observe," Captain Hopkins kidded.

Otello smiled agreement. He moved back to a distant tree stump and sat down to watch.

Captain Hopkins set an empty whiskey bottle on a tree stump. "Okay, Eli. Stand about here and see if you can bust up that old bottle," Captain Hopkins instructed as he placed Eli fifty yards from the bottle. Eli agreed and withdrew the gun from his waistband. Eli hefted the gun and acted as if he knew what he was doing.

Eli held the heavy revolver in his hand and took careful aim. The weight of the gun caused him to drop the sights beneath the whiskey bottle target seconds before he pulled the trigger. The gun went off and jumped in his hand so wildly that the ball missed the bottle and everything else—except it almost killed a jackass grazing on a hillside above them.

"This ain't gonna be easy," Eli sighed to himself.

"You have to work with it, Eli. It's just like anything else. Once you get used to it it'll be as natural as sleeping."

Eli looked cynical and raised the heavy revolver, this time holding it with two hands. Once more he squeezed the trigger, slowly. The gun exploded but only jumped a few inches and Eli was delighted to see the ball kick up dirt a few feet from the bottle. The bottle wobbled slightly, as a dirt clod hit it.

"Hey Cap'n. Did you see that?" Eli exclaimed, happily.

"Yep. If that had been a man you would have missed him by only thirty feet," Captain Hopkins chuckled.

Eli frowned at the Captain as he took careful aim one more time. He made sure he was steady and, slowly, squeezed off a round.

The gun exploded and sent the ball into the tree stump blowing powdered wood fifty feet in all directions. A wood chip hit the bottle and knocked it over.

"Hot doggety! I did it, Cap'n. Look at that," Eli jumped for joy.

"Yep. If he'd been standing on a tree stump you'd of knocked him down for sure," The Captain said as he picked at his fingernails with his whittling knife.

"You know, Cap'n. A gun just don't feel natural in my hand. I held a pick axe handle so long it's all I really feel like I know exactly how to use."

"Well, for your sake, you'd better make that gun mighty comfortable unless you changed your mind about doing what you've been intending to do."

Eli shook his head as he stormed over to the bottle. He picked it up and placed it on the stump.

Eli turned and stomped back to the firing position. He wheeled and fired the last three rounds from the gun. One round went wide ricocheting off trees cutting down small branches. The second round missed so completely its trajectory could not be seen or heard. The third round cracked into the middle of the bottle blowing it into a thousand pieces of useless glass.

"No, sir. I ain't changed my mind one little bit. Not one little bit!" Eli blew the smoke from the barrel as it oozed into the air. He looked at the Captain and waited for the Captain's approval.

"Lucky shot," Captain Hopkins kidded.

Eli shook his head "No."

"The last shot was a good one, Eli, but I expect the Joshua brothers will give you one chance—maybe. I do know they aren't going to hold still."

"I know that, but I don't expect them to be no better than me, if as good. I've got reasons for this they don't have. I've got the necessary meaning to do it and I believe I've got the good Lord behind me, Cap'n," Eli insisted.

Captain Hopkins half-smiled. "Yes. Well, I don't know much about the Lord but I heard it said he works in some mysterious ways."

"I expect his strong hand to guide me," Eli was convinced.

"Yes. That's fine, Eli. Meanwhile, I'd feel better if you practiced with that gun more and counted on providence less," Captain said as he took the gun from Eli and began to reload it.

Eli studied the Captain's face. He saw the disapproval there. "You think this to be a godless quest, Cap'n?"

"What I think I have already outlined. Now here let's keep at it," Captain Hopkins handed Eli the reloaded gun.

"I want you to know, Cap'n that I never wanted things to be this way. I was happy . . . real happy."

"I understand, Eli."

"It's not godless bloodlust, Cap'n. If I thought there was another way to be at peace inside . . . . "

"Will vengeance bring you peace, Eli?"

"I can't read but my mother memorized the bible to me, Cap'n. There's a lot of gettin' even in the bible. There's an eye for an eye and all that."

"As I remember it also says, "Thou shalt not kill"."

Eli was confused for only a moment.

"Them words do mix me up sometimes."

"Second thoughts, Eli?"

Eli gathered his composure and looked at the Captain with a steady gaze. "No, Sir! You help me with this here gun and the Lord will provide a time to use it," Eli said with absolute certainty.

The Captain shook his head in amazement. "I'm not making fun of your religion, Eli. I just don't happen to believe in those things. Well, except when the high winds are on the open sea and my ship is being tossed around like a cork. I respect you and that's enough," the Captain offered. He paused and looked deadly serious. "It's just . . . just that you can't proceed with the slightest bit of doubt."

"I don't doubt none, Captain."

"Oh? The bartender you shot at was in your face. You missed him by five feet."

Eli had to ponder the wisdom in the Captain's words. "I don't know how that happened. I swear I don't!"

"I do. You did not have a sure hand."

Eli slowly nodded agreement. "I expect that's true, Cap'n. But good God almighty knows I'll have one when it comes to the Joshua brothers!"

"Oh? Are you sure?"

"I'm not straight all together about what's gonna' happen. I just know I'll do right by Lydia when the time comes," Eli explained as he took the reloaded gun from Captain Hopkins.

Captain Hopkins walked over and set up three more whiskey bottles on the tree stump.

"Eli, for your sake, I hope there is a God and I hope he's on your side," Captain Hopkins sighed and stepped aside.

"Oh don't worry, Cap'n. There is . . . and he is!" Eli concluded as he turned and emptied the revolver.

This time Eli held the gun steady. This time he made himself take a liking to the feel of it. He squeezed off six rounds. Four balls went wide, the other two hit two bottles squarely, blowing them to pieces.

"It's true enough that when the anger boils up inside your hand is steady, Eli," Captain Hopkins observed.

"That may be so Cap'n. But I don't know if I'm suited to this enterprise. I ain't angry all the time like I was months ago. It comes and goes like a summer wind," Eli paused and looked sad.

"How do I know if it'll be there when I need it? I just can't keep it burning hot all the time."

"Maybe that's why some people rely on providence to right things for them. I do know that you're a decent man, Eli Llynne. From what I know of these Joshua brothers that isn't so about them. There will be no hesitating when they see you."

Eli nodded his head in agreement. He gritted his teeth as he thought about the Joshua brothers. When they were hot on his mind he had no trouble hating them enough to kill them, easily.

It was when he had time to cool out and go about life's normal patterns that the white hot hatred began to fade. At times, he wondered if he would be able to do what he had to do when it came time to do it.

"It seems to me that the evil I've seen in life is as constant and unflagging as midnight must be on the other side of the moon. It is the good that seems to waver not because good is inherently weaker than evil, but because good, decent men ponder the true mysteries of life. They weigh and measure their deeds daily. While good men ponder their moral compasses, evil men have their rudders battened down to one course without thought of consequences to man or beast."

"I expect that's true enough, Cap'n."

"Yes. If you are still intent on this course, you must steel yourself to be as unmoving and as free of doubt as they will be," He paused and looked stern. "Or you must abandon this course now."

"I know, Cap'n. I get confused sometimes. Sometimes I see my Mother. My mother used to come into my room and read bible stories. She believed because these were hard times and mean men there was no call for me to be that way. In my head she impressed on me that killin' was a bad thing. Though we lived with killin' in a manner of speaking every day, I promised her I would never kill a man. It's hard to dishonor her memory . . . 'cept when I'm real angered up."

"I understand. I went to sea against my parents wishes. It has been hard to live with that all these years. It's a helluva thing you have to live with, Eli. I don't envy you a bit. Whatever you do decide to do, . . . if you do it with a sure hand . . . I will give you my word I'll stand shoulder to shoulder with you on it," Captain Hopkins insisted firmly.

Eli gave the Captain a determined look. He thought it over a long moment. "A sure hand, Cap'n. A sure hand."

The Captain looked at Eli and his strong gray eyes did not waver.

Eli put his strong hand firmly on Captain Hopkin's shoulder and stared deep into his eyes.

A silent prayer of thanks for the blessing of friendship passed between them.

Otello watched them for a long moment until he dared to join in their radiant camaraderie.

CHAPTER THIRTEEN

The mountain pass was much steeper than Jules had figured and the first light snow of winter was dusting the trail ahead. Everyone they passed warned them it was too late in the year to head over the crude pass through the mountains. The same pass that had trapped The Donner Party five years before. Jules had heard the tales of The Donner Party that had been trapped in this in the winter of '46-'47. Jules suspected the tales of cannibalism were just made up story telling to scare off forty-niners. Yet the graphic stories of the grisly doings of the Donner party made even Jules pause and think—but for only a moment.

In his mind nothing was going to deter the Joshua brothers from heading toward the gold fields the soonest way possible. Jules was damned determined that he would not let the heavier snowfalls to come catch him anywhere near these parts if he could help it.

The Missouri Merchant had purchased a fine team of horses. Yet, even their strength, could not move the overloaded wagon through the steepest parts of the higher elevations without considerable help.

Jules, with his usual beneficence, solved the problem by putting his brothers, except for Sly who was delirious with a raging fever, in a jury-rigged harness. He even made the wounded Big John get out of the wagon and help pull. James was the only man sitting a horse. Jules had him pull on the wagon with a guy rope tied to his saddle.

Jules sat atop the driver's seat and urged them on with the most foul curses known to man. Jules whipped the horses, and, occasionally, his brothers. Except Big John and Matthew whom he took pains to miss.

The cold mountain air hinted of a bad winter not many days away. It made Jules more determined than ever to push on faster and faster.

"Pull damnit, pull!" Jules urged his brothers and the horses up the narrow mountain trail.

Horsemen, riding alone, passed them and looked at Jules and his brothers, suspiciously. Jules with his unkempt appearance and unsightly demeanor did not fit, at all, in the driver's seat of a merchant's wagon.

If there had been law in these parts, or if people had minded their own business less, Jules would surely have been arrested.

Jules did not like the hard looks of some of the horsemen and what they implied. As they moved closer to California, there were more and more people passing by asking too many questions. Jules didn't like people to begin with and when they started asking questions, he didn't like them double. He kept his colt loose in his belt and his eyes wide open to watch for any man with a star. He decided that he would have to unload the wagon and merchandise at the first available opportunity.

The old Murphy wagon creaked and groaned as it strained to make it up the steep grade. In addition to the steepness, the trail was narrow and snaky. A fast-moving mountain river roared by seven hundred feet below. Loose rock and gravel tumbled down the mountainside toward the river. An occasional boulder would dislodge itself and come pounding down the mountainside, narrowly, missing the wagon. On the descent of a steep hillside, Jules would lock the wheels of the wagon and they would let it slide. The slide would cut deep grooves in the trail with the locked wheels, as had many wagons who had gone before.

"I don't like this none," Zack huffed. "I say we take these here horses and leave this wagon. We can pack most of this stuff in."

"We ain't leaving nothin'. You just keep on keeping on. It ain't much further to the other side now!" Jules ordered. He pointed to the other side of the grade and an old signpost that pointed to Sacramento.

The high Sierra Nevada Mountains were ablaze with late autumn foliage. Scattered among the high mountain pine were young aspen trees with leaves shining like gold nuggets hanging to every limb. A herd of white-tail deer paused and watched the intruders then scampered away. The high sky was devoid of clouds and competed with the high mountain lakes for the most dazzling shade of blue possible.

It would have been breathtaking scenery for someone who cared the least bit about the natural beauty of the world. Jules saw only a trail that would take him to the gold fields of California. It would not have mattered to him if his surroundings were as barren as the moon, so long as they served their purpose.

Everybody that passed them, had tales of rich strikes.

In Jules' mind, California was a big gold field where a man just reached down and picked up a fortune.

Jules already had a small sack full of golddust and small nuggets from returning Argonauts who bought his stolen dry goods. Jules enjoyed selling goods for far more than they were worth. He figured that after he struck it rich in the gold fields, he would become a merchant.

Jules' hopes of ever reaching California were diminished by the fact that they were making only three to five miles a day. The slow pace was, partly due, to the steep mountain trails and, partly, to the fact that Big John's shoulder still hurt him and Sly was, completely bedridden with a fever.

Jules was so frustrated that he, finally, concluded he would have to go on alone. His only problem would be to convince his brothers he wasn't abandoning them.

"I'm mightily worried about Sly's fever," Jules said as he feigned a look of deep concern.

"It should'a broken by now," Zack offered.

"I thought we might pass a good doctor on this trail but that don't seem likely," Jules said as he looked up at the sky, prayerfully.

"That one horse doctor shore didn't do us no good," Big John grumped.

"Yep. We'd better see to some help, I suppose." Jules hesitated and spit out the side of the wagon.

"I reckon I'd better take a horse and go on ahead. They say they's some camps up the trail that might have a doctor. Maybe I can get him to come back this way for enough money." Jules pulled the wagon over to a small clearing by the trail.

"I can go, Jules. I know this horse good," James offered.

Jules took on his mean countenance. "I said I was goin' up ahead, James, and that's all there is to it," Jules snapped as he dismounted the wagon.

Matthew and Big John were suspicious of Jules' intentions. Their concern for Ezekiel made them more than favorable to Jules' suggestion.

"Well, how long you gonna be gone? How far you gonna be goin'?" Big John asked.

"We need every man jack to get over these mountains, Jules," Matthew added.

"Well now, how would I know how long? I don't know what's up there except what all these dudes been tellin' us and half of all that is outright lies."

"Matthew has a point, Jules," Big John said.

"Oh he dies? Well I might get lost up there, 'jest as easy as not. It 'shore ain't like I want to do this!" Jules took James' horse.

Matthew and Big John looked doubtful.

"Don't you worry, Matthew. I fully intend to pull my load unless I git lost. Now 'iffen I do, I want you to sell all that stuff in the wagon and bring my share to that town . . . . .what's the name of that town where that man got that big nugget he showed us?" Jules asked himself as he took a bolt of silk from the wagon.

"Samora or something like that," Zack said. He scratched his beard disturbing a half dozen contented fleas. "What's that there cloth for, Jules?"

Jules stuffed the silk in his saddlebags. "It's for tradin' for a doctor. That's what! Okay? Samora you say?"

"Snora . . . I think," Zack replied.

"No. It was more like . . . Snorea . . . Sonora. Sonora! That's it. If something happens and I get caught up in something I'll meet you boys in Sonora."

"Sonora? Whereabouts in Sonora, Jules?" Zack looked worried.

"At the best saloon in town," Jules concluded.

His brothers' faces showed their doubts as Jules turned the horse's head west and started to ride off.

Big John grabbed the reins of the horse. He looked Jules hard in the eyes.

Matthew moved up behind him and lent support.

"Jules, don't you get lost out there. It ain't right you riding off like this unless you fully intend to get a doctor. 'Iffen you don't come back with a doctor Sly might not make it.' Big John paused and looked Jules hard in the eye. "You understand, Jules?"

"That's so, Jules!" Matthew added.

"I told you both what to do, John . . . Matthew. Now I expect you to do it. I done said what I'm gonna' do and that's that!" Jules snapped as he jerked the reins from Big John's hands.

Big John was still not well from his injury or he would not have let them go.

"And the same doctor is gonna' make you well, Big John. I promise. Now ain't I done well so far? Ain't that wagon full of good things that bring money? You think you could do that, Matthew?" Jules challenged.

"You 'jest do what you say and we'll have no cause to fuss," Matthew insisted.

"Ain't I always?"

Jules smirked as he spurred the horse and rode away before Matthew or Big John could reply.

Sly eased up in the back of the wagon just as Jules rode away. "What's he doin', John?" Sly mumbled weakly.

"He's goin' to get you a doctor. Now lay back down," Big John replied.

"No, John! No! You shouldn't of let him go. You shouldn't have let him go. You know he ain't coming back. Now we's really in it."

Matthew and Big John looked at each other. Their eyes were in agreement with Sly.

Big John held his sore shoulder as he eased himself out of the harness. He started to mount a horse and chase after Jules. He got ten yards before the pain in his arm told him how futile his effort was. Slowly, he walked back to where Matthew and James were standing.

"You want me to go after him, John?" Matthew wondered aloud.

"No! No,'iffen he don't come back, I'll kill him with my bare hands. I swear it. I know he's my blood but I'll kill him, so help me, God!" Big John swore.

James and Zack stepped back from Big John's anger. They nodded agreement as they watched the small figure of Jules Joshua disappearing on the western horizon.

CHAPTER FOURTEEN

Spring 1852

Mokelumne Hill—California Gold Fields

Mokelumne Hill or "Mok" Hill as it was called by the miners was perhaps the nastiest of gold towns, with the possible exception of Bodie. In the spring of 1852 when Eli and company arrived there, miners were being killed, in violent arguments—or convenient accidents—at the rate of five to eleven a week.

"Mok" hill was, in actuality, several hills all with their hidebound ethnic or racial groups encamped to suit themselves. Excluding others who crossed the unmarked international boundaries at their peril.

Not all hills were equal with "Frenchman's Hill" being the most unequal. Argonauts in their cups, considered it their divine right and civil duty to, on occasion, go to "Frenchman's Hill" and cleanse it of every "Keskeydee" found there. These "occasions" were, mostly when the Frenchmen were panning out more high grade dust and nuggets than anybody else.

"Moke Hill" had about the same mixture of nationalities as most camps, but was exceptional for the large, nationalistic, French population.

Frenchie had heard tales of "Frenchman's Hill", and could not wait to see it. He almost cried as he saw the tri-color flying from the flag pole on a distant hill. He waxed melancholy as he smelled the scents of French cooking that wafted into his big homesick nostrils.

"Well boys, this is where I leave you for awhile. I shall get a *petite coquette*, a bottle of *appellation' extraordinaire'*, a small room and see you in two or three days," Frenchie said as he, joyfully, leaped from the wagon into the crowded, dusty street and moved at a fast pace toward the saloon.

Otello, Scotty, Eli and Captain Hopkins laughed together.

"We leave for Sonora on Monday with or without you, Frenchie," Captain Hopkins cautioned.

"Ah, *wee*! But I 'weel be there, *Mon Capitan'*. If not, I have died one very happy mon'." Frenchie headed for the saloon that had a French flag in the window.

Eli and the others looked at each other and shrugged.

"A draught of ale does sound good," Scotty said.

"Yes it does, Scotty. Otello? Eli?" Captain Hopkins asked.

"If it's all the same to you, I think I'll find a spot to practice some more," Eli said as he fondled the handle of his revolver.

"I expect I need it more than him," Otello said.

"Amen! From the looks of this place you won't be having to go far," Scotty mused aloud.

"They're a right ripe looking bunch, alright. I hope Frenchie is careful with his comport. Everyone here seems a might edgy," Captain Hopkins observed.

"Frenchie, careful? Those do not be two words that go along with him well," Scotty laughed.

"Aye, but, perhaps in this place . . . ," Captain Hopkins did not get the words out of his mouth before Frenchie came tumbling backwards out of the doors of the saloon.

Blood poured from a big gash in Frenchie's head as he fell into the thick mud of the dirt street.

Eli was the first to his side. "My God, Frenchie! What happened?" Eli asked as he tried to revive the unconscious Frenchman.

"The goddamn frog tried to buy a drink in a white man's saloon! You his friend?"

A huge oak tree of a man, holding a broken whiskey bottle, looked down at Eli and snarled. Eli took a deep breath and blew it out hard before he replied.

"Yes. Yes, he's my friend." Eli stood up. Eli, a big man himself, had to bend his neck to look up in this giant's face.

"Well, you don't look like a frog. Are you?"

"No. I don't think I'm a frog and neither is he. It ain't your business but he's of french extraction."

"Right. A goddamned frog! I can smell a damn Frenchman a mile away. When he opens his frog mouth and starts talking, I know it for sure. Now you'd best move him on up to Frenchman's Hill. Up to those frog saloons where he and all the other frogs can blow garlic into each others faces."

"Come on, Eli. I'll help the laddie," Scotty said as he stepped up and knelt down beside Frenchie. Frenchie wobbled to his feet. He stood up, weakly. A mean-looking bunch of men gathered around him.

Eli didn't like backing down from any fight, but he did not want to lose one here. Eli had to save himself to fight another time, another place. He looked at Otello.

Otello was uncertain also.

"Thanks, Scotty," Eli replied as he backed off and knelt down to help lift Frenchie.

"Ah, a Scotsman. A kinsman. Welcome to Moke Hill. I'm Little Tom. Little Thomas Mc Dowell." Little Tom's face turned pleasant. He offered Scotty his hand.

Scotty shook his head "No."

"You'd be a friend to this frog but not to a kinsman?" Little Tom became angry again. He looked at Otello. "Who are you, boy? Don't look at me with them damn strange eyes. What is you anyways?"

"None of your goddamn business!" Otello snapped.

"Now that's a lie. Everything here is my business. I expect you a "keskydee" too. Well hell, one more don't make no never mind!" Little Tom held out the broken whiskey bottle.

Frenchie shook Eli and Scotty off and got to his feet.

"No kinsman of mine be found fighting with broken whiskey

bottles," Scotty snapped.

Little Tom looked at the broken bottle in his hand. He shrugged and tossed it into the street. He looked a little meek for a moment before he turned angry once more. "With frogs you got to fight dirty. They don't know what fair is."

Little Tom growled just as Frenchie hit him square on the jaw with his fist.

Little Tom smirked. He planted his huge fist into Frenchie's face and sent Frenchie reeling to the ground.

Seconds later, two miners came out of the shadows and kicked Frenchie in the stomach with their boots. Frenchie doubled over in pain.

Eli, still, hesitated.

Otello looked at him and waited for him to lead.

Frenchie looked up at Eli in agony. He spit blood and tried to get to his feet.

Eli sighed hard and grabbed one miner by the collar. With one motion he lifted the medium-sized man off the ground and threw him hard against a wall. The man did not have time to protest before he was silenced forever.

Otello leaped into the fray. He took two of them down to the street in a tumbling wrestle hold.

Another of Little Tom's friends leaped on Scotty's back.

Eli did not hesitate this time. With his huge left hand, Eli grabbed the kicker by the shoulder. He turned his face around.

Eli hit him with a fisted right hand that sent him to the ground with blood spurting from both nostrils.

A dozen of Little Tom's friends now poured out of the saloon and joined the fight. The first one out of the door ran into Scotty's fists.

Eli backed Scotty up.

Otello joined them to form a phalanx of formidable presence.

Captain Hopkins bit down on the stem of his pipe as he pondering stripping his coat and joining in.

The decision was made for him.

In a matter of minutes, an all out brawl ensued. The fight was joined by people from half a mile down the street who had no particular interest in who was fighting over what.

Some fought because their friends were involved. Some fought because a relative was involved. Some fought to pick up nuggets knocked loose in the fray.

Most, just fought for the hell of it.

"See all this trouble a goddamn Frenchman caused! I'm goin' to see he don't cause no more!" Little Tom advanced on Frenchie who was just getting to his feet.

Eli moved in between Little Tom and Frenchie.

Frenchie wobbled with double vision.

Captain Hopkins picked up an axe handle, from a nearby general store, and stood behind Eli.

"I thought using things wasn't fair?" Little Tom challenged as he looked at the axe handle.

"You want to back off? You want to cool this thing down?" Eli replied.

"Yep! Sure." Little Tom grinned just before he hit Eli full in the face with his fist.

Eli fell, hard, to the street. Eli was down only a moment before he was pummeled by three other men.

Otello stepped in between two of the men and took blows meant for Eli.

Captain Hopkins broke the axe handle over Little Tom's head. It seemed to have no immediate effect.

Little Tom hit Captain Hopkins with two quick punches that sent him reeling into the water trough in front of the general store.

Captain Hopkins, quickly, shook it off. He grabbed another axe handle and moved back to the fray.

Scotty was buried under a pile of five men. Frenchie was on the ground on top of two men but four others were hitting him in the back.

Captain Hopkins saw the glint of a knife blade raised above someone's head poised to strike Eli. Quickly, Captain Hopkins pushed his way by two men obscuring his vision until he spotted the man holding the knife. With all his strength he swung the axe handle at the man's neck. The axe handle broke off as it smashed into the man's head and dropped him to the ground. Moments later, the knife fell, harmlessly, at his side.

Eli paused a moment to smile "thanks" to the Captain.

The Captain could not reply. A pistol butt blow from a gun sent him sprawling on the ground. He fought with all his strength to stay conscious. He lost.

Otello turned to help. He was dropped by a rifle stock that cracked into the back of his neck. He dropped hard to the earth.

Scotty had put up a good fight but there were too many. He was groggy and a few moments from passing out. Hard blows continually rained on his head from several different directions.

Eli was bleeding from his nose and mouth and had already spit one tooth in the street.

Frenchie's cut had bled so much into his eyes that he was almost blind. Half his punches went wild as he swung at shadows.

Matters, were now, extremely serious.

No one knew where the first shot came from.

The loud report of the gun caused everyone to freeze a moment. Everyone saw the miner fall to the street with half his head blown off.

Now, what had begun as a bare-knuckle brawl, descended into a devil's rain of gunfire and hot lead.

Bullets came from every direction and everyone who had a gun—and that was most everybody—was shooting without regard to who or what or where.

The fact that most of these shooters were miners and not gunman was all that saved many a man that day.

Eli had never known such a feeling. Men were dropping all around him, yet his colt remained in his belt. It was as if he were in a bad dream that he wanted to go away. The loud report of gunfire only inches from his ears seemed distant. He wasn't afraid. He just did not have the right anger to kill any of these men.

Eli saw the bullets hit and tear into the flesh of men that

dropped around him—but his hand would not move to his gun. Scotty had found cover.

Frenchie was still struggling to his feet.

Captain Hopkins was no where to be seen. A huge shadow fell on Eli's face. He looked up to see the grinning countenance of Little Tom.

Little Tom looked puzzled. He looked at the colt in Eli's belt, then looked at Eli's face.

"You some kind of sissy boy or something? You got a colt there doncha'?" Little Tom looked confused.

"This kind of killin' ain't right," Eli gritted his teeth.

"Oh? So what are you going to do about it? I'll kill you, Mister. I'll kill you and what's yours!"

"What did you say?" Eli was suddenly angry.

"I said, I'm going to kill you. You and what's yours!" Little Tom repeated.

"The hell you say! Nobody is ever gonna' kill what's mine again!" Eli pulled the colt from his belt. He pushed it at Little Tom's face.

Little Tom looked fearful as Eli cocked the hammer.

Eli looked deep into Little Tom's eyes. Eli did not know this man. Eli was angered at him. He was not angered enough to kill. Eli's hand was unsure. He, slowly, lowered the gun. He shoved Little Tom hard to the ground. He started to turn and walk away. Little Tom could not believe it. Quickly, he pulled a long barrelled colt from his belt. He leaped to his feet. He brought his gun level with Eli's face.

Eli watched with almost detached fascination as the long shiny barrel moved to his eye level.

Little Tom wasn't sure what Eli was up to as he cocked the hammer of the gun. "You want to die 'jest like that? You not gonna' use that there gun?"

Eli stared, quietly. He showed no fear and that scared the hell out of Little Tom.

"You're crazy, Mister. But you oughta' know if you put a gun to a man's face you'd better be pullin' the trigger cause you ain't gettin' no more chances! You sick or tryin' to pull somethin' crazy, Mister?" Little Tom truly did not understand Eli. Little Tom shook his head in wonder. Then he scowled as he looked down at Eli's gun. "That's a fine gun but it ain't your'n is it? You just a fancy pants in a man's clothes. You's better off dead." Little Tom started to fire. He was unable to pull the trigger as Otello put a bullet in his left ear.

Little Tom fell to the ground dead.

Otello looked at Eli in disbelief. "He was going to shoot you for sure, Mister Eli. Are you alright?"

Captain Hopkins appeared out of the gunsmoke. He looked at Otello then at Eli.

"Good work, Otello. I thought Eli was a goner for sure. What happened, Eli?"

Eli shook his head, slowly. "I don't know Cap'n. Thank you, Otello." The words were barely out of Eli's mouth when two dozen of Little Tom's friends gathered around his dead body. They looked at their fallen companion then at Eli. They all raised their guns and readied themselves to shoot Eli and the others dead.

Just then, scores of Frenchmen poured out of their French saloons, like water through a broken dam. The Frenchmen had guns at the ready and they formed a human wall between Eli and Little Tom's friends.

There was a long moment of forced tension before Captain Hopkins broke it. "I think there has been enough trouble for one afternoon, gentlemen. Anyone caring to indulge, I'll be buying a round of drinks for the house in that saloon." Captain Hopkins offered.

There was a lot of grumbling and posturing but, finally, all agreed. They disbursed, almost as quickly as they had gathered, heading for the free drinks.

"I'm sorry we were a little late getting the message are you hurt, Mon'?"

The biggest of the Frenchmen said as he brushed Frenchie off.

"No! No. *Merci*! You came in time. But I do not understand. I saw the tri-color hanging in the window of that saloon?" Frenchie shook his head.

"Oh, *Wee*. This is Little Tom's idea of a joke. Frenchmen come into town, stop there and he has his fight. Little Tom is not much too happy when he is not fighting. I am Maurice Treadway," he offered his hand.

"I am Louis... Frenchie. They call me Frenchie," Frenchie laughed.

"*Wee*. A second name for us all," Maurice laughed also. "Come. Come with me to a real French Saloon. Turn your nose to the wind. Can you not smell the delicious smells from the kitchen?" Maurice motioned everyone to follow him down the street to his saloon.

Everyone followed along except Captain Hopkins. He paused to leave enough money with the saloon bartender to keep his promise to the miners. They toasted his generosity as he moved to join Eli and the others—worried to his soul about Eli's mental health.

"*Wee*. I believe I have died and gone to heaven." Frenchie went through the doors of the saloon with his nose in the smelling position.

Once inside, two lovely ladies grabbed him by each arm and dabbed at his wounds with perfumed handkerchiefs. One kissed him on the neck.

"Ah *Wee*. I know for sure I have died and gone to heaven," Frenchie said as he put his arms around the ladies and disappeared into the crowd at the bar.

Eli, Otello and Scotty stood in the background and shared their friend's happiness quietly. They were soon joined by Captain Hopkins. "I think we should find a bar that flies no countries flag and have the best part of a bottle amongst us," Captain Hopkins said as he looked at Eli with concern.

"Aye, Captain. There's enough bars in this town to have one for every man and his horse," Scotty agreed.

Eli was quiet for a moment before he replied. "I would like to have the honor of buying it."

Scotty and Otello laughed and moved to a water trough to wash the blood off their hands and face.

Captain Hopkins and Eli stood alone in the street.

"Captain, I intend to go on alone now. After seeing what you saw back there . . . I hope you understand."

"Damnit, Eli! We've already come through hell and damnation together and we're not splitting up now."

Eli disagreed with his eyes.

"We're friends. It is the way of friends to stand by one other. Now, no more of this going alone stuff!" Captain Hopkins boomed.

"I am a coward. I shoulda' blown that man's head off! I coulda' got everybody kilt! . . . I ain't got the sure hand, Cap'n," Eli said as he dabbed at the blood on his mouth with his dirty bandanna.

"A coward? You, Eli? No, but maybe shootin' isn't your way. You were plenty good with your fists."

"I won't be stopping the Joshua brothers with my fists!"

Captain Hopkins nodded understanding. "A man isn't an empty whiskey bottle is he, Eli?"

"No, sir. I saw deep into his eyes. I felt his breath. He was a livin' person."

"It's still not too late to consider a sailors' life, Eli. We can go back to San Francisco anytime."

"No, sir! Shootin' Little Tom was one thing. Shootin' the Joshua brothers is another! It ain't nuthin' I can't handle." Eli tried to assure himself.

"My friend, you'd better get it straight quick. I don't know these boys you are after. I do believe they are going to let you have only one chance. If that."

Eli pulled the shiny colt from his belt. He hefted it in his hand. He replaced it. "I expect that's all I want. I expect that's all I deserve."

Captain Hopkins look worried.

Scotty and Otello rejoined them. "I hope all the camps aren't like this one. Maybe the next one doesn't like Scotsmen," Scotty mused aloud.

"The talk is they're having some trouble with the Mexicans down in Sonora. You should be alright and so should the Frenchman," Captain Hopkins replied as he looked at Otello and wondered.

Otello did not reveal any emotion.

"Aye but do you ever think we'll be able to get Frenchie to leave "Moke Hill?"," Scotty chuckled.

"Yes. As soon as he's had a fling the gold fever will hit him. I know it's beginning to hit me," Captain Hopkins said as he looked deep into Eli's eyes. "Do you want to look around here some more, Eli?"

"No. It's Sonora. It's something I feel inside, Cap'n."

"Then Sonora it is, Eli. But tonight why don't we see if Frenchie is right about french cooking. Particularly the desserts," Captain Hopkins said, hungrily.

They began walking toward the French sector.

Otello hung back and followed Eli.

They paused and looked at the bodies of the dead men that littered the street. They studied the indifference of people who passed by. People going about normal business as if nothing had happened.

Eli had respect for the living and dead. He looked at the hard faces of the prospectors. He thought about their callousness. He knew some had come by their hardness because of circumstance, some by temperament. He knew to do what he had to do, he would have to become as hard as the hardest of them.

Otello watched his friend observing the miners. Otello thought he knew what Eli was thinking. He wondered on such things, himself.

CHAPTER FIFTEEN

Jules rode straight into California as fast as he could. There was no thought of stopping for a doctor.

He figured his brothers would find some way to fend for themselves. There was no thought of anything but getting to Sonora as fast as possible. All the tales of the vast riches just lying around had his mind buzzing with selfish thoughts. He loved his brothers as much as his heart could love. He also loved the thought of what money could bring. Jules had a mean streak as wide as any man who ever lived but he also had a deep and abiding loyalty toward his brothers. The only time his mind was troubled was when these two emotions were in conflict.

Jules was tired and his horse was a little lame. Jules cursed the animal for its lameness as he pulled up to take a brief rest in a wilderness meadow by a mountain brook.

Jules dismounted and watched as the horse drank from the brook. He yawned and stretched, then took a long drink form the brook, downstream from where the horse drank. He tied the horse to a branch and sat down beneath an old oak tree. The high noon sun was warm on his face and, before he knew it, he was fast asleep. Moments later, he was visited by the dream. The dream that haunted him almost every night of his life:

"You slothful, slacker! Look at this pitiful fifty cents in script! It ain't worth twenty cents in real money you done brought home, boy!" Ephraim Joshua, Jules' father, drove his huge fist full into Jules' young mouth. Jules reeled backwards and hit the cold wood wall hard. He could not get his breath for a long moment.

Jules was eleven years old and was supposed to be the

breadwinner for the Joshua family of ten. His two sisters were frail, sickly asthmatics and could not tolerate the mines.

The other brothers were not quite old enough to be "Trappers". Except for James who was older but not half as big as Jules and Ezekiel, his identical twin, in all respects except courage.

"Goddamn you boy! How in the hell do you expect us to keep body and soul together bringing home this pittance? Huh? Huh? Say something, boy!" Ephraim towered over Jules and glared down at him.

Jules let the blood from his bleeding gums pour through his fingers. He stared up at his father with white-hot hatred in his soul. Finally, Jules eased back up on his feet.

His father had broken both legs in a mining accident and they had not healed properly. As a result, he had limited mobility in his legs, but his arms and fists were as hard as the coal he had mined for twenty years.

Jules spit out two teeth and frowned at his father. He looked at his mother, Miriam, for support. Miriam's eyes said she wanted to help but she backed into the shadows instead.

"This ain't even gonna' git us one days rations at the company store. If it weren't past dark I'd have your young ass back down there doin' some real mining!"

Jules did not reply but looked into the frightened eyes of his brothers who cowered in the corner. Big John was only five, and big for his age. But he was the most frightened of them all.

"Don't hit me no more, Pa!" Jules challenged.

"What?"

"I said don't hit me no more. I done been hit enough. I done been hit too many times."

"You tellin' me what to do, boy?"

"No, Pa. But you know I done as good at minin' as anybody my age done. Even more sometimes!"

"Except, Eli Llynne. He's out done you everytime. Every day he makes twice your quota and he makes cash money. You know that?"

"Yes, Pa."

"Then goddamnit you'd better listen up and start producing or I'll be hittin' you a lot more than I am now! You hear?" Ephraim Joshua backhanded his son.

Jules fell backwards against a wall deep in the shadows of the small shack where Miriam cowered in a corner.

Miriam looked at her son and almost cried. She took her apron and dabbed the blood away from his mouth.

"Now don't go coddling the boy, Miriam. He's near to a sissy boy now, anyways."

"You don't hit him anymore. Please, Ephraim? Please?"

"Stay out of this, woman! I done told you not to interfere in my disciplinin'. So 'jest shut up!"

Ephraim hobbled over to Jules and clenched his fists.

Jules looked at him with hard eyes.

"I told you I don't want you to hit on me anymore, Pa!"

Miriam stepped in between them. "Please, Ephraim He's bleeding bad."

Ephraim grabbed Miriam by the hair and threw her to the floor. "Shut up, woman! Shut up!" Ephraim growled.

Jules looked at his mother prostrate on the floor and then looked at his father with unyielding hatred.

"You best not touch my Momma no more!"

Ephraim looked stunned before he broke into a mocking cackle. "What?"

"There's been too much hittin' 'round here. I ain't lettin' you do it no more," Jules said calmly, coldly.

"You best watch your mouth, boy. You don't have no say 'bout nothin' in this here house! You hear me?"

"I hear you," Jules paused. He looked at the fear in his brothers' eyes. He looked at his mother's terrified face. "I hear'd you. You hear'd me?"

"Ha!" Ephraim started to scoff until he saw the look in Jules' eyes. "You best be wiping that look 'offen your face before I bust you up like I ain't never done it 'afore!"

"No, sir!"

"No, sir what?"

"No, sir. I ain't doin' nothin' 'til I know, you know, I mean what I done said!"

Ephraim's face turned malevolent. He unhooked the buckle of his thick leather belt. He pulled it loose from his pants and began whipping Jules hard.

The sturdy leather belt stung Jules' face and back. Jules did not let out so much as a whimper.

Miriam could take it no more. She stepped in between Jules and Ephraim.

Ephraim whipped her harder than he did Jules.

Jules eyed a miners pickaxe. He hesitated a moment. His Mother's screams prodded him to action.

Calmly, with measured detachment, Jules lifted the pick axe and drove it into his father's chest.

Ephraim looked at him in disbelief before he hobbled backwards and fell against the wall.

Jules followed him and pulled the pick axe from his chest.

His father's blood spurted out of the wound and drenched Jules from head to toe.

Miriam started to run toward Jules. "No, son! No!"

Jules raised the pick axe high. He glared at his mother. "Shut up, woman!"

Jules said just before he drove the pick axe deep into his fathers head—killing him with more joy than remorse.

The dream was broken by the horse licking Jules face.

"What? What? What the devil?" Jules jumped up and drew his Colt. He looked at the benign expression on the horses' face and almost chuckled. He mounted the horse and rode hard into Mokelumne Hill.

Jules pulled up in front of the hotel in "Mok Hill". He dismounted and stood on the boardwalk. He looked up and down the street with delight in his eyes. He took in the sights and sounds of people busy about the business of finding gold. It was the happiest he had ever been in his life.

He paused as he watched undertakers loading a wagon with bodies wrapped in canvas. He could see dark stains in the dirt.

There was still a hint of gunsmoke in the air. Jules cursed the lame horse, again, for not having been fast enough to get him here in time to join the fray.

The horse looked at Jules with tired, angry eyes. If the horse had been a gunman, Jules would have been dead many times over.

Jules took the bolt of silk from his saddlebags. He moved, quickly, down the boardwalk to a general store. He wanted to get outfitted for mining as fast a possible. He had studied a crude map of the gold trail and he figured to prospect his way all the way south to Sonora, unless, he hit it rich before then.

The proprietor of the store saw him coming and licked his chops.

"Yes sir? What can I do for you?" The proprietor asked almost prayfully.

"I need prospecting gear. The best there is but not nothin' fancy," Jules insisted.

"Will this be dust, ore or cash money?"

"It don't matter. I got all three. Plus I got this here bolt of imported silk goods."

The proprietor's eyes lit up like new silver dollars. He took the bolt of cloth and fondled it, carefully. "How did you come by this?"

"I . . . I found it on the trail. There was an indian fight. It musta' dropped outta' a wagon or somethin'."

"I see. Well it's not the finest quality but . . . hhhmmmmm . . . let's see."

"Don't be flim-flamming me, Mister. That's right good dry goods. Maybe I'll go somewhere else."

The proprietor laughed.

Jules drew his colt and shook it, angrily, at the proprietor. "What the hell you laughing at?"

"You don't understand, Mister. There ain't no other place. Now you want to do business or what?"

Jules holstered the gun. He grinned. "You just treat me fairly and we don't have no trouble."

"Yes. I see. Well, I can give you a most complete package for less than $3,000.00," the proprietor hedged a moment. "An even trade for the silk?"

Jules balked, slightly, then shrugged. The proprietor knew he had his catch.

"You show me what you got. Then we'll see."

"Of course. Step this way."

Jules followed the man to the back of the store where two mules stood tied to a rail. He watched as the proprietor pointed to the animals with some pride.

"They're already packed and fully equipped for your convenience. Take your pick. They're both good animals," The proprietor offered.

Jules walked over and looked at the animals' teeth and legs. He inspected the bundles tied to the animals backs. He, finally, picked the larger one.

"I got everything I need to do fancy prospectin'?"

"This is the finest equipment west of the Mississippi."

"This don't look like much."

"Well, I assure you, it's a fair exchange. And if you come by anymore silk . . . accidently . . . you bring it to me, okay?"

Jules paused. He looked at a sleek stallion with a fancy saddle tied to another rail.

"I want that horse. Then we's even."

"Oh, no! That's my horse."

Jules pulled his gun and shoved it into the proprietors face. "You take me for a fool? You think I don't know `nuthin'? You think I don't know how hard it is to get silk dry goods in these parts? I outta' shoot you dead for cheatin' me, Mister!"

The proprietor swallowed hard. "Yes. Yes, of course! You take the horse and both mules."

Jules put the gun away. He looked at the proprietor with contempt. "I ain't taking both mules. That ain't a fair exchange. I ain't no crook, Mister!"

The proprietor nodded half-hearted agreement.

Jules led the animals around to the front of the store where his horse was tied.

Once there, Jules transferred his belongings to the saddlebags of the new horse. He smiled as he mounted the handsome animal.

It was near dark and he decided to set up camp just outside of town. He wanted to be as close to the streams and placer deposits— and as far away from hard-rock mining as possible.

Jules rode several miles outside of town. He headed into a grove of pine trees almost to the top of one of the high hills around "Mok Hill". He saw no one else around and figured this would be a good place to start. He was dismounting his horse when the gun butt cracked him on the back of the head.

Jules never saw the man who hit him and stripped him of his money. He lay on the ground unconscious the whole night.

It was five minutes before daylight when Jules regained his consciousness, cursing.

Slowly, he got to his feet and found that his assailant had taken everything except a small wad of bills he had in his boot. His head hurt and he was cold as he looked around his environs. He cursed the bad luck that had found him in this position. He had no idea what he would do until he spied a small tent stuck back in a ravine a hundred yards away.

There was a handsome chestnut mare and a black stallion tied to a willow tree ten yards from the tent. Jules knew, immediately, what had to be done.

Jules watched the camp for a few minutes and was happy to see no sign of activity. His heavy boots cracked the leaves and fallen branches more loudly than Jules wanted as he crept down close to the horses. The horses were nervous and they made Jules nervous. He had never ridden bareback, but he knew he didn't have time to saddle one of these fidgety animals.

Suddenly, Jules heard a stirring in the tent and saw shadows of a man outlined by the light from a kerosene lantern. He hesitated for an instant then untied the mare. He stepped on a tree stump and jumped on the mare's back. The horse balked and whinnied. Jules kicked it in the sides and, finally, got it headed full speed out of the camp.

A sleepy, young prospector came out of his tent with nothing on but a revolver. Jules was out of range by the time the prospector could line him up in his sights. The prospector fired until he emptied his gun, anyway. The loud report of the revolver echoed down the ravine long after Jules was out of sight over a hill.

The prospector retrieved another gun from his tent.

The prospector didn't stop for his pants. He leaped on the stallion's back and headed after Jules.

Jules was having a hard time riding the mare at full speed without a saddle. He had to rein her back a little. He let her out again when a bullet whizzed past his ear.

"Goddamnit!" Jules swore as he looked over his shoulder and saw the prospector bearing down on him. The prospector was a better horseman than Jules and the stallion was much faster than the mare.

Jules knew the prospector would be on him in a matter of minutes. Jules only hope was that the prospector would be out of bullets when he caught up. Jules was lucky, the prospector fired his last shot wide when he was still a tenth of a mile away. Jules looked back and watched the prospector try to fire. He was delighted that the gun clicked empty.

Jules grinned and pulled the mare up. He could see the prospector was a man smaller than he.

The prospector slowed the stallion as he turned the gun around. He held it in his hand like a hammer. When the prospector was right beside Jules, he swung the gun at Jules' head.

Jules grabbed the prospector's arm.

The momentum carried them both off their horses' backs to the ground.

Jules got in the first punch. Once both men were on their feet, Jules hit the prospector full on the mouth with his fist, sending the man reeling back into the cold mountain stream.

Jules hesitated a moment to laugh at the site of the naked man splashing around in the water. Then Jules picked up a big rock and moved toward him. The prospector saw Jules approaching and picked up a small tree limb.

They danced around each other, for a moment, before Jules threw the rock at the prospector's head. The prospector swung the branch wildly. Jules grabbed it and pulled the man to the ground.

The prospector released the branch and got up before Jules could hit him with another rock.

"My horse was stole. I was gonna pay you sometime later for your'n," Jules chortled.

"That's a likely story. You know horse thievin's a hanging offense in these parts," the prospector replied.

"I suppose they have to catch you to hang you," Jules grinned, showing his uneven rotten teeth.

"I suppose," the prospector replied. He moved toward the stallion as Jules kept backing him up.

"Well, I ain't catched yet, and I ain't intending to be catched." Jules picked up the prospector's gun by the barrel.

"I got friends all over this camp, stranger."

"Now that's funny. You seemed to be out there all by your lonesome."

"Look. Take the mare. Just take it and leave!"

"But I like the stallion. Can I have it, too?"

The prospector now had his back up against the stallion. Jules was only five feet away.

"No, you bastard!" The prospector shouted as he took a swing at Jules.

The swing was wide as Jules leaned out of the way. Jules brought the gun butt down, hard, on the man's head.

The prospector fell to the ground and didn't move. Jules started to raise the gun to hit him again. He stopped when he saw the two horsemen come over the top of the hill at full gallop.

Jules tried to jump on the stallion's back but slid off. The stallion shied away from him. Jules ran up to the mare and tried to jump on her back.

He slipped again and fell to the ground.

The riders were only a hundred feet away now and Jules could see the anger in their faces.

The prospector hadn't lied. He did have friends. Jules took off running on foot as the horsemen bore down on him. He realized how stupid that was when he heard the horses' hoofs bearing down on his back.

Jules made it to the mountain stream. He was about to pick up a rock when the rope fell over his shoulders. He tried, unsuccessfully, to get it loose.

He gasped in fear as the rope was pulled tight around him and he was jerked, violently, to the ground.

CHAPTER SIXTEEN

As Eli stood on a high hill overlooking the road to Sonora, he fondled Lydia's Celtic Crucifix. He let himself wax melancholy for only a moment before he put it back into his pocket. He looked at the jagged edges of the distant snow-covered Sierra's and felt the warm wind at his back.

Eli marveled at this place called California.

The distance covered by a day's ride could make the difference between a hard winter or a strange extended indian summer.

Here, in late autumn, there was still lingering foliage on many trees and the bright sun felt good on his face. He smiled as he saw a weathered bird house hanging from a big oak tree limb. A bluebird sat on the perch looking for food. Eli thought that they were as confused by the seasons in this wonderful land as he was.

As he watched the bird, he fought off a flood of memories. The memory of the first Spring he had spent with his bride.

In the dirt, dust, grime and drudgery that was his life as a coal miner, Eli had one bright shining reality—Lydia.

From the first day he saw her until she agreed to marry him, he went into a stupid, bashful boyish stupor everytime she was near. He never knew what she saw in him. He only knew he thanked God everyday that she saw something.

Eli loved Lydia more than life because without her his life had little meaning or direction. The pain of rising in darkness to descend into darkness to exit in darkness to make meager wages, would have been too much to bear without her beauty to come home to.

Lydia was a small-framed woman. She had been sick with scarlet fever and many thought she would die. The sickness left her sensitive to cold but Eli never thought of her as weak. She used to resent it when he tried to defer to her or do anything she thought was condescending. She would not accept help from anyone to do anything her hand found to do.

Most of all, Lydia hated violence.

Lydia's family, of proud Irish stock, was known as the "Fighting Flynns".

Lydia's father and four brothers would fight at the drop of a word they didn't like or look they thought was provoking. And if a fight didn't come their way when they were in their cups they would go looking for it.

Her father and three of her brothers, including her favorite, John the youngest, were blown to pieces in a shotgun duel. The brother who survived lost an arm and later died of alcohol poisoning.

For that reason, Lydia would not let Eli keep a hunting rifle in the house or go around mean-spirited people who partook of strong drink. It was hard for Eli to keep faithful to Lydia's desires in this regard. A coal mining camp was chock-full of silver-back gorilla's with big chips on their shoulders. Avoiding fights in such a place was a full-time endeavor for Eli. But such was his love for Lydia he did as she asked.

After a time, Eli saw the wisdom of such a policy. Many of his friends and acquaintances were killed or maimed by stupid fights for reasons that were lost in the heat of the fighting.

Because Eli was a big man who put out more than his quota every day no one dared call him a coward. Though he heard mumbling behind his back, no one said it to his face.

Lydia was good at making the best of small things. She could take remnants of material and make the loveliest dresses or curtains for the windows or fine sturdy shirts for Eli to wear.

She did things with spices that made bland food into zesty meals Eli devoured with gusto.

Lydia was so sensitive to life that she, once nursed a bird that had fallen from a nest back to health. Eli had marveled at the care she had given that animal. For six weeks she had delighted in watching it grow strong. He remembered coming home one day to see her crying. When she wiped away her tears she told him a young boy wielding his birthday shotgun had shot the bird dead that afternoon.

Eli insisted on going to the boy's house, taking away his gun and rendering him a good spanking.

Lydia would have none of that. She told Eli she had already admonished the boy and obtained his sworn oath he would not ever shoot a defenseless animal again.

Eli did not like her solution but it was her bluebird and her justice to mete out.

That night Lydia had fixed Eli a hearty meal and acted as if nothing had ever happened.

She never spoke of it again.

But Eli saw the light in her eyes everytime she saw a bird on the wing and he wondered by what grace she had never uttered an angry word or said an unkind thing about anyone.

It was a constant marvel to Eli that God made warm, decent, loving people like Lydia and allowed them to live in such a cold, hostile world.

It was a great and constant sadness that the same God allowed such beauty to die

At times, Eli risked the blasphemy of being angry with God. There was a bitterness in his soul that could not reconcile the death of innocence. To Eli's mind, it wasn't fair to let innocent bluebirds be born into a world, nurture them until they were grown, then blow them away like they were chaff.

He loved Lydia so much it hurt his great heart to remember and he forced the remembrance from his mind.

Once Eli shook the remembrance from his mind, he pulled the Colt from his waistband. He studied it.

Eli stroked the barrel with the ends of his fingers. He played with it, trying to make it familiar to his hand. It still did not feel comfortable. Eli's huge hands were made for hard honest labor. They did not take easily to the handling of weapons.

Eli had seen Otello's "sure hand" in the Moke Hill fight. Eli was determined to get his mind set that way—or else.

Captain Hopkins moved up, quietly, behind Eli. He put his hand, gently, on Eli's shoulder. "Well my friend, have the events of yesterday caused you to rethink anything, about anything?"

Eli shuddered with confusion. "I just don't understand this constant confusion inside my bones. God knows, a man shouldn't doubt what he knows is the right thing to do!"

"Maybe that means it's not the right thing."

"No, sir! I could never believe that!"

"She must have been an exceptional woman, Eli. I understand. Anyway, tomorrow we'll be in Sonora. We've all come a long way. Aye, Eli?"

"Yes sir, Cap'n. I hope all of you strike it rich. No men are more deserving. I really wish well for you," Eli said, sincerely.

"Aye, and you too, Eli. We'll file a claim under everyone's name. I'll have all the right papers drawn up proper. We'll get to digging right away, just as soon as we hit town and find where it's best."

"Cap'n, you know I won't be prospectin'. Not for awhile, anyways."

"Well I understand that, Eli, but while you're looking, you might as well do a little digging. Maybe they ain't there yet. Tell you what. You help us dig and we'll help you look. How's that?"

Eli shook his head in admiration.

"You're a lot like my father. He was always working at flim flaming me, too."

"Flim flam? Me? Why I mean everything I say and do to be in the interest of my men. You know, you never were discharged from the Silver Cloud. Officially, Eli that makes you my charge," Captain Hopkins said as he looked serious. He broke into a boisterous laugh before he looked serious once more.

"We come a long way, Captain. I tell you, truly, I never knowed I'd get this far. I do thank you, sir."

"Thank me? It was I who live because you were there when I needed you. I fully intend to be there when you need me."

"You are a good and true friend. I would not want to put you at risk," Eli turned and looked hard into The Captain's eyes. "I ain't got the sure hand yet!"

"I see. Your friend, Otello. He seems quite ready?"

"That's God's truth, alright . . . .and that's comin' to me. It'll come to me soon enough!" Eli tried to convince himself.

"I won't lie to you, Eli. You know full well my feelings on the matter."

"Yes, sir. I do."

"I hope those men aren't in Sonora and I hope they never get there. You suffered a most grievous loss and you have every right to be mad as hell. But you're contemplating killing six men or getting yourself killed. It's not rational, son. Even if it made sense it would be foolish. There are six of them, Eli! That's against the odds. You're going after pure vengeance. That's against God's law!'" Captain Hopkins concluded like a fire and brimstone minister.

Eli took a deep breath and blew it out before replying. "I done told you about the good book. It's done said that a man has a right to take an eye for an eye."

"Isn't that an old testament doctrine? As I remember, didn't the new testament change all that?" Captain Hopkins probed.

"No matter, I reckon that's something I'll have to work out with the Lord and myself. I ain't quite set on what I'll do, Captain, 'iffen I do find 'em. Iffen' there was any law to speak of out here . . . if a man could look to or depend on the law . . . it might be something different. But they just can't go scot free after what they did. That just wouldn't be right, nohow!" Eli assured himself.

Captain Hopkins sighed hard. "In that you may have a solid point."

Neither of them paid much attention to the hooting and hollering going on in the streets of "Mok Hill" below them.

"I had to tell you my concerns, my dear friend. Now that is done, I will stand beside you which ever course you take," Captain Hopkins said, sincerely.

Eli nodded agreement. He looked sad for a long moment.

"As I said, I ain't exactly fixed on what I might do myself. Out here in the sunshine, what they done don't seem as mean a thing as it did back there . . . but it's still mean enough, alright."

"I've noticed the air has been good for your asthma."

"Yes, sir. I done healed up some. Maybe I done healed up a lot. It's mighty good weather here."

"Aye, that it is! A man could settle here and do well even without a strike."

"I tell you, Cap'n. For myself, I'm powerful sure. It's thoughts of her that make my hand hesitate. Lydia was a peaceable woman who didn't cotton to guns. It's like she's tellin' me maybe this ain't right somehow."

"The Lord works in mysterious ways. I still have hopes of getting you back on my ship. A long voyage has a way of making a man forget many things."

Eli tried to frown but, finally, had to break into a smile. "You old horse trader. You ain't gettin' me back out there where a man can't see or smell a tree and has to walk like a stumblebum."

Captain Hopkins laughed and Eli laughed with him.

Eli fondled the Celtic Crucifix.

Captain Hopkins looked away to the horizon.

"I tell you Cap'n. It's knowin' what she would want that tears me apart inside. I have to get this troublin' out of my soul before I go on. No man should be at risk beside me until I done that."

"That's for me to decide."

"She was a quiet woman. She loved pretty, wonderful, happy things. She would not let me hunt for food. She would not allow guns in the house. Like I told you, I can not do anything that would dishonor her memory. I swear, when I know . . . for sure .. what she wants then there will be no hesitatin'."

"I understand."

"I'm sorry, Cap'n but I don't see how anyone can understand."

Captain Hopkins looked angry for a moment. He held his finger out and pointed to the East. "Understand? Understand the need for vengeance? To make things right? Me what was press-ganged into the navy. Who saw his brothers press-ganged. Who was shipped out to sea before he had a whisker on his face? A man who was never allowed to see his parents grow old and die. Never allowed to return to his homeland again. I have a bitterness in my soul also, but I do not pretend to know what it's like to lose such a love as yours. Alas, I deeply regret, I never had a chance to know such a happiness," Captain Hopkins heaved a heavy sigh.

"I do not know but what it would have been better that I not known it," Eli replied, sadly.

Captain Hopkins nodded, knowingly.

Had Eli turned and walked down the hill, he would have seen Jules Joshua being led down the street of "Mok Hill" at the end of a rope. He would have seen the miner's yelling for Jules to be whipped. He would have seen the proprietor of the general store spit in Jule's face.

He would have seen the one-room shanty of a jail where Jules was placed to await hanging at the pleasure of the miners.

CHAPTER SEVENTEEN

The Joshua brothers were mad as hell at Jules. It was over three weeks since he rode off looking for a doctor and they hadn't seen hide or hair of him since.

It had taken a super-human effort on Big John's part to get them through the mountains before the heavy late November snows fell. They had just made it to the foothills leading to the gold country when the first winter storm closed the pass behind them for the winter.

Big John's shoulder was healing well and Sly's fever had broken. They should have been a happy bunch. Their anger at Jules stopped them from enjoying the fact that they were out of the rugged Sierra Nevada mountains and into the heart of the California gold country.

They had no idea where Sonora was, but they figured Jules wasn't there anyway.

They all figured Jules was where the richest strike was at the time. They were determined to find out exactly where that was.

Big John had a strange feeling in his gut as he pulled the wagon off on a side street of "Mok Hill". There was a nervous edge to the town that made him uneasy. He dismounted the wagon and looked around, carefully.

"You think maybe we should go on down to Sonora and look for Jules?" Sly pondered as he pulled on a one dollar cigar he had taken off the merchant's cold body. "Well, he done left us behind, but maybe he got into some kind of trouble," Zack said as he eyed the pretty little dance hall girl walking into a nearby saloon.

"Well, I got to admit he done right good by us. This stuff is worth a powerful lot of money even if we don't find gold,"

Sly said as he looked over the dry goods in the wagon. "We sell all this and then we can do prospecting on the way down to Sonora?"

"You get prospectin' 'offen your mind." Big John took the big cigar from Sly's mouth. He stomped it out in the dirt. He noticed the dark red blood stains in the black-orange dust.

"It don't make no never mind. Jules done left us and if he run into some trouble he better be ready to explain it. Now let's see what we can get for this stuff and get rid of this wagon. Don't nobody say muthin' to nobody, I'll do the talkin'," Big John huffed.

"Yeah. Let's go outfit ourselves and get right at it. I can smell the gold around here," James said.

"I told you boys. No prospectin' 'til we know what's happened to Jules. There's a store right there. Bring the wagon 'round back, Ezekiel. I want rid of it!" Big John ordered.

Sly, looked at the smashed cigar. He grumped as he drove the wagon to the rear of the store.

They had no way of knowing it was the store that Jules had visited only three days before.

The proprietor looked at Jules' twin brother Sly as he came through the door and turned pale.

Big John noticed the man's pallor and was suspicious. "Something wrong, mister?"

"Oh, no! Nothing. How can I help you?" He chortled.

Big John shrugged. "We want to sell you some merchandise and be outfitted for gold finding."

"I'm almost at full inventory."

Big John looked doubtful. "Be that as it may, the five of us need prospectin' stuff. Good stuff. The wagon's out back. You take a look at the fine merchandise we brung you and maybe your "inventory" ain't as full up as you think!"

The proprietor knew, the moment he saw the wagon, who he was dealing with. The wagon belonged to Harold Messinger, the Missouri Merchant who was to deliver the goods weeks ago. The proprietor had suspected the bolt of cloth Jules had given him was stolen.

Now he knew for sure.

He examined the material, nervously, as the Joshua brother's looked on.

Big John did not like the man's manner. "Maybe you better tell us what's ailing you, Mister."

"Nothing! I just don't believe I can handle all this merchandise right now. As I said, I really have a full inventory."

Big John towered over the proprietor and looked deep into his eyes. "I seen your store. There ain't nothin' this good in there. You tell me what's goin' on. You tell me now! I mean it, you hear!"

The other brothers gathered around.

The merchant, pointed to a pack mule tied to a railing. "Why don't you just take that mule-pack there. It's all there. That is all you need for some right fine prospecting."

Sly's eyes lit up. He inspected the mule-pack. "This is all we need, eh? Cause if it ain't, we know where to come to make it right," Sly grinned.

"Yes, sir. If anything is unsatisfactory you bring it back and Marvin Richards . . . that's me . . . I'm Marvin Richards . . . I will make good on it. Yes sir, don't you worry none."

"I don't worry none but you shore seem worried 'bout something. You get away from that mule 'til we find out what's goin' on, Ezekiel." Big John put his huge hand on Marvin's throat. "Now you best not be talkin' down to me. You think I'm a hick or something? You been looking at us like we was dead men since we come through that door!" Big John threatened.

"No. Nothing . . . nothing like that. Not you . . . this gentleman," Marvin pointed to Sly, "If he had an eye patch he would favor, mightily, a man they're fixin' to hang, that's all." The merchant choked.

"Jules! Jules? They fixin' to hang Jules?" Big John choked the man harder.

"Oh, my God! You must be his kin. I swear it's none of my doin'!" Marvin chortled.

Big John grabbed Marvin by the shirt collar and pulled him across the counter. "Why? Why are they goin' to hang my brother? Why?"

"I told you. I didn't have nothing to do with it. He stole Bullfrog Smith's horse. They ain't no doubt about it. They'll hang him in the morning for sure . . . unless they get drunk enough to do it tonight," Marvin gasped.

Big John thought it over and let Marvin go.

"Damn! Now why would Jules steal a horse? He had money. Damn him!" Big John mumbled to himself. "Where they holding him, Mister? Where's this here jail house at?"

"Well, it ain't exactly a jail. We ain't big enough yet."

"Where?" Big John closed his massive hand around Marvin's throat, again.

"Three blocks down the street and up the hill. They got a little one room jail. Well it ain't exactly a jail, it's John Thomas' old tool shed," Marvin chortled.

"You got a 'Closed' sign?" Big John asked coolly.

"Right over there."

"Put it in the window, Sly. Marvin's closed for the day." Big John reached beneath Marvin's shirt and removed a big money belt. He released Marvin. He smiled as he counted out the huge sum it contained.

"Hotdamn we's rich now!" Sly exclaimed.

"You boys unload that merchandise. Marvin here is going to make out a piece of paper sayin' he bought all that stuff proper and legal. Ain't you Marvin?"

Marvin rubbed his throat. He started to object but, begrudgingly, made out the bill of sale.

Big John took it and looked at it as if he could read. He put it in his pocket. "Thank you, Marvin. It's a pleasure doin' business with you," Big John said as he brought his revolver down on Marvin's head. Marvin staggered, then dropped to the floor unconscious.

Once the wagon was empty, Matthew and Zack unhooked the horses. They helped themselves to saddles and made them ready to ride.

Big John sat in a corner and thought things over. He was less mad at Jules as he counted the money. "Ezekiel, you go down to the Livery and get us four more horses. The best they got. All you boys meet me at that there tool shed in an hour. Understand?"

"John, we ain't gonna risk getting shot over Jules. You know he done left us out there on that trail," Sly interrupted.

"We don't know what might of happened to him. Maybe he got waylaid by bushwhackers. It don't make no never mind. He's kin. Blood kin and he ain't hangin'!" Big John insisted as he pulled Marvin's body behind the counter.

"Blood kin don't leave blood kin behind like he left us. It ain't right. It 'jest ain't right, nohow," Matthew added.

"Shut up, Matthew! Just do as I told you! Do it now!" Big John glared at Sly. Sly backed his way out of the back door with his three brothers close behind.

Jules alternated between feverish sweating and violent cold shivers. The ramshackle tool shed the miners called a jail leaked cold rain that added to his fear.

Jules knew the law in these parts was whatever the miners said it was. He knew, to them, horse stealing was worse than murder. It was a hanging offense. Jules knew as soon as they got in the mood or drunk enough, they would come for him.

The one man left to guard him had gone into a tent about twenty yards away from the tool shed to get out of the rain.

Jules rammed his body against the old boards of the shack hoping they would give way. He only succeeded in hurting his arm. He started to sit down in the corner when his ear picked up a familiar voice.

"Jules? Jules you in there?" Big John whispered through a crack in the boards.

"John? Hot damn! It's you." Jules voice took on a seductive tone.

Big John waited to let Jules stew for awhile before he would reply.

"Big John I swear, before God Almighty, I tried to come back to get you. John, I had a doctor and everything but I was robbed and beaten and I had to steal a horse and they come after me . . . I swear, I was coming with help, John," Jules almost cried.

"That ain't exactly what we heard, Jules," Big John, finally replied.

"Well whatever you heard ain't the truth. You know I had merchandise worth some money. Well that merchant he set me up. You know I ain't stupid enough to steal a horse in these parts lessen' I has to!"

"Well, that does make some sense. I told the others you got waylaid by bushwhackers. Ain't that like I told you?" Big John yelled at Sly who hung his head, shamefully.

"How many they got guarding this place?"

"One man. Only one and he's in that tent, most probably half drunk." Jules peeked through the cracks and pointed toward the tent.

"Sly, you go down and take care of him," Big John instructed. He unholstered his revolver and aimed at the iron lock on the door.

Sly shrugged and moved off down the hill. It was slippery and he fell down twice.

Big John was about to shoot the lock off when Matthew spoke up.

"You shoot that gun and them other miners might come on up here, John. Hold on. Let's try to pry it open first," Matthew said, nervously.

Big John thought about it a moment and nodded agreement.

"You see anything 'round here strong enough?" John asked as he and James began looking around. James picked up a rusty old pick axe.

"Here, see if you can work it with this."

James handed the pick axe to Big John.

Big John stuck the end in the lock joint and began to pry.

"Hurry up, John. No tellin' when somebody might take a mind to come up here," Jules urged as he peered through the cracks.

"Damnit. I'm doin' the best I know how," Big John snapped as he grunted at his work. The lock jerked back and forth as Big John worked at it but didn't budge. Big John gave it two more hard tries, then the pick handle snapped off in his hand.

"I'm shooting the damn thing off right now," Big John said as he pulled out his revolver.

"Wait!" Matthew ordered. He pulled John around to see Sly coming up the hill with a frightened looking miner in front of him.

"He's got the key and he says it don't make no never mind to him if he let's Jules out. 'Cause they ain't paying him anyway," Sly grinned.

"That's right. I never would of got into this if Bullfrog Smith hadn't made me. I don't put store in hanging a man for stealing a horse. Besides he got it back shore 'nough." The grizzled Old Timer shook as he pulled out a small ring of keys.

"Hurry up old man!" Sly snarled.

The old man, nervously, unlocked the door and Jules came out in a hurry.

"You got me a horse?" Jules snapped.

"Jules! We got all the prospecting stuff. Now we can go to Sonora and get right at it!" Sly stopped when he saw the angry look in Jules' eye.

"You boys done good. Damn good! Let's get the hell out of here!" Jules instructed as he and the others started to leave. Jules hesitated a moment, turned to the old timer and grinned. "My brother don't know when to shut his mouth. It's a real bad habit."

"I didn't hear nothin', Mister. I don't care where you're going or what you'd be doin'. It ain't like I'm a real lawman or nothin'. Hell, I'm nobody. I'm just the town drunk and your business ain't no never mind to me," The Old Timer choked.

"I understand. You just go inside here and let me lock you up so's we can get a head start," Jules said with a smile.

"Yes sir," the Old Timer replied as he moved inside the

shack.

Jules motioned for the others to leave him and the old timer alone.

After they left Jules stepped inside the shack behind the old timer.

Once inside the shack, Jules pistol-whipped the old man's head as calmly as if he were polishing his boots. Then he returned outside and slapped Sly in the face.

"You don't never say nuthin' to anybody about where we's goin' or what we's doin'! If anybody comes after us over this, I'll kill you, Ezekiel!" Jules glared at Sly.

Sly rubbed his face and glared at Jules.

"Now come on. Let's ride out of here," Jules ordered as they ran to their horses, mounted them and rode hard through the heavy cold rain out of town.

Moments later the old timer took his last gurgling breath.

CHAPTER EIGHTEEN

Those who "came to see the elephant" were part adventurer, part dreamer, and part fool. "Coming to see the elephant," as the cynical joke of the time went, was to be like the farmer whose consuming passion in life was to see a real live elephant. When a circus finally came to town, he rushed so fast to "see the elephant" he almost killed himself. Near death he exclaimed, "I might be dying but I done seen the elephant."

The lure of the gold, but possibly more powerful, the lure of being in on a great adventure drew men from every walk of life to the California gold fields. Scattered among the legions of claim jumpers, hardened criminals and scalawags of every kind, were educated gentlemen who gave up comfortable lives for the physical and intellectual deprivations of the gold country.

Of all the rude awakenings to slap the foolhardy adventurer to reality—loneliness was the most rude.

Of the hundred thousand 49ers scattered throughout the gold fields, only a smattering were women. In the history of the world no finer place existed for a homely cocoon of a woman to turn into a social butterfly. Miners, long tired of "seeing the elephant" wanted to see anything in female form. Indeed, many a lonesome miner was found cuddled up with a bear cub, a friendly sow or whatever warm body was handy.

A woman need not be a prostitute to make it big. She could make a fortune if she could sing halfway decent or read letters or provide the most meager entertainment. Even educated men had deprivations in the gold field because of the lack of books. They too succumbed to the most outlandish types of entertainment to pass the time through the long wet, lonely winters—when there was no gold and no adventure to found.

For the few who struck it rich California was the fabled "El Dorado". For the majority of the others it was a mean-spirited hell.

If you didn't like the smell of canvas and wet muslin and men who disdained bathing. If you were outraged by people who communicated by cursing.

If you were bothered by hunger, thievery, sudden death and dirty clothes so stiff they could stand alone. Worst of all, if you couldn't tolerate eating your own cooking—you didn't belong coming to see this elephant.

The hunger for a diversion drove the 49ers to do things they knew were not right in polite society. They really didn't give a damn so long as it provided relief from the reality that they had failed themselves. Or, more profoundly, the folks back home.

The medium sized grizzly bear was not, particularly, in the mood for fighting, but the miners were in the mood for sport. They prodded him into the corral with pitchforks and knives.

The horse had been of good stock and a fine animal when younger but was now slowed by age. The bear was straight out of the high country woods and had been captured while feeding on the miner's garbage.

The bear walked out to the middle of the corral He stood up on its hind quarters, roared and postured before he sat down and picked bugs off his chest.

Eli, Otello, Frenchie, Scotty and the Captain rode into the outskirts of Sonora.

They were, instantly, drawn to the buzz of activity at a corral on the edge of town.

"It's a damn bear in the ring with a stallion. What kind of sport is this?" Captain Hopkins wondered as he pulled the wagon over and off the road.

A grizzled old miner looked at them, skeptically, before he spoke.

"Why, we're celebrating Rattlesnake's strike. Get down and have a drink with us!" He held up a jug to Captain Hopkins.

Captain Hopkins took a drink and passed it on to the others. He watched the horse circle the corral whinnying and kicking up dust, as the bear seemed disinterested.

"Hard as horses are to come by, you'd think they'd put a man in there instead," Eli offered.

"Don't worry. `iffen it goes long enough, old Rattlesnake will get in there and fight them both," the old timer chuckled.

The bear was jolted back to his feet by the crack of a whip. The whip was wielded by a huge barrel-chested man. Each stroke of the whip tore small pieces of the bear's fur. The bear lashed out with its paw and struck the horse on its left hind quarter.

The horse kicked out with its hind legs and just missed the bear's head. The bear reared up and growled then advanced, backing the horse into a corner. The horse raised up on its hind legs as the bear took three swipes with its huge paws and narrowly missed.

"You fella's just getting in, eh? Come down by Moke hill? Didja' hear about all that trouble over there? Look's like you just got into the gold country?" The old timer looked them over.

"Is it that apparent we're greenhorns? Yes, we heard about it. Not a proper place to raise a family is it?" Captain Hopkins smiled.

"Yep! Nothin' personal, but tenderfeet have a certain air `bout `em," the old timer chuckled.

Eli, who had been watching the spectacle with increasing irritation, jumped down from the wagon and made his way over to the side of the corral.

Scotty followed him and grabbed him by the arm.

"You couldn't be thinking of interfering in this?"

"I got enough personal trouble to be interfering in another man's business, Scotty," Eli put one foot on the lower corral railing.

Otello moved up behind them and watched the spectacle quietly.

The horse was bleeding badly and was now running about the corral kicking wildly and whinnying in pain. The bear loped across the corral at an angle to intercept the horse.

Stella came out of nowhere and leaped onto the fence. She paused a moment before she started to leap into the corral.

Eli recognized her immediately. He couldn't believe his eyes as she started toward the struggling animals.

"Sue? No . . . Stella! Stella from San Francisco!" Eli stood frozen a long moment. Then he saw the bear look toward her. Eli jumped the rail and started to move to help her. A big hand grabbed his shoulder and yanked him back.

"Where the hell you going, Mister?" the big barrel-chested man holding the whip growled.

"I'm going to get Stella out of there, that's where!" Eli tried to pull away.

"Another goddamn psalm singer out to spoil the fun," the big man grumped. He planted his fist in Eli's face sending Eli reeling to the ground.

Otello jumped on the man's back before he could swing again.

The big man hit Otello across the face with the butt of the whip.

Otello felt his teeth loosen. He spit blood and had to release his grip.

Eli got up off the ground and butted the big man in the stomach. They tumbled to the dust and rolled over and over wrestling for the whip.

Otello moved to help Eli. Two other men grabbed Otello's arms and held him back. Otello shook one loose and busted his jaw with a left cross.

"Lordy mercy. Then two greenhorns has attacked old Rattlesnake. They'll be kilt for sure," a miner mused aloud.

Captain Hopkins slowly walked over to the fight. Rattlesnake and Eli were on their feet now.

Scotty and Frenchie started to interfere.

Captain Hopkins motioned for them to back off. "Let Eli finish it, gentlemen!"

Eli saw the bear was only a few feet from Stella.

So did Otello. Otello wrestled free from the other man. He

downed him with one blow, then rushed in between rattlesnake and Eli. "You go, Mister Eli. I'll stand here for you."

Rattlesnake started to laugh.

He stopped laughing when Otello broke his nose with a punch in the face.

Eli did not hesitate. He turned and ran full out toward Stella and the bear.

The bear took a swipe at Stella's head and just missed. Eli swooped in before the bear took another swing. Eli picked Stella up and carried her out of the corral.

Instead of thanking him, she clawed at Eli's eyes and kicked at his shins. "What are you doing you crazy bastard! Who the hell are you?"

"I'm Eli. From when we was together in Frisco. Don't you remember me?" Eli looked puzzled.

Stella stared at him with contempt. "And why would I remember you?"

"We were . . . you and I . . . were . . ."

"Look, Mister. I don't know who you are but you'd better stay the hell out of this!" Stella looked at Eli and, for an instant, seemed to recognize him. "Now step back so I can go get my horse!"

"It ain't your horse anymore, Stella!" Rattlesnake stepped up and spit blood as he backed away from Otello.

"The hell it ain't, Rattlesnake!"

"The hell it is! Your pardner lost it in poker before he got himself shot. It's mine and you best be leavin' him alone!" Rattlesnake glowered.

"Sam caught you cheating, Rattlesnake. Everybody here knows you're a cheat and a liar. If I was a man I'd break your head open and feed what little is inside it to the crows! But no matter. You ain't killing my horse this day!" Stella put her face as high up Rattlesnake's chest as it would reach.

Eli had never seen such beauty and fire altogether in one woman. He had not remembered her being as pretty as she looked this day. Eli looked at her with a consuming wonder of disbelief and attraction.

"Look, Woman! You're just a fandango whore who thinks she's somebody. But you ain't nobody here! We's been working hard and this is our time to have some fun. You just get out of the way and let us be. There's too much money on this entertainment to let anything mess with it. Unless you want to take the place of the horse? Now that would be worth money to see!" Rattlesnake chuckled.

"Look, Mister. You don't have no business callin' her those names," Eli stuck his nose in it.

Rattlesnake and Stella looked at Eli in disbelief.

"Who the hell are you?" They both asked.

"I told you. I'm Eli Llynne. We met in Frisco."

"You and four thousand others," Rattlesnake laughed.

Stella slapped him.

Rattlesnake clinched his fist and started to deck her.

Eli stepped between them. "I'll be happy to pay cash money for the horse, Rattlesnake. I'll pay more than a fair price."

Rattlesnake looked at Eli with contempt. "If you don't get out of my way you ain't going to be among the livin' in a minute, so 'iffen you got cash money, you'd better name your inheritors."

Rattlesnake pushed himself into Eli's face.

Eli shoved him away so hard, Rattlesnake fell into the Sonora mud.

When Rattlesnake got up, his face was as red as an overheated locomotive boiler. "I'm gonna to kill you, Mister! I'm gonna kill you real dead!" Rattlesnake wrapped his whip around Eli's neck. Eli could barely breathe as the hard leather cut into his windpipe.

Otello started to interfere.

Eli waved him off.

"It's Eli's fight, Otello," Captain Hopkins held Otello back.

Otello was not so sure. He watched as Eli started slipping to his knees. He would not wait much longer.

Eli grimaced. He gasped for breath. He reached back and grabbed Rattlesnake's hair. He pulled with all his might.

Rattlesnake squeezed the whip harder. Eli was almost on the ground. His face was turning blue.

Otello started to step in. He was only inches away, when Eli gave one more pull.

The pull yanked Rattlesnake over Eli's back.

Rattlesnake flew through the air. He hit hard against the corral railing. He grunted and groaned—then lay motionless.

Those who watched were impressed with Eli's strength. Rattlesnake weighed in at over three hundred pounds.

Eli clinched his fists and advanced to beat Rattlesnake to death.

"Hold on, Mister!" Someone put a gun to Eli's head.

Eli froze.

"Put that gun down, Mister!" Captain Hopkins stepped in. He put a revolver against the man's ear.

Rattlesnake's friend started to ignore him.

Captain Hopkin's cocked the hammer.

Rattlesnake's friend lowered his gun.

Rattlesnake looked up at Eli with respect. He looked at Captain Hopkin's gun. "You got an upper hand for now, Mister, but what are you gonna do when you have to put that gun down?" Rattlesnake snarled.

"Who do you have your money on?" Eli challenged.

"What?"

"Which one? The horse or the bear?"

Rattlesnake looked confused for a moment. "Why hell, it's on the bear. That's my bear. He ain't lost a fight yet," Rattlesnake said with pride.

"I'll bet one hundred against title to the horse, that I can take that bear."

"Well hell, Mister, you're crazier than I figured," Rattlesnake laughed. "I'll take that bet and add a hundred of dust to go with it. But you can't use no guns!"

"Just my knife," Eli offered.

Rattlesnake looked at the crowd. They all seemed to like the idea. He nodded agreement.

Eli extended his hand and helped Rattlesnake to his feet.

"Eli, you aren't intending on getting in there with that bear?" Captain Hopkins cautioned.

Stella looked at Eli as if she was impressed by his strength but not his wisdom. "You done enough, Mister. You don't have to do no more. Rattlesnake has no right to be using *MY* horse like this. Somebody give me a gun and I'll take care of the bear," She said.

"That ain't the way it's gonna' be, Stella." Rattlesnake insisted.

Stella turned and looked at her horse. It whinnied as it backed into a corner of the corral. "The hell it ain't!" She grabbed for the gun in Eli's belt.

Eli stopped her hand. She swung at him with the other hand. Eli grabbed it. She kicked at him. He managed to dodge all but a few of the swiftest kicks.

Their eyes met in fiery disagreement before Eli's eyes won the argument.

Eli waited until she had settled down, somewhat, before he released his grip. She growled at him and rubbed her wrists.

Eli shook his head in wonder and rubbed his shins. "You hold the stakes for me, Stella?" Eli handed her his money.

Stella hesitated, then took it.

"Yes. I will. And I'll put two hundred of mine with it. On the bear!" she growled.

"You're covered," Captain Hopkins said.

"I'll bet another hundred in dust that he ain't never coming back. Not on two legs he ain't!" Rattlesnake chuckled with glee.

Captain Hopkins gave Eli a look of encouragement. "All bets on my friend are covered," he said and was soon surrounded by a mob of bettors.

"Eli, I'm lots better with a knife than you," Otello said.

"That may be so. But I done started this, so I expect I"d better get at finishing it," Eli said. He took a deep breath. He pulled a long knife from his belt and leaped over the corral rail.

It looked like a very bad bet for Eli as the bear, now frothing at the mouth, backed the frightened horse into a corner. The horse banged up against the corral railing. He was busting boards loose when the bear's claws ripped into its side.

Rattlesnake was pleased.

The horse reared up and hammered at the fence with its front legs. The bear bit into the horse's flank. The horse bucked the bear off.

The horse kicked out with both legs, cracking the bear squarely on the side of the head.

The bear staggered back as Eli approached with his large hunting knife drawn. The bear looked confused as Eli danced in between him and the horse.

Eli eased toward the latch on the gate. The bear snarled as Eli lifted the latch and swung the gate open. The horse paused and stared at the opening for a long moment, then turned and galloped, whinnying with joy into the hills.

The bear growled in frustration. He reared and stomped. He charged Eli.

The huge paws hit the hardpan dirt of the corral cracking small rocks and sending debris flying. Large gobs of froth poured out of both sides of the red-eyed bear's huge jaws.

Eli was drenched with sweat and the knife handle was slippery. He swallowed hard as the bear's foul breath blew into his face.

The bear took a swipe at Eli's face with its huge paw. Eli ducked. The bear reared up and roared so loud it hurt Eli's ears.

Eli wiped his hands and tried to get a tight grip on the knife handle.

Eli could hear the chants and taunts of the miners in the back of his mind. He was sad that most of them were chanting for the bear.

The bear swiped at him again. This time the claws tore into Eli's chest. The blood poured from the wound and soaked his thick clothing. Eli felt weak. He almost lost control of the slippery knife handle. The bear's shiny white teeth were inches from Eli's throat.

Eli placed both hands on the handle of the knife and thrust at the bear. He did not know if he had wounded the bear or not. The bear's huge paw slammed into the side of his head and knocked Eli, to the ground semi-conscious.

Eli's eyes were covered with blood. He could barely see the bear rear up on its hind legs once again. Eli probed the dust for his knife.

The ground shook as the bear seemed to descend toward him.

Eli braced himself for the pain the bears claws would soon deliver.

The pain never came as the bear fell over into a heap—Eli's knife buried in its heart.

Eli was too blood-soaked and weak to rejoice. He slumped and almost fell.

Rattlesnake watched his bear fall into a lifeless heap in the middle of the ring. He shook his head in disbelief. He looked at Captain Hopkins. "No hard feelings. Rattlesnake is a gambling man who knows how to win and knows how to lose," he turned to Stella. "Okay, Stella?"

"Go to hell, Rattlesnake!" Stella said.

Otello did not hear them. He was already at Eli's side. He looked at the blood and Eli's stillness. He feared for his friend's life. He turned and called out for help.

"Well, Stella. Looks like your hero needs some nursing," Rattlesnake chuckled.

"You heard the, Lady. Go to hell!" Captain Hopkins stepped in. "Is there a Doctor hereabouts?"

There was general laughter among the group.

"Ha! Ha! Looks like I'm not the one goin' to hell. That would be anyone lookin' for a doctor in this place, for sure," Rattlesnake growled.

"No! We have to get Eli some help," Captain Hopkins insisted.

"Well Stella here knows old Doc Bullock. He can cure anything so long as you got the price of a bottle of sippin' whiskey." Rattlesnake chuckled.

Captain Hopkins looked for Stella. She had moved to Eli's side. He followed after her.

Scotty and Frenchie followed also.

Rattlesnake watched them go. He spit and stomped off down the street to the nearest saloon.

Eli was bleeding badly and Stella was, at first, shocked by the sight. She took a deep breath and regained her composure as Captain Hopkins moved up behind her.

Stella looked up at Captain Hopkins. "Please, my buckboard is right over there. Bring it up. We have to get him to Doctor Bullock!" Stella insisted.

"Scotty, bring it up!" Captain Hopkins said.

Scotty moved to get it without replying.

"Hey, Mister. Can you hear me?" Stella tried to comfort him.

Eli nodded a weak "Yes."

"You are really something else, Mister. I sure hope you haven't gone and gotten yourself 'kilt. It was a good horse but it wasn't worth a man's life."

Eli looked at her with hurt and disappointment. "You don't remember me?"

"Eli," Captain Hopkins leaned down and whispered in Stella's ear.

"Uhhhmmm, yes. Eli, isn't it? Of course I do."

Eli seemed pleased.

Stella did not have the heart to tell him she hardly ever looked at men's faces, much less remembered their names.

"Did I get him?" Eli asked hoarsely.

"Him?"

"The bear. Did I get him?" Eli tried not to grimace in pain.

Stella looked at Eli with cautious respect. The last thing she wanted was to owe a man anything. She figured she owed Eli some simple courtesies. "Yes. He's lying over there looking, I must say, a lot better than you."

Eli smiled as he looked up at her shiny auburn hair and sparkling green eyes.

The afternoon sun formed an angelic halo around her. She smelled of Spring flowers and her touch was soothing. Her alabaster skin was flawless. She radiated beauty and vitality. The pain burned through his body, but her soft presence eased it, considerably.

Eli was slipping into unconsciousness but he didn't care. The vision of loveliness before his eyes was so pleasurable he could ignore the intense pain.

Stella's beauty was the last thing Eli remembered until he woke up in a large feather bed, on red satin sheets beneath a red velvet canopy—with a grizzled old man looking into his eyes.

"He's comin' 'round." Doc Bullock said as Stella moved up beside the bed. "If the fever breaks he should make it. Don't let him try to move too much. Those ribs is cracked up and down. If he moves too fast he'll just bust 'em up all over again."

Eli tried to get up.

Doc Bullock shoved him back down. "I just told you mister. Don't be movin' too much!"

"Who? . . . what happened? What am I doing here . . . . "

"This is Doc Bullock. He's been tending to you for a week now. Don't be givin' him any trouble," Stella insisted.

Eli started to object. The pain made him ease back on his pillow.

Doc Bullock frowned a moment, then he broke into a loud laugh. "You are one lucky man. You beat the bear and the infection. We have yet to see if you break the fever."

Eli sighed hard and eased back on the over-stuffed feather pillow.

Eli looked at Doc Bullock with eyes that he still could not focus well.

"Eli? Eli Llynne is that your handle?" Doc Bullock asked.

Eli nodded "Yes."

"Well, you're a might daffy for my tastes, Eli. But what you did with that bear is already a legend in these parts."

"I don't understand?"

"You best not let it go to your head. I got you patched together as best I could. I told Stella I'm mostly a horse doctor. I don't make no guarantees 'bout humans. Stella thinks there is merit to you, so I'll go along with her judgement."

"Stella said that?"

"You heard the doctor. Just lie still and don't make any sudden movements." Stella stepped up. She was dressed in the finest silk dress Eli had ever seen.

"My friends? Otello? The Cap'n?"

"They are in tents just down the street. They'll be by later," Stella said.

"No! Not for a little while yet. Friends is stressin'. I don't want him stressin' them ribs!" Doc Bullock insisted.

Eli looked about the fancy appointments of the boudoir. There were thick couches covered with red velvet and gold-backed chairs. The walls were covered with fancy embroidered wall paper on which were hung paintings in golden frames. The bed posts of his bed were thick mahogany and there were statues of naked people all about.

"A week? I've been out a week?" Eli wondered aloud.

"Closer to ten days. How do you feel? " Doc Bullock asked.

"It hurts to breath, Doc." Eli grimaced. "It's okay. I done breathed like this before."

"Yes. I saw evidence of an old injury. I understand. Then you know it hurts worse when you try to laugh" Doc chuckled.

Eli tried to laugh. He stopped as sharp pains shot through his chest. He nodded agreement.

"Well I'll leave him in your tender care, Stella. He's mighty spry so I'd keep a close eye on him,"

Doc paused. "Where were you and your friends planning on locating, Eli?" Doc wondered as he stroked his beard.

"Wherever we can along the river."

"Well, as you can tell this is a mighty edgy town. When you get well you're welcome on my side of the river. Just so long as you keep a proper distance and respect my diggings."

"Thank you, Doc."

"You'll thank me by getting well and making people think I really know what I'm doin'. If the gold plays out I might make a buck or two at this doctorin' thing," he smiled. "Welcome to Sonora, Eli," he said just before he left.

Stella chuckled at the thought.

Eli looked at Stella with admiration. She did not return his look as she turned and walked away.

"Yea. Welcome to Sonora indeed," Eli grimaced in pain with each shallow breath.

Stella watched his courage and wondered.

CHAPTER NINETEEN

There were hundreds of abandoned mining shafts filled with the darkened hopes and dreams of countless miners between Moke Hill and Sonora. The Joshua brothers used half of them to hide and evade the small posse. The posse had started out in hot pursuit but soon decided the offense was not great enough to be away from their diggings more than two days.

Besides, they had sobered up.

Jules was anxious to get to mining as soon as possible. His britches were itching to start digging but he had enough sense to be cautious. He did not like the way bad news seemed to get around in these loosely connected mining camps. He decided, to be on the safe side, it was a good idea to lay low for a month or so. He also thought it would be better to travel in groups of two so people looking for six brothers would be put off the trail.

"Sly, you and Big John go on ahead. James and Matthew will ride together. Zack will ride with me. We'll meet up in Sonora in thirty days. I hear Spring comes early in these parts. We'll get to serious diggin' then. Don't be tellin' nobody you is brothers. We gonna' lay low for a little while. So don't be drawin' no unnecessary attention to yourself," Jules instructed.

"I don't think we need worry 'bout those miners, Jules. They're more interested in their diggin's than chasin' us," Big John objected.

"Well maybe so and maybe not. But we's jest gonna' take no chances. Now jest find a saloon in Sonora and I'll be lookin' for your horses tied up out front. John why don't you give me the money you got for that merchandise and I'll count out shares," Jules grinned.

"No! Not this time, Jules. I'll count out the shares and I'll be keeping the most of it until we meet up!" Big John was adamant. Jules looked at him and then at Matthew.

"He's right, Jules. Nobody is happy with what's been goin' on with you. Maybe you was bushwhacked and maybe not. But we're jest gonna' see what we're gonna see for awhile!" Matthew was equally adamant.

"Is that a fact? Okay. Give me my share and I'll be goin'," Jules paused and looked malevolent. "Maybe you don't want to meet up. Is that it?"

"Nobody said that. We're 'jest movin' a little slower and watchin' a little longer," Big John said.

"After what I done for you all, that's your final word on it, Big John? Matthew?"

Big John and Matthew nodded agreement.

Jules turned his head in disgust as Big John counted out a handful of bills and gave them to Jules and the rest. "I see," Jules said. He took the money and tried not to look hateful. "You headin' up the family now, John?"

"I ain't said that. Jules."

"No? I heard you different."

"That ain't my intentions, Jules."

"Well I'm gonna' think on it and maybe I'll meet up with you boys," he looked at Big John and Matthew hard. He jerked his horse around. ". . . and maybe I won't!" Jules spit into the wind, then rode off at full gallop.

The others watched as he rode away.

"You done, done it now, John. He's gone and not comin' back for shore!" Sly chortled.

Big John moved up beside Sly. He looked at him a moment before he slammed a fist into Sly's mouth and knocked him off his horse. "I'm damned tired of your stupid mouth! You keep it shut from here on out or I'll bust you every time! Now get up and let's get goin'!" Big John's fiery eyes made his point with the others.

"Which way are we headed, John?" Zack wondered.

"We're gonna' do like Jules said. It makes sense to ride out, two by two. Matthew you ride with me. Zack and James ride off that way. We'll see you in Sonora in thirty days. Some saloon 'bout the middle of town. Be there," Big John said.

Matthew nodded agreement.

James shrugged, then joined Zack. They rode off Southeast.

Sly, rubbed traces of blood from the corner of his mouth. He spit red through his teeth. For an instant, his hand passed over the butt of his gun.

Big John looked at him with a stern dare.

Sly eased off. "Two by two don't leave nobody for me 'iffen Zack rides with you?"

"That be true, brother. You ride back 'aways from us."

"How far back?"

"Back so I don't see your face for sometime!"

Sly was not comfortable with that thought, but he would bide his time. He spit blood once more and nodded agreement.

Big John waited a moment before he led them Southwest.

From the bushes in the hills above them, Jules watched them go and smiled. He then turned his horse's head to the gold fields of Sonora.

CHAPTER TWENTY

Eli watched Stella's every move out of the corner of his eyes. It was now almost two months since his encounter with the bear and his fever had broken.

Eli was much better, though he was still weak. It didn't hurt to breathe anymore but it hurt to cough. Every once in awhile dust would blow in through an open window and fill his lungs. The dust would aggravate his miner's asthma and he would have to cough. Stella would watch his pain until she could stand it no longer. Finally, she would turn away and move into another room.

"How is the horse doing, Stella?" Eli asked one bright morning in the late Spring of 1852.

"Bear? He's doing a lot like you. He's scarred but getting around fine. I do owe you many thanks for that."

"Bear? You named him "Bear?"."

"Of course."

"You don't owe me anything. You saved my life. I owe you." Eli looked at her with unashamed fondness. She looked a little embarrassed.

"Look, I know this has been hard on you. Keepin' a man under a woman's roof ain't seemly. Captain Hopkins has set a place for me at his claim. I think I'd best be goin' there."

"You aren't going anywhere until Doc says you can and he ain't said you can. This ain't the East and I'm no sunbonnet woman. I don't give a damn about phony appearances or what anybody thinks. You're in the West, Eli. Drop all those pretentious Eastern manners!"

Eli was dazzled by her. Nothing in his experience prepared him for such a confident woman. Eli had never met a man, much less a woman, who had so much brazen energy.

"Don't you worry none, the minute Doc says it's okay, I'll make sure to see to it you're gone out of here soon enough!"

Eli sighed hard. "It shore enough ain't the East. But I do feel almost one hundred per cent, Stella. I thank you, but I best be goin'." Eli forced himself to get up.

"You are a stubborn man, Eli Llynne. That's what got you hurt. But I do things the proper way. You and I don't know nuthin' about the human body. Doc says them ribs still ain't right so you just stay put and quit talking so much it slows the healin'!"

"You're a strong-willed woman, Stella. You remind me of my Lydia."

"You sure don't know anything about flattering a woman, Eli Llynne."

"I'm sorry. I don't understand?"

"Well if I have to explain it to you then it doesn't work right. You should know that a woman wants to be special in her own right . . . not compared to someone else. Any man with half a brain should know that," Stella said.

Eli thought it over a moment. "I only know'd one woman. I never had much time to learn much about proper courtin'. I'm sorry."

For the first time since he had known her, Stella looked at Eli with genuine affection. "You really don't know do you?" She sighed.

Eli shrugged.

"Well then it's high time you learned."

"I don't understand."

"I'm sick and tired of crude men. You know what I did for a living, Eli?"

"Yes, Ma'am . . . but I don't . . . I don't hold that against you none."

"Well I don't give a good damn if you do or not! That's way more than past over 'cause I got enough money to carry me 'til doomsday. I can buy anything I want. But there is one thing I can't buy. You know what that is, Eli?"

Eli was too fascinated by her to reply.

"A gentleman. A refined man who knows how to treat a lady. You're about as crude a hick as I've ever seen but you have possibilities," Stella paused and looked at him like an auctioneer inspecting a prize bull. "Would you mind if I taught you a few things?" she asked with a gentle voice he had never heard her use.

"Why, no. No, Ma'am."

"First stop calling me, "Ma'am!"

"Yes Ma'am . . . I mean. Yes, Stella."

"You understand I'm not doing this just for my sake but for the sake of any other women . . . god help them . . . you might meet up with?" Stella moved to a closet and brought Eli a fancy suit. "Do you feel up to dressing in this?"

Eli looked at the suit and looked puzzled. "My goodness! I ain't never seen nice clothes like that. Not even for Sunday meetin'."

"I think not. This was worn by a New Orleans Dandy. There were two bullet holes in it I had re-weaved. If I let you wear it, don't get it ventilated again. Okay?"

"Oh? I wouldn't presume . . ."

"Take it! It's yours."

Eli, reluctantly, took the suit.

"Put it on. There's shirts and unders in those drawers over there. When you're properly dressed, join me in the sitting room." Stella paused and looked Eli up and down. "We'll continue the lesson there," Stella said and left the room.

Eli felt even more awkward as he dressed in a nice smelling, neatly ironed set of clothes. He had never been dressed so well. He felt slightly uncomfortable as he moved into the other room to rejoin Stella.

Stella tried to hide her approval, but her eyes showed she liked what she saw.

Eli Llynne was a handsome man of striking bearing. His ice-blue eyes sparkled soft and kind in certain light.

His thick dark hair had a slight curl in it. His muscular chest seemed to want to burst from the fancy shirt. His huge biceps made the coat sleeves bulge to breaking. His huge hands could crush her skull, but Stella had felt a softness in them. "Please, sir. Won't you join me over here by this window," Stella said.

Eli moved to the window and looked outside to see a flower bed.

"Does that give you any ideas?" Stella wondered aloud.

Eli stared at the flower bed for a long moment before the light went on in his head. He smiled as he leaned out the window. He picked several of the prettiest flowers. He, proudly, offered them to Stella. She refused to take them.

"I don't understand," Eli said.

"Think about it!" Stella insisted.

Eli thought about it until he got a headache. "I'm sorry, Ma'am. I thought you wanted flowers?"

"Just like that? Just pick 'em and shove 'em in my face. Is that it?"

Eli looked dumfounded for a moment, then his face brightened. "*Och hyd atat-ti, Ddum, na ddam-mor dros dir! Pa beth y'ngedir i ohiriaw,*" Eli said proudly in Welsh.

"What in God's name was that?" Stella almost laughed.

Eli looked insulted. He stepped back and tried not to be angry. "It is poetry what was taught me as a child. It was my father's last words. It's Welsh. The english meanin' is, 'God, why does not the sea not cover the land? Why are we left to linger?'"

"I see," Stella said. She did not know what to think or how to reply.

"It is all the poetry I know. I'm sorry."

"Well! I thank you for the sentiments. I believe they were truly felt."

"Yes, Ma'am."

"That "Ma'am" thing again, Eli!"

"Yes . . . Stella."

"Much better."

"Thank you, Ma'am."

They looked at each other for a moment before they both broke into laughter.

The pain from Eli's broken ribs made him stop laughing first. "I know you'd expect more personal sentiments from a gentleman caller. I'm sorry I'm not expert in that particular way . . . . Stella," Eli apologized.

Stella smiled. She moved close to him. "Well give it a try. Maybe you're better at it than you think."

"Oh, Miss Stella if you knew how hard that comes to me."

"Try. Just say whatever comes to mind."

Eli would have rather pulled a basket laden with ten tons of coal. He stepped back and grimaced.

"It's Spring, Eli. The earth is coming alive again. Can't you feel that rebirth in your soul?"

Eli took a deep breath and blew it out hard.

"Aaahhmmm. Oh! Madame, I hope you will accept these flowers as a token of my . . . my esteem?" Eli said, haltingly.

"And?"

"And? Ahhmmm! Ahhmmm! Jesus, Stella, this is hard! I never had a chance to give Lydia . . . flowers!"

"I told you, this isn't about her or any other woman."

Eli glowered in anger. He started to turn and walk away. "This ain't no good idea, 'atall!"

"You quit when a job is half finished, Eli?"

"I ain't no actin' person!"

"That's true enough but you almost had it," Stella cooed.

Eli turned and looked doubtful. "I don't like playin' no fool, Stella!"

"You thought that was what I was up to?"

"Yes, Ma'am!"

"You could not be more wrong! I was just trying to help you manage a little better in the world outside. Forget it! Okay?'" Stella fumed. She turned to leave.

Eli watched her go. He felt beholden to her for her help. He felt a long lost feeling inside. He did not want her to leave. "You stay if you want and I'll try one more time."

Stella stopped. She thought it over. She, slowly, turned. She walked back by his side. She looked at the flowers. "That was a good try because it was heart felt. I was not mocking you, Eli. I would not do that Ever! Understand?" Stella looked at him with mellow eyes. Eyes that revealed a deep affection.

Eli looked into her eyes and liked what he saw. Stella was right. It was Spring and he was chock full of the juices of life. It took all his restraint not to pull her into his arms. "I know of a Lady's need for poetic things. I ain't the hick you take me for. When I set my mind to it, I can be the things a woman wants. I don't think it has much to do with fancy clothes."

Eli unbuttoned his starched collar. He moved close to Stella.

"My! My! I think we're getting there," Stella smiled.

Eli started to reach out for her.

Stella danced away.

Eli sighed hard. His breath approached the temperature of steam.

"Nobody is asking for the Song of Solomon. Here! Give me the flowers." Stella took the flowers and stepped back. She paused a moment then held them out and approached him with a curtsy. "My, Lady. These are for you. They are the first flowers of spring and they are lovely, but their beauty is a pale imitation of yours."

"Yes, Ma'am. Those are pretty words but they ain't mine." Eli insisted.

"Oh? Then think of me as a teacher." Stella shoved the flowers back into Eli's hands. "It's your turn!"

Eli's huge frame quivered with indecision. Eli would have rather fought another bear than go through this emotional strain. "Aahhmmm, Madame. Madame . . . oh, my, Stella . . . I'm sorry. This ain't my kind of thing. I'm sorry!"

"You're hopeless.! All men are hopeless!" Stella turned her back on him. She thought it over. She turned and looked deep into his eyes. "Then you can go!"

"Ma'am?"

"I said you can go! Leave. Go join your crude friends. Remain crude and unpolished. So be it! I have done all I can. All I will!" Stella moved to the front door and opened it.

"I don't understand. You said the Doctor said it wasn't time."

"Maybe you aren't as sick as I thought. Just go!"

Eli hesitated. He looked deep into her eyes. Stella had the most compelling green eyes. Eyes with an enchanting emerald cast. Eyes that pulled you inside and made you stay awhile. Eyes that could catch a man's soul if he let his linger on them too long.

"I don't want to go," Eli said coolly.

"What?"

"I don't care if I am well enough. I'm, sayin' I don't want to go," Eli gathered his strength.

Stella's revealing eyes could not hide her amusement—her admiration. Her desire. "I said you are leaving!"

Eli took a deep breath and blew it out hard.

"No, Ma'am!"

"Oh? Well we'll see about that, Mister!" Stella moved to a bureau drawer. She started to withdraw a pistol.

Eli pulled her hand away and slammed the drawer.

She growled and spewed at him. She raised her hand to hit him.

He grabbed her hand and stopped it. He put his other hand, gently, on her shoulder.

She looked up at him with a false anger that Eli sensed was inviting.

Eli let her go. He looked deep into her eyes and smiled with affection. "Maybe you could learn to let a man have his head. Maybe then he could show you in his own way. Will you give me a chance to do that?"

Stella shrugged. She watched as Eli pulled a small box of his belongings out from under the bed.

Eli unwrapped something from a cloth. He hid it behind his back as he approached her. He stopped in front of her and stood tall. "Madame Stella! This is for you. I carved it for you to show respect for what you done to help me through my sickness. I keep special feelin's for you and for all that you have done for me," Eli said firmly.

Stella looked at the carved Welsh "Love Spoon" in Eli's hand. She held back a moment. She studied the strength in his manner. Stella took the "Love Spoon" and looked it over.

The spoon was of normal size but the stem widened into half an arm's length. The long wide stem was carved with a wooden cage in which were six wooden balls. It was adorned with single hearts with some room left for adding others. At the very end was a Celtic Cross.

It was exquisite workmanship that made Stella wonder how and when he had carved it. She decided that didn't matter and her long ingrained cynicism melted the moment she held it in her hands.

"My God! It's beautiful. It really is."

"This is how my people express their deep feelings. The hearts were meant to tell you how I feel. I did not presume to carve two side by side."

Stella was dumfounded. No man had ever recited more beautiful poetry. She had to step back and gather her thoughts.

"I'm sorry. Did I offend you in some manner?"

"No! No. Not at all." Stella studied the spoon. "The cage, Eli? The cage and balls inside?"

Eli looked a little embarrassed. "Some say it has a meaning of captive love or a wish for many children."

"I see. What was your meaning?"

Eli stepped up close to her. He gathered his courage and looked at her with unashamed affection.

"I meant both."

Stella's hard eyes mellowed. She turned her head away from him. She fought back tears.

Eli touched her shoulders gently. He turned her slowly. He drew his face close to hers. "I thought I would never have any room inside myself for anyone ever again but I have the most honorable feelin's for you. I would be most proud if you would consent to being my wife," Eli said with unashamed courage and conviction.

For the first time since he had known her, Stella looked dumfounded. She almost fainted.

"I'm sorry. I'm sorry. I didn't mean it. I just was lookin' for somethin' to say and I kept on sayin' it!" Eli tried to assure her.

"You didn't?"

"I didn't?"

"Mean it?"

"No, Ma'am. It ain't exactly like . . . . "

"You intend to breach a promise, sir?"

"Ma'am?"

"A proposal of marriage as I recall?"

"No! But I didn't. It weren't exactly like that. I mean . . . I . . ."

"Oh, shut up you big lug! Yes! Yes, I'll marry you!" Stella threw her arms around his neck and kissed him hard.

Eli lost himself in the warmth of her kisses. In a long moment of tenderness, all the pain in his body was gone—and much of the hurt from his soul.

CHAPTER TWENTY ONE

Late Spring, 1852

Jules waited in the saloon in the dark shadows toward the back. He sipped a beer and watched as his brothers came through the swinging doors. He was surprised they had not gotten lost over the weeks without him to guide them around. He had hoped to strike it rich and not have to crawl back to them. Instead, he had spent the better part of the month trying to avoid some mexicans he had tried, unsuccessfully, to rob.

"We seen your horse tied up outside, Jules. We knowed you'd be here. Good to see you brother!" Sly exclaimed as he and Big John approached.

"Well it's damn good to see you boys didn't 'git lost! Now sit down and have a beer and . . . let's see . . . everybody is here but Matthew . . . is he still mad at me? Are you still mad at me, John?"

"Nobody is mad at you, Jules. Matthew is outside. He'll be along," Big John replied as he picked up a beer. He downed the big glass with one gulp.

Matthew was outside tying his horse up when his eyeballs almost fell out of their sockets. He watched in utter amazement as he saw Eli and a pretty woman, holding hands and laughing as they crossed the street to the county court house. He stared for what seemed like forever, until he was sure of what he was seeing.

Matthew was sure. It was Eli. It could not be, but it was. He ran inside the saloon and stood before Jules, breathless. "Jules! Jules! Everybody come here quick!" Matthew shouted.

"Hold on, Matthew. What's got you so spooked?" Jules almost laughed.

"Eli! Eli Llynne! He's out there Jules. I done seen him!"

Jules looked doubtful. He started to laugh. The look in Matthew's frightened eyes told him it might be worth a look. He got up from the table and moved to the doors. He looked out into the street.

The others followed Jules' eyes as they all fell on Eli and Stella moving across the street. They turned and looked at each other in disbelief.

"It can't be Eli, Jules. It can't be. But 'iffen it ain't, it's his twin brother," Sly choked.

Jules stared for a long moment. He cursed under his breath "He ain't got no twin brother. That's him. I not only see him, I smell him. It can't be, but it is. It shore as hell it is!" Jules growled.

"He didn't see us. We can ride out and get lost on down the road. They say there's good diggin's at Mariposa," Sly offered.

"My, God! If that is him, maybe that's the thing to do," Zack agreed.

"We ain't goin' nowhere else. This is as far as we go. 'Iffen that is Eli and I'm sayin' it is, he's a dead man for shore this time!" Jules glared at Zack, then at Big John. "I thought he had a whole mountain on him?"

Zack moved into the shadows.

"That's right, Jules! He had to be dead. No man could of lived with all that rock on him!" Big John apologized.

"Well he did, didn't he?"

Big John looked contrite.

"This time I'll show you how to do it!"

"Here?" Sly wondered.

"No, stupid! Not here! Not now. First we find out where he's stayin' and who he's with. Then we do it. Follow them, Sly, and mind you do it good. Don't you let them see you. We'll set up out in that oak grove. You come back to us there," Jules instructed as he grit his teeth so hard a chip broke loose from a molar.

Eli felt a cold chill on the back of his neck. He did not want to startle Stella. He took a quick look back up the street.

It seemed to be free of danger.

Eli could not shake the familiar feeling of dread. He held his soon to be wife's sweet hand, tighter.

Stella looked at new bonnets in store windows.

Eli turned and looked up the street again. This time, he strained his clear blue eyes to find what his soul told him should be there.

"They're here. I know it. They're here," he thought to himself.

"Eli? Are you alright? Don't tell me the bright light of day is giving you cold feet?" Stella looked concerned.

"No! No, what I said I mean. I mean to marry you if you'll have me."

"I felt a shiver in your hand."

"It's just the hurt that bear put on me. I ain't exactly well yet. You sure you want half a man?"

"You aren't half a man." Stella gripped his hand tightly. "I have a confession to make. Doc said you were ready to leave weeks ago. It was me that kept you there." Stella looked embarrassed.

Eli smiled at her and touched her face lovingly. "Now I know I have to marry you. I surely don't want to be a kept man anymore," he laughed.

Stella smiled thinly.

They walked awhile quietly.

Stella stopped and looked deep into his eyes. "I wasn't entirely honest with you. You have a right to get out if you want. I'll step aside if you want to leave now," Stella said firmly.

Eli looked at her with love in his eyes. "It was pure luck that brought me you when I never thought I could ever have such things again. No man or woman will ever take you away from me. If you still want me I will have you as my wife."

Stella thought it over. "Maybe? Maybe I'll give you a trial run." Stella turned and looked at him with love brimming in her eyes.

They embraced in the street oblivious of the turned heads that looked at them. Some with censure, some with amusement— and some with profound envy.

CHAPTER TWENTY TWO

"It's good to see that light in your eyes, Eli. You seem to be more at ease. I'll be delighted to be best man at your wedding," Captain Hopkins said. He smiled and lit his pipe. He blew out a large cloud of smoke that wafted out of the tent and across his recently filed claim.

The light from the kerosene lantern illuminated Eli's face. A face that lacked much of the spring steel tension of days past. A face, still strong, but lit by eyes more mischievous than mean. A face no longer taunt with the agony of a tortured soul.

Captain Hopkins was pleased to see the pain gone from it. "Does this mean you have decided that vengeance is the Lord's?"

"No! No, I ain't forgot. That just ain't been uppermost in my mind of late."

Captain Hopkins lit his pipe.

"I see. I welcome the peace it seems to have brought you," Captain Hopkins paused and puffed on his pipe. "Stella is one remarkable woman. I'm happy for you."

"I thank you for that, Cap'n. She speaks well of you," Eli heaved a sigh and sipped black coffee for a long moment. "I expect when I'm a married man I won't go looking for trouble. Stella is almost as much against guns and killin' as Lydia was."

"I understand."

"If they show up or I hear tell of 'em, then that's somethin' else," Eli convinced himself.

"A sensible attitude. Meanwhile there is gold to be extracted from this good land. I took the liberty of filing you and Otello a share of the claim."

"That's mighty nice, Cap'n, but I ain't done nothin' to deserve that," Eli insisted.

"Consider it a wedding gift, Eli."

"A wedding gift? It don't really seem real, Cap'n. It don't seem right somehow."

"Oh? Is the groom getting cold feet?"

"I didn't come all this way for no wedding but I got one comin' sure enough."

"Eli you think too much. Take it as a blessing and don't question it."

"Yes, sir. I do . . . then I don't," Eli grimaced. "It ain't nothin' I can't handle."

"Oh? Then what is that look of doubt I see in those eyes all about?"

"You show me where to stand and I'll hold up the whole damn world on my shoulders, Cap'n!"

"I see. A modern day Atlas."

"A what?" Otello wondered.

"A mythical hero."

"You gonna' teach me that too, Cap'n?"

"Yes, Otello."

"Did you see them alphabets I wrote for you?"

"Yes, Otello. You are making remarkable progress."

Otello smiled.

Eli spoke as if they weren't there. "I want Stella more than anything."

Captain Hopkins nodded agreement. "I do believe she is yours, sir."

Eli looked pleased then very sad. "I don't have no room inside to lose her, Cap'n."

"I understand. But you have chosen the proper course. You can have a good life here, Eli."

"I thought that too."

"And?"

Eli paced as he thought it over.

"I see 'em, Cap'n! I see 'em in my dreams and there's times on waking there's a presence of 'em all about me!"

"Time will heal that malady, Eli."

"Sometimes I think I can feel them surrounding me, Cap'n. I feel it in my bones today. They've either been here or they're on their way."

"If they are, *WE* will all deal with it!"

"It ain't exactly like that and it ain't nothin' I can't handle, Cap'n!"

"Eli! You hold so much inside that huge chest. You are not alone! Otello and Scotty and Frenchie and I, are more than a match for the Joshua Brothers. As a matter of fact, I welcome such a showdown."

"I have prayed for it many times, Cap'n!"

"There, then it's settled."

"No, sir!"

"What then?"

"I can fight them easy enough."

"Yes?"

"As long as I have this feelin' . . . this feelin' that they're nearby, I won't be marryin', Cap'n."

Captain Hopkins studied the determined look on Eli's face. He nodded agreement. "And, Stella? She will wait until this feeling goes?"

The tension came back to Eli's face. He did not need to reply.

"The Joshua brothers are like a biblical pestilence on your soul, Eli. My take is, you won't have any peace until you are rid of them," Captain Hopkins paused and looked deep into his friend's eyes. "If you go after them you'll lose her."

Eli nodded sad agreement.

"It's some kind of dilemma, alright," Captain Hopkins paused to light his pipe.

"A what, Cap'n?"

"Dilemma? Essentially a choice between equally disagreeable alternatives."

Eli waited on further explanation.

"I can't decide for you, Eli."

"No, sir. I know that. I think I done decided, anyhow."
"Don't!"
"Sir?"
"Don't ride off alone in the night, like you did in San Francisco. Not if you consider me a friend."

Eli looked very hurt. "You are and always will be my friend, Cap'n!"

"Not if you do what I think you're planning on doing."

"Hells bells, Cap'n! I have to do what comes to me straight. Crooked thinking makes my head hurt!"

"With due respect, what happened in Pennslyvannia is three thousand miles and now almost two years behind you, Eli. This country is wide open. You could have a wonderful new beginning here, with Stella. I want that for you. I want to help you have it. What if you're wrong and those Joshua Brothers are already dead? Good god, Man! Men that mean are bound to get themselves killed by somebody! Please, let the past rest. Let's all make California our bright new home." Captain Hopkins hoped aloud.

Eli took a deep breath and blew it out hard.

"I know that, Captain. I been thinking mightily on it. I was raised a religious man. I prayed some on it, too. Maybe it is too long. I don't feel so much hurt inside as before but there's still a powerful lot in there! I know I done got this gold fever. But maybe it's wrong to think about myself and Stella, about us striking it rich with Lydia lying cold in those Pennsylvania hills. I don't know, Captain. I just know my thinking gets all crooked, sometimes . . . . . but it ain't nothin' I can't handle."

Captain Hopkins did not like to see the pain return to his friends face.

He knew by the look in Eli's eyes when he spoke of Stella, why it was there. ". . . 'for I will wear my heart on my sleeve, for daws to peck at . . . ' Alas, at times, do we all!"

"Sir?"

"Oh, just a little Shakespeare. When I don't have the answers, sometimes he does."

"Shakespeare, Cap'n?" Otello's eyes lit up as he moved close to Captain Hopkins.

"Shakespeare? Yes. Yes my dear, Otello. Eli and I were discussing, much ado about nothing," Captain Hopkins chuckled.

Eli looked puzzled.

Otello shrugged.

"Otello, tell Eli about the worth of this claim. I want us to cool his itchy feet!" Captain Hopkins said.

"Yes, sir, Cap'n. Look at what I sluiced out today!" Otello poured a bag of gold dust on a piece of paper.

Eli watched the sparkling metal with wonder. "I've been a miner all my life but I never did see anything come out of the earth as pretty as that," Eli sighed.

"Well one fifth of it is yours. The three of us share with Frenchie and Scotty. Early tomorrow morning we'll double, maybe triple this take."

Captain Hopkins paused and looked directly at Eli. "I don't believe it's a sin to dream of a good life, Eli."

Eli looked at Otello.

Otello's eyes were glazed over with gold fever.

"There is a whole lot of magical soul healin' in this stuff, Cap'n." Otello mused aloud.

"Amen, Otello!" Captain Hopkins reached into a locker and withdrew a bottle of scotch whiskey. He poured them each a glass. He raised his to toast. "To a new life in a golden new world! To a great happiness to come. To my friend, Otello. To my friend, Eli," Captain Hopkins paused for effect. ". . . and to his bride."

Otello toasted with delight.

Eli held back. He thought it over. Finally, he lifted his glass and joined in the toast.

They did not see the shadowy figure of Sly Joshua watching them from the trees high on the hill above. Sly watched awhile longer then mounted his horse and rode to the oak grove where his brother's waited.

"They's got tents crowded in only a few yards from the river.

There's thirty camps surrounding them. They got a sluice box set up and there's miners all around. Eli's with Otello and three others."

"Otello? Otello Jones?" Jules growled.

Sly swallowed hard and nodded agreement.

"Well, God almighty! Did the whole damn mining company come this here way?" Jules fumed. "Who else?"

"One's an older man. The other two about Eli's age. They don't look like no gunfighters or nothing. But it's him, Jules. For sure. I still don't believe it, but it's him," Sly reported.

"You know which tent Eli's livin' in?" Jules asked.

"He's got the small one closest the river. I seen him putting his stuff in there. It's right beside a tent with an old man wearing a sailor's hat."

"A sailor?"

"He don't look like he'd be no trouble at all. Don't none of them look like it."

"Oh? Like they was no trouble back in Pennslyvannia. Is that it?"

Sly moved behind Big John.

Jules let his anger dissipate. He thought it over. "We go down after dark when the moon is behind some clouds. All of us gonna put one bullet into him so there's no doubt. If any of his friends get in the way we kill them too. Here try this on," Jules threw Sly a wide-brimmed Mexican sombrero.

"Why, Jules? Where'd you get this silly looking hat?"

"I stole them off some sleeping Mexicans. Just put it on."

Sly frowned but put the wide-brimmed hat on.

"Now that will make just the right silhouette in the moonlight. All those other miners gonna' believe the Mexicans done killed another white man. So we get rid of Eli once and for all and we get rid of some Mexicans and there's more gold for everybody!" Jules was delighted with himself.

"Jules, that's one fine and dandy idea!" Sly exclaimed.

Big John was not so sure. He picked up a Mexican hat and tried it on. It was too small by three hat sizes.

James took it and it dropped down over his ears.

Matthew put it on. It fit well. With his sun-tanned face and dark mustache, he looked like a "Bandito".

Jules was pleased. "So you think I might still have any ideas, brother John?" Jules growled.

"I never thought otherwise, Jules. I jest had to practice some cautions."

"Am I in charge?"

"Yes, Jules. You're in charge."

"Fine. Now when we get there we don't call each other by our names, no matter what. We all call each other `Jose or Pedro, if we need to say anything. We're going to have to stay here long after he's dead so no one is gonna say we done nuthin'!" Jules held some goldust in his hand.

"Where'd you get that, Jules?" Sly looked at the goldust with envy.

"This is half an ounce of dust in just one day's panning. That's why we stayin' here. That's why there ain't gonna' be no mistakes at this killin'!" Jules insisted. "This golden land is ours if we `jest want it bad enough. When Eli's gone, these "Mexicans" can help us thin out some other competition," Jules grinned as he put on his sombrero.

"Hot damn, Jules! You shore got brains. I'm shore glad I'm your brother," Sly said with genuine admiration.

The other brothers nodded agreement except for Big John and Matthew.

Jules gave them a withering look and waited.

Big John, and Matthew, finally, nodded agreement.

CHAPTER TWENTY THREE

It was a beautiful dawn that Stella greeted with a light heart. A heart she had forced herself to purge of dark suspicions and bad memories. Her nature, born out of hardship, was to accept life with a jaundiced eye. She never liked it that way. She was happier being of blithe spirit and hopeful outlook.

Her first marriage to Sam, the gambling drunk who was shot by Rattlesnake for cheating at cards, had been a miserable one. He was not only a drunk and a cheat but a woman-beater, as well. It was sinful to be glad someone was dead, but Stella was not unhappy Sam was no longer among the living.

She had never wanted to love another man, or amy man. She knew she was a rare commodity in this land of few women and she had delighted in it.

A poor Irish girl whose parents came to America as indentured servants in "Black 47", Stella had been proud of her independence.

She had delighted in her ability to make money hand over fist in the fancy parlors of San Francisco. She prided herself that she was not a "Fandango" woman who was shipped in by a Spanish white slave trader and kept in bondage forever; or a pitiful chinese whore, forced by cruel taskmasters, to lay on her back in the dark alleys and take on all comers for pennies.

Stella considered herself a "high-class sporting woman" and she made sure she got the top rate paid for female charms in this part of the world.

Sam had been a mistake made over too much champagne and too much melancholy. Melancholy and self-pity after her parents had returned the money she had sent them.

Her parents had not believed she had made so money in any

respectable calling. They were right. Their rejection hurt, nevertheless, and Sam was there to take advantage of it. She never loved him—not like she loved Eli Llynne.

Stella had hardened her heart to endure the callous emotional approach necessary to be successful in her business. She really had not loved anyone. She thought of love as a cynical emotion used by silver-tongued liars to enslave gullible women.

But she knew she loved Eli Llynne.

Eli filled her every thought with bright hopes of an honest tomorrow. A tomorrow where she could send money home to her parents—and they might send back love.

Stella let her heart melt, reluctantly, but well. Eli was all that Sam was not or could never have been. Eli inspired trust, and if anything was too trustworthy.

She knew he would never hurt her. She knew he would work hard at honest labor for her. For that, she would love Eli honestly, deeply and completely.

Her only concern was that Eli might hold her past against her.

She felt good as she thought of how he ignored the looks of scorn. Looks of scorn directed at her and him by the bluenose snobs who lived on the hill—many the direct descendants of claim jumpers and whores.

Eli knew she was a former dancehall girl, but all she ever got from him was love and kindness.

Stella was not used to such tender treatment from men and it had taken some getting used to. But his gentle, slow hand and comforting manner had made the difference.

She was as giddy as a schoolgirl as she prepared a surprise breakfast to take to him at the diggings.

She loved him with all her heart. She vowed that she would do everything within her power to make him a good wife.

"You're doing that like a veteran," Captain Hopkins said as he watched Eli dig the ore and wash it in the sluice box.

"Cap'n, this beats the devil out of coal mining. Look, I got a thimble full of gold already. This land is solid gold, sure enough," Eli laughed.

"I know. I've got about as much as you, and Frenchie and Scotty about the same also. Otello even more. Between us we got almost nine ounces. I've made a whole lot worse wages for a day's work."

"Oh Lord! I know I have. That's for sure." Eli sighed hard. He dug into the rocky soil. He threw the gravel into the running water and caressed it lovingly with his hands.

"I'll be fixing supper tonight. We'll rotate like we do everything else. I might even put a little meat in the beans," Captain Hopkins kidded as he moved to the sluicebox to check the hours' earnings.

Eli watched the Captain as he walked away. He was glad he was fortunate enough to be in Captain Hopkins' company and blessed to be called his friend.

Eli's thoughts, now, were good, soul-satisfying thoughts. He felt a little guilty that his sorrow over the loss of Lydia, now, always lost out to thoughts of the happiness brought to him by Stella and gold.

But he took comfort in believing that, that was what God had ordained for him. That putting the past away was, now, a healthy thing to do. That he could always remember Lydia fondly and speak of her with respect.

Yet, he would steel himself to not look back so much now—as he would look forward.

He was thankful that God had let his hard heart open to love again. Love that healed his wounds inside and out. Love that he accepted, daily, with sincere prayers of thanksgiving.

As his thoughts leaned toward the excitement of this new life, he looked to the clear blue California sky then at the gold in his pan. He watched his friends laughing as they filled their sacks with gold dust.

He paused and whispered a silent prayer asking God to forgive him for his previous angry blasphemy. To forget his mean-spirited anger. For this golden day, Eli was not angry with God or anyone in God's creation.

The day passed with good fortune piled on good fortune.

Among the slivers of fine golddust, Eli found a nugget as big as a man's fist that weighed in at over two pounds.

In one golden rock, found in a instant beneath the bright, sunlit sky, was near as much money as a coal miner would make in five years toiling in the darkness.

"*Myn yn Brain!* Cap'n! Stella and I are going to have the biggest wedding there ever was. My share of this rock must be enough to buy a great house."

"A great house? Next you'll be talking about wee feet pattering about," Scotty shuddered.

They all laughed until Stella interrupted them. "And what is so funny about children's feet?" Stella feigned anger.

Scotty stepped back with his hands up.

The Captain laughed.

Frenchie shrugged.

Eli turned and looked at her with admiration.

"Don't listen to Scotty. He's an old bachelor beyond hope," Eli greeted her.

"Well then maybe he shouldn't share this food I brought you. We wouldn't want him to be poisoned by a woman's touch," Stella kidded.

Scotty looked at the steaming food beneath the checkered cloth.

"I expect to have a bunch of the little lads and lassie's myself, anyday now." Scotty offered, contritely.

"Well, I hope you'll be marrying the poor lady first," Stella replied.

They all laughed before they joined in a sumptuous feast.

Stella studied the huge gold nugget as they ate. She did not like the fact it was big enough to attract the eye.

"If it's alright with the others, I want you to take that home and hide it in a safe place," Eli said.

The others nodded agreement.

Stella put it in her apron and stuffed a handkerchief behind it. Then she gathered the biscuit-swept, morsel-less plates and turned to go home.

"Do I expect you for supper tonight?" Stella addressed Eli.

"The diggings goin' mighty good."

"If you aren't home by dark, expect the door to be latched," Stella said firmly as she turned and left them.

When she was out of earshot, they all gave Eli looks of mock contempt and pretended to dance and mimicked the behavior of women.

"You better be home tonight "honey" or else there ain't no lovin' for you!" Scotty kidded.

"But darlin' you're my only love. Please don't lock the door, Mon, Cheri! It's all those big ugly men's fault," Frenchie sighed.

"It's a marvel of creation how a love bug can cower a mighty man," Captain Hopkins mused aloud.

"Amen, Cap'n!" Otello said with wonder.

They laughed together as good friends laugh when they share the communion of brotherhood and admiration. Communion that comes from trust, understanding and well-deserved respect.

Sly Joshua almost fell off the hillside as he saw the sparkle from the nugget Stella put into her apron pocket. He mounted his horse and rode as hard as he could to tell Jules the news.

CHAPTER TWENTY FOUR

The day went quickly, as it does when hands are busy at a work of joy. The daylight faded much too fast to suit these new miners. They were, now, totally smitten with gold fever. With each new ounce of dust and each new nugget that went into their pokes, Eli and his friends became more and more caught up in the lure of riches yet to be found.

The darkness had been upon them for several hours, before they deemed it too dark to continue.

Stella looked out of her window at the darkness and the empty road that led toward the diggings. She looked at the cold meal she had prepared and sighed hard. She knew Eli would not be home until late if at all this night.

Stella worried about the new, distant look on Eli's face.

She had seen it many times before.

It was the look of a man consumed with gold fever. She had been consumed by it once herself. It was a fever for which there was no tonic except time and misfortune. Or discovery of a fortune so great the fever vanished into a rich man's sense of well being.

Though Stella knew Eli was doing it to the greatest extent for her, she did not like the intensity of it. She had seen men leave their wives and families to pursue the gold bug. She had seen men killed over tiny specks of goldust. She hoped, in her heart, it was a passing thing with Eli.

She took the nugget from her apron and looked at it. The glisten of the gold specks in the nugget told her the fever would not pass any time soon.

Stella looked for a safe place to hide it. She felt the heft of it in her hand and, for a moment, remembered how the fever had affected her.

Outside, she thought she heard horses. She listened intently, but heard nothing. She found a small strongbox and placed the nugget inside. She locked it and placed it under some dirty clothes in the darkest corner of her closet.

Once again, she thought she heard noises.

Stella opened her door and peered outside. She saw nothing but darkness. Slowly, she closed the door and locked it.

From his position in the deepest, most dark shadows, Sly Joshua watched and waited.

Captain Hopkins fixed a hearty meal and they all shared the food. Food surrounded by a good days earnings that provoked laughter. Laughter of the kind derived more from wonder than merriment.

Captain Hopkins had known wealth, but not the others. He had known its pleasures and pitfalls. There would be time enough for tales of caution. Tonight he watched with quiet delight as they shared a drink of whiskey. Whiskey and tall tales about how much more gold they would find.

They sat in the glow of a kerosene lantern with the wick turned up full. The bright light added to the sparkle of their days bounty. The gleam of the gold was so dazzling it seemed possible they had already found all the gold in the world.

The Captain was deep in his cups and at his tall tale telling best.

That was saying something because Captain Hopkins was one great teller of tales.

As the night wore on, they drank way too much. They did not care this night. This was a night full of marvelous things to be savored. Fabulous, long-awaited things. Wonderful, joyful things to make up for all the endless, empty, hungry nights that had gone before.

Captain Hopkins, reluctantly, called an end to his share of the festivities around midnight. He lifted one final toast. As they drank it, their eyes were bright with camaraderie. Captain Hopkins was so into his cups, he hugged them all dearly. He chuckled, turned and departed with a fond, "Adieu!"

Captain Hopkins cursed as he stumbled out into the cold night. A man who kept his feet in high seas, wobbled under the whiskey induced fog.

He was drunker than he knew.

In the darkness he could not fully get his bearings. All the tents looked alike. He looked into two tents. He rubbed his eyes and weaved at the third tent. He knew it was not his, but it was available. He lurched inside Eli's tent in a stupor and passed out.

Eli followed only a few minutes later. He looked at the Captain, already deep in sleep.

Eli thought it best not to disturb his friend. He covered the Captain with a blanket. He moved to take the Captain's tent up the hill.

Frenchie and Scotty passed out on the threshold of their respective tents.

Otello sat in the main tent surrounded by the gold. He could not help staring at it. He did not stare with lust, but with satisfaction. Here before him, was the means to an end. With his share he could fulfill his boyhood dream of finding his parents.

Otello delighted in the memory of the Captain's promise to help him find his parents. This very night the Captain had renewed that promise. This very night the Captain had shown him a page in the book he had never seen before. A page with the scribbled note:

"For Desdemona, my beloved.

Max,

New Orleans."

Otello wondered if his father's name was "Max.". He wondered if Desdemona was his mother's name. He wondered what sort of place was this "New Orleans". It was not much to go on, but it was a place to begin.

Captain Hopkins said he knew New Orleans, well. He had served, for a brief time, on a river boat there.

He promised to take Otello there this year or sooner if the claim played out.

That thought made Otello's heart almost as happy as did the glow from the gold.

It was 4:30 a.m. and a heavy mist hung over the ravine as the Joshua brothers, except for Sly, looking ridiculous in their Mexican get-ups, crept into camp. Jules held them up as they were halfway down the hill. He pointed to the small tent closest to the river.

"That's where Sly said Eli put his things," Jules whispered.

"Let me take him, Jules!" James hoped.

"Ssssshhhh!" Jules instructed.

Jules paused. He sniffed the wind. There was none. He drew his revolver and made his way in the moonless darkness toward the tent. His brothers waited until he was almost there, before they followed behind.

They were almost to the tent, when James tripped and tumbled down the hill. He crashed into the river with a big splash.

Jules cursed under his breath and ran the rest of the way to Eli's tent. He could barely make out the figure in the tent. As he watched, the man stirred a little from the noise.

Jules waited a moment until the man was still. He licked his lips. He aimed his gun at the middle of the figure and fired all six rounds.

The bullets tore into Captain Hopkins' body killing him before he could raise the slightest protest.

Eli, Scotty and Frenchie were awakened almost simultaneously by the shots.

Eli, instinctively, knew something terrible had happened. He felt the same terrible sting in his heart he felt long ago. The feeling he hoped he'd never feel again.

In the darkness Eli had trouble finding his gun. Then he remembered he wasn't in his tent. He heard the sound of three more shots being fired. Shots that echoed up and down the river. The river where his tent and Captain Hopkins were. Eli gritted his teeth and cursed as he found one of Captain Hopkin's guns. He ran out of the tent and full bore down the hill.

The other Joshua brothers emptied their guns into Captain Hopkin's dead body, believing they were making sure Eli was dead. Scotty was first out of his tent with a gun. He peered into the darkness and saw nothing.

"Aye! I knew there'd be claim jumpers, but not this soon. Come on you godless bastards!" Scotty grumbled as he peered into the darkness. He tried to pick out the figures of the men firing the shots in the darkness. The figures weren't clear except for Mexican hats. Scotty could make out where the muzzle flashes came from. He took aim and he fired in that direction. His first two shots were wide. His third grazed James in the left eye. James fell to his knees and fired back.

Scotty's gun jammed as James pulled down on him. Scotty cursed James as James grinned, sardonically. Before James could pull the trigger Eli stepped in between Scotty and James.

"Kill the son-of-a-bitch, Eli! Kill him!" Scotty grimaced in pain.

James looked at Eli in disbelief.

Eli stood there with the colt aimed at James' gut and did not pull the trigger.

"Eli Llynne? Man we thought we'd done `kilt you!" James pulled the trigger on his gun.

Eli saw the muzzle flash as if it were in a dream. The bullet whizzed by his head, so close he could hear the whine.

"Eli? Shoot him! What the hell is wrong with you! They must be the Joshua brother's. They `kilt your wife!" Scotty paused as he looked toward Captain Hopkin's tent. "And . . . . "

James pulled the trigger on his gun only to have it click empty. He, quickly, broke the chamber to reload.

Eli held his gun unable to pull the trigger.

There before him was a man who had helped kill Lydia. Eli reached for the anger to fire. He saw the man's eyes. He let the hate, Stella had almost killed, fill his soul.

"We was all friends once, Eli, You're a god-fearing man. You don't do no senseless killin'," James begged.

"... and ... good God almighty, Laddie! They done kilt the Captain!" Scotty cried.

Eli heard Scotty's voice coming at him from some murky distance. Like a fog horn blasting through dense fog, Scotty's words burst into his confused mind. The slow hand—the reluctant anger—the hesitation passed into oblivion with those words.

The words were barely out of Scotty's mouth before Eli raised the barrel of his gun.

Now, Eli looked at James with eyes devoid of compassion.

"Good lord you ain't really gonna' ... ," James was unable to finish.

Eli fired all six rounds into James' mouth. The bullets tore James' head off at the neck line.

Jules watched James plunge headless into the river. He saw Eli standing tall. He began running up the hill away from him.

Big John and Matthew followed, quickly.

Frenchie was now out of his tent firing.

Eli reloaded his revolver.

Otello, in the main tent, had thought the gun shots might be some drunken celebration. When they continued, he decided to investigate. He poked his head out of the main tent. A bullet almost took off his nose. He grabbed a gun and eased into the darkness toward the muzzle flashes.

Big John, Matthew, and Zack returned the fire as they made their way up the hill to their horses. It was so dark the shots went wild and every hit was a lucky one. One lucky shot by Big John hit Frenchie in his big heart and stopped it instantly.

Frenchie fell over and rolled past Eli.

Eli swore as he fired at the fleeing shadows. "I can't see you but I know who you are. It's you, Jules Joshua. I know it. *Dialls! Dialls!* Damn you! Damn you! God damn you to hell!"

Eli fired in all directions, aiming more at sound than substance.

"Damnit! It wasn't him. We missed Eli again. Damn!" Jules cursed as he reached the top of the hill. "Damn that man. He's accursed by God!" Jules fired at the general area of Eli's voice.

Eli's revolver was empty. He grabbed for the shotgun lying by the sluice box. He began maneuvering himself up the hill for a close-in shot.

Big John fired his last two rounds down the hill at Eli's approaching shadow. One bullet whizzed over Eli's head. The other hit Scotty in the knee, shattering it.

Scotty cried out in pain and fell over, almost rolling into the river.

Eli was, momentarily, distracted. He did not see a long shadow step out from behind a tree. He heard a gunshot only a few feet away. He felt a sting in his elbow. The bullet fired by Zack grazed his forearm. It caused him to drop the shotgun.

Otello's eyes picked up the flash of Zack's gun. He saw the outline of a sombrero. He fired one shot at the outline of the hat. He fired a second shot six inches lower. One bullet put a window in the sombrero. The second bullet hit Zack right between the eyes. He fell dead at Jules' feet.

Eli shook off the pain. He picked up the shotgun with a blood soaked hand. He ran towards Jules. He paused to pick up a knife embedded in a stump. In his rage it occurred to him, shooting was too good for Jules.

"Good Lord! I could see the whites of Eli's eyes clean up here! I never seen a man that mad!" Matthew shivered.

"He ain't near as mad as me!" Jules growled. He looked at Zack's body. He seemed almost sad.

Seconds later, Otello opened up with a pistol. A bullet tore off a piece of Jules' right ear. Another took off his sombrero.

Suddenly gunfire erupted all around them. In every direction they looked, miners from adjacent claims were joining in the fray.

Jules did not bother to see if Zack was dead. He stepped over him and mounted his horse.

Big John glared at Jules. He checked to see if Zack was dead before he mounted his horse.

"We got to check on the James, Jules. He might just be wounded," Big John insisted.

Jules looked at the approaching miners and cursed under his breath. "He's already in hell and that's where we'll be 'iffen we don't git!" Jules yanked the reins and turned his horses' head.

"We gonna leave without killin' Eli?" Big John wondered.

Jules looked around a moment. Bullets whizzed about their head as he glared at Big John. "No! You stay here and do it for me. Just like you did in Pennslyvannia, you goddamned idiot!" Jules said as he turned his horse's head and goaded it into a gallop.

Split-seconds later, his remaining brothers followed.

Eli heard the horses galloping away. He ran up the hill after them trying to fire the empty shotgun. He held the knife high over his head. "You bastard, Jules Joshua! I know it's you. I know it. I'll kill you for sure this time! You ain't ridin' free this time! I'll kill you. I'll kill you, I'll kill you!" Eli screamed at the darkness long after the riders had gone.

Stella watched the doorknob as it rattled. She got the shotgun off the wall mount and aimed it at the door. The door hesitated. Someone's boot kicked at it. It held. The boot kicked at it again. It still held. Before the boot could kick again, Stella fired both barrels at the door. The blast from the shotgun tore a large melon-sized hole that smoldered from the heat of the lead pellets.

Stella was surprised to see she had missed the kicker.

She was more surprised when she saw Sly Joshua walk inside. Stella tried, frantically, to reload the gun. Sly grabbed it by the barrel. He slammed his pistol against Stella's head knocking her to the floor. "Now you tell me where that nugget is and I won't shoot your head off."

"I don't know what you're talking about. Get the hell out of my house!"

"My goodness where does Eli find these handsome women? I swear he's done had two and I ain't never had any. Now that just ain't fair, nohow!"

"Who are you? No, I don't care who you are. Just get the hell out of here!"

"Now that ain't polite!"

"Eli will be here soon. You better 'git while you can."

"I don't think so. I think my brother done shot him plum dead by now," Sly said. He grinned as he pulled a knife and pointed it at Stella's face. "Now where is that nugget or do I cut that pretty face?"

Stella spit in his eyes.

Eli's rage was unrelenting. He ran into the night cursing the darkness an hour after Jules was gone.

Eli finally stopped. He leaned back against a tree and gathered his breath. He drove the knife blade deep into the guts of the oak.

Otello had followed at a short distance. He eased up beside his friend.

Eli looked at Otello with the meanest eyes Otello had ever seen.

"The horses. Where are the horses?" Eli demanded.

"In the corral, Mister Eli."

"Well don't just stand there. Go get them, Goddmanit!"

Otello stepped back only a half pace before he stepped up again. "No, sir!"

"What?"

"It's too dark tonight, Mister Eli. Besides we got to get help for Mister Scotty. We'll get a posse and get them at first light."

Eli glared at Otello. He let his anger cool only a degree. "It ain't nuthin' I can't handle. *YOU* help, Scotty. I'm going for my horse!" Eli pushed past Otello.

"What about the Cap'n?" Otello posed.

Eli stopped. He turned and looked back at Otello. "He is alive?"

"I don't know. I just thought we'd better see for sure."

"You're just tryin' to stall me, Otello. You best just keep the hell out of my way. You best tell everybody that!"

Otello nodded understanding. The withering look in Eli's eye demanded no less. "You want me to tell, Stella?"

Eli stopped. He froze. He felt a sickening feeling in his gut. "Stella? Stella! Oh, God no!" Eli's thoughts raced as he ran full speed toward the corral.

A mile ahead, Jules and Big John pulled their horses to a stop in front of Stella's house.

Seconds later, they barged through the empty doorway. Jules was not surprised to see Sly cutting at Stella's dress as she kicked and screamed at him.

"What the hell are you doin' Sly? You ain't supposed to be doin' that! Where is that gold you done told us about?"

Jules motioned for Big John to pull Sly off of Stella.

Big John lifted him and threw him against a wall.

"I don't know. I was just tryin' to ask her. You got no call throwin' me around!" Sly grumped.

Stella took the opportunity to break for the door. Jules tackled her just outside of it.

Stella clawed his face. Jules flinched as he felt the blood from her scratches ooze down his face. He grimaced as he felt the familiar sting. "God almighty! All you bitches fight the same!" Jules picked her up. He threw her on the floor hard. "You boys take a long walk. I'm gonna' talk to Miss Stella here about a few matters," Jules said.

"You want us to leave you alone, Jules?" Sly wondered.

"That's what I said ain't it? Now git!"

Big John saw the look in Jules eyes.

He nodded agreement and motioned for the others to follow him outside.

Jules waited until they left and closed the door. He looked down at Stella who lay on the floor, slightly dazed. "I'm damned tired of Eli Llynne's women scratching at my eyeballs! The word around town is that you're a sporting woman. Well why don't I just sample me some of that stuff you been sellin' to everybody else?" Jules unbuckled his belt.

"You go to hell! Touch me and I'll kill you!" Stella kicked out at him.

Jules grabbed her feet and drug her across the floor. He reached down and tore her dress from around her shoulders—exposing her ample bosom.

Jules eyes lit up with lust. He tore away the rest of the dress, ignoring Stella's flashing claws, until she was naked before him.

"Now you uppity whore we'll see what's what!" Jules let his pants fall to the floor.

Stella took desperate swings at Jules. He fought them off. With his overpowering strength, he forced her down and still. He eased himself upon her.

"No! No! I'd rather die! I'd rather die!" Stella screamed as she felt his foul breath on her face.

"So I ain't good enough for you, is that it? Well that don't bother me none." Jules stopped as Stella tore away the patch covering his eye.

A look of complete revulsion crossed her face as she stared at Jules.

"You bitch! Yea, that's what the other Miss Llynne did to me! Ain't very pretty is it?"

"You're the ugliest, most foul beast of a man I've ever seen. Get your disgusting hands off of me! You'll never have me. You'll have to kill me first!"

Jules reached down and picked up his revolver. He stuck the cold barrel next to her head. "Hell, Lady, I'd rather have your cooperation, but a man has to take his satisfaction however he can 'git it." Jules cocked the hammer of the revolver.

Stella spit in his face just before Jules pulled the trigger.

CHAPTER TWENTY FIVE

Eli's hands shook as he watched Doc Bullock tend to Stella. She had lay unconscious for three days without moving. So distraught was Eli, that he had not bothered to clean up the clutter and debris left behind by Jules' successful search for the gold.

Eli had not eaten in days and cared not to eat again unless she moved.

The wound left by Jules' bullet was not deep. To look at the small scar on the outside, you would not think it a mortal wound. It was the inside where he could not see that worried Doc Bullock.

"As I told you, this is not my specialty. I've done all I know how to do. All I can suggest is we send to Sacramento or San Francisco for a specialist. I don't think she can be moved," Doc Bullock said sadly. He looked around the room at the mess. "My, God. What animals! You say you knew these men?"

Eli looked at Otello who stood a few feet behind him. Their eyes met in mutual disdain for the Joshua brothers.

"Yes. Yes, I knew them. Do you know a special doctor in particular in Sacramento or San Francisco?" Eli's voice was calm, belying his inner turmoil.

"Yes. I believe so. But they are very expensive. I have a little money. I could help you out some."

"No. No thank you, Doc. Tell me, do you know a good nursemaid in these parts?" Eli asked calmly.

"Why yes. As a matter of fact, Carmalita, my wife is well schooled in nursing techniques. Some believe she is a better Doctor than I am."

"That will be fine. Please have her move in, in the morning."

"Move in? In the morning? I don't understand?"

"I have to go away for awhile. I need Carmalita's help to look after Stella. I need your help to go to Sacramento or San Francisco . . . or hell if you have to, to find help for Stella. I expect to have the money to pay you in awhile," Eli insisted.

"I'm sorry. It would be a rather large sum. We would have to pay for the travel and whatever special medicines. Where could you get that kind of money?"

"Would a two pound nugget take care of it?"

"Yes. Yes, of course, but where . . . . "

"From those who took it from me."

"I see," Doc Bulloch saw the look in Eli's eye and did not doubt his word.

Otello stepped forward and put a large sack of gold dust mixed with some nuggets on a table. "Everyone has thrown in most of their shares, Eli. There's over twenty thousand here. Is that enough, Doc?"

Doc Bulloch started to nod agreement.

Eli stopped him. "No! No. Payment for this will come from those responsible. You send for the special doctor. You get Carmelita in here. I will see to payment."

Doc Bulloch looked at Otello.

Otello shrugged.

"Whatever you say, Eli. I know you mean to do what you say but I would need five thousand up front," Doc almost apologized.

Eli looked at Otello. "Is my share that much?"

"That much and more," Otello replied.

"Then it's settled," Eli paused and looked hard at Doc Bulloch. "I'm counting on you, Doc. Stella is counting on you," Eli said.

He stepped past Doc toward Stella's bedside. He stood quietly and looked down at her without revealing any emotion.

Otello motioned for he and Doc Bulloch to leave the room.

Doc Bulloch agreed and they eased out leaving Eli alone with Stella.

Once they were gone, Eli knelt beside the bed. He reached out and gently touched her silky auburn hair. His fingers touched her forehead and recoiled at the intensity of her fever. He lifted her small hand in his and kissed it, tenderly. He said a silent prayer and got to his feet.

He took the revolver from his belt and checked it. He shoved it back down in his belt and strode out of the room with giant steps. He walked past Doc Bulloch and Otello without saying a word.

Otello waited until Eli was outside before he spoke. He pointed to the sack of gold. "You take that gold. In case, well just in case, you use all of it to help, Stella. You understand?"

"Yes. Yes I do. You goin' with him?"

Otello sighed hard. "If he'll have me."

Doc Bulloch smiled, "God speed to you both."

Otello tipped his hat to Doc Bulloch. He turned and moved out of the room. Once outside, he saw Eli already astride his horse. He saw the negative look in Eli's eyes. He looked back just as forcibly.

"There's no need arguing. This is my hunt too!"

"Is that right?"

"Yes, sir. Cap'n Hopkins was as much a father as any man I ever knowed."

Eli grimaced and almost looked sympathetic. "You do what you like. Just stay the hell out of my way! Understand?" Eli insisted. He wheeled his horse around. He galloped off before Otello could reply.

Otello waited until Eli was almost out of sight before he mounted his horse and followed.

Doctor Bullock had watched out of the window as Eli and Otello spoke. In all his days, Doc Bullock had never seen the countenance of a man change so quickly. When Doc Bullock first knew Eli he thought he was an almost laughable tenderfoot. Everything Eli did had a tentative quality that made Doc Bullock wonder if Eli wasn't a mite timid. As he watched the purposeful way Eli mounted his horse and the stern set of his jaw this day, he knew that whatever man had been hidden inside that tenderfoot was loose now.

Now Eli was a determined man. A man without hesitation. A menacing fury of a man. God help anybody who got in his way. Doc Bulloch looked at the immovable Stella. He wiped her forehead. He wondered if even the best Doctors in the world could help.

On his way out of town, Eli stopped at the cemetery. He, reverently, walked over to the graves of his dead friends and removed his hat.

Eli looked at them for a long moment before he put his hat back on.

As Eli stood by the two graves of his friends, he thought of Frenchie's laughter but he thought more of Captain Hopkin's friendship. In Eli's estimation, no finer man, no better friend ever lived.

Eli, quietly, swore an oath that he would find Jules Joshua wherever he was, however long it took. Find him without any stops, without any reservations, without any doubt.

Jules Joshua had cost Eli everything he loved in life twice now and that was enough. There would be no consideration given to the biblical admonition that vengeance was the Lord's.

The Lord had, had his chance—now it was Eli's turn.

God had stood by and let Lydia die. Eli's two friends, Captain Hopkins and Frenchie were now dead. Scotty had lost the use of a leg, and Eli's beloved Stella lay in a coma.

Eli was, once again, angry with God. Steeped with an anger that passed all understanding.

What money Eli had not given Doc Bulloch he had posted to an address in France, Frenchie had left behind.

Eli took only enough money to last him a few weeks. He expected to have found the Joshua brothers in that time, or be dead, or both. Eli had used some of the money to buy a new Navy Colt revolver to match the one he had purchased in San Francisco.

Eli also bought what was said to be the fastest horse in Sonora.

As he stood over Captain Hopkin's grave, he took a knife and carved two notches in the butt of one the guns. One for each of the dead Joshua brothers.

He swore on the grave of his dead friends that he would not let himself rest until he had carved four more notches in it. Eli bowed his head in silent prayer for the souls of his friends. He stuffed one revolver deep into his waistband and the other in its holster. Eli had found the Joshua brothers' camp and witnesses had told him they were headed north. He mounted his horse and rode out of Sonora at full gallop.

Otello watched from the top of a high hill. He waited until Eli galloped off. Then he moved to the graveyard and paid his respects to his lost friends.

Eli had his problems with horses but he liked this one. He sat this one well and it carried him without the discomfort he felt with others. It was a strong horse ready to gallop at a rider's pleasure. Eli would save that strength until needed.

The road out of Sonora was full of people coming and going and just getting in the way. Eli he had to slow himself many times. No matter what speed he maintained, his eyes were always searching. His senses were always fully alert. His gun hand was ever ready.

As he rode, he felt the strangest sensation in his trigger finger. His huge hand, that had been so ill at ease with a gun, now itched to hold it. His backbone, that had sagged from doubt, was as straight as an iron rod. His ears, that had listened to confusing philosophies, now perked only to hear the voice of his adversaries.

Eli almost shot a stranger who looked a little like one of the Joshua brothers.

Otello had seen the incident and now followed Eli somewhat closer.

Jules Joshua pulled his horse up, turned in the saddle and looked down the long road behind him.

He was concerned that they had not seen any signs of Eli in the week they had been running. He wanted to believe that he had doubled back and criss-crossed his trail enough to have lost Eli. But he knew better. This time Eli would not relent. This time Eli would find him. This time it would be over, one way or the other, for good.

"How long we gonna keep runnin' from this man, Jules? Hell, he's only one or two at the most!" Big John grumped as he turned in his saddle.

"We don't know that. He had three friends at the shoot-out. Besides all them other miners. Maybe they got friends too. He mighta' hired a bunch more."

"How could he? He's more poor than us. We got all his gold," Sly said.

"How did he get to California? How did he survive in the coal mine landslide?"

Jules looked, scornfully, at Big John.

Big John was not intimidated. "Hell, don't ask me questions like that! All I know is he's accursed. He's of the devil himself. That's how! He should be dead three times over."

"Well he ain't, is he?" Jules spit into the wind. The wind blew it back in his face.

"That may be so, but I'm saying I'm tired of running. I'm way past damn good and tired! I want to kill him quick and find me some gold like everybody else!" Big John was just short of mutiny.

So was Matthew and Jules knew it.

Jules looked at the glint of rebellion in their eyes. He thought it over for a long moment before he backed off. "Yep! I'm tired too. I figure we done strung it out enough so that we can pick our spot now. We gonna ride on up by Hornitos. I hear tell they're doing hardrock mining over there. You can wash the river a hundred years and not do as good as you can with one good mother lode. Besides, the best spots in the river is already staked," Jules sighed.

Matthew and the others looked very worried.

"You talking about going down inside the ground again, Jules?" Matthew shuddered.

Jules looked at him in disgust. "You boys seen that river. I told you all the good spots is taken in this here country. We know about hard rock mining. It's just like coal except, it's better. Now you know they need some hard rock miners so that's where we'll be goin' and that's, that!" Jules snapped.

Big John shifted in his saddle. "No!"

"No?" Jules looked hard at Big John. His hand moved to the handle of his gun.

Big John put his hand on his gun. He glared at Jules. "That's just what Eli will be thinkin', Jules."

Jules looked at Big John and grinned. "I hope so, John. I'm counting on it," Jules said. He grinned, sardonically. He turned his horse to head for Hornitos.

Eli lay on his right side. He was unable to turn on the two foot wide straw mattress in the room crammed full of miners. It was too cold and rainy to sleep outside so he had purchased a bed in a ramshackle bedding house.

It hurt his sense of fair play to pay five dollars to sleep in such a miserable manner.

Jammed in such close quarters—thick with the dank aroma of human mold.

Eli had refused to pay the two dollars extra for a thin blanket, so he shivered from the cold. The closeness of the room and the cold made his cough come back. He tried but could not suppress it. He coughed loud enough to awake an old man sleeping right beside him.

The old man yawned and stretched himself awake. He studied Eli's face and nodded knowingly. "Here, drink this!" The old man shoved a bottle in Eli's face.

Eli started to ignore the old man but he felt another cough forming in his throat. He took the bottle and pulled down a drink of the very green corn whiskey. "Thanks." Eli handed the bottle back.

The old man took the bottle. He smiled, then took a drink himself. He studied Eli's face. "That's a coal miner's cough?"

Eli could barely make out the man's face in the dark. "I suppose. What's it to you?"

"Well hell, Mister! It ain't nothin' to me. 'Cept I know it when I hear it!" The old man took another swig of whiskey. He offered it to Eli.

Eli took the bottle. He pulled down three long swallows. He handed it back. "I thought I was over it. That's all!"

"It don't never go away completely. Out here it's better, but it's always there, waiting on a crowded place like this," the old man paused and looked around the room. "Have another." He handed the bottle back to Eli.

"I ain't here to make no friends," Eli insisted.

"You ain't tellin' me nothin' I don't know, Mister."

Eli almost laughed. He took the bottle. He took two long pulls. The liquid was hot and bitter but it also felt soothing to his throat. "That's mighty kind of you. It goes down easier now. The tickle has gone away a mite," Eli felt a certain kinship with the old man.

"I'm an old anthracite miner from Kentucky," The old man volunteered.

"I worked in Pottsville, Pennsylvania. Schuylkill county mines. About ten thousand years ago, I reckon," Eli mused aloud.

"Scottish?"

"No! Welsh."

"The Welsh is good hard rock miners. I'll bet you could get on easy over around Hornitos."

"Hornitos? What's a Hornitos?"

"It's mostly Mexicans that don't know too much about hard rock mining. They're trying to hire people who do. Seems there's a good sized find over there," The old man said as he studied Eli's hard eyes.

"I don't ever want to go below the earth again as long as I live," Eli insisted. He lay back on his side and prepared to go to sleep.

"I can understand that. That's why you don't see me over there. I can sluice enough to keep me in whiskey though it's a mite green sometimes."

"That it is!" Eli agreed. "I'll thank you for the spirits and say, goodnight," Eli turned his back on the old man.

"They's paying good wages. I hear tell hard rock miners are coming from all over . . . even Pennsylvannia to hire on," The old man babbled on.

"What did you say?" Eli jumped to his feet.

The old man dropped the bottle and looked scared. "Nuthin', Mister! Just that the whiskey is a mite green. I'm sorry. I can't afford the good stuff."

"No! What did you say about miner's from Pennslyvannia going to Hornitos?"

"Yes, sir. People from all over is hiring on. Maybe some of your folks from pennsly . . . . "

"*Myn yn brain!* By the cross, that's it! That's it for sure!" Eli exclaimed triumphantly.

"Yes, sir. I suppose it is?"

"No! You don't understand," Eli paused. He gathered his stuff as a thrill of discovery ran the length of his spine. He looked at The Old man and smiled a smile of victory. "Of course! Hornitos. Hard rock mining. They found placer mining not to their liking so what else would they do? Thank you! Thank you, old timer. Thank you very much!" Eli shook the old man's hand.

"Well don't mention it. Maybe, if you don't mind, you could help me get another jug. Maybe we could get the real stuff . . . some imported whiskey . . . and do some real celebrating."

Eli reached into his pants pockets and withdrew a five dollar gold piece. "I wish I could give you more. But for now, I hope this helps you as much as I hope you've helped me." Eli handed the old timer the money.

"That's fine. Just fine!" The old timer took long pulls from the bottle. "Nice drinkin' with you. You take it easy, Mister. God speed to you wherever it is you're goin'."

Eli did not reply.

As the old man shook his head in wonder, Eli leaped over a dozen sleeping miners and bounded out the boarding house without looking back.

In a darkened corner of the room, Otello watched until Eli was gone. Then he moved over to where the old man sat sipping on his bottle of whiskey.

"Can I speak with you?" Otello asked.

The old man looked up at Otello. He looked scared a moment. He watched Otello smile, then he relaxed. "Don't have much left, but you're welcome to a pull," he offered Otello the bottle.

Otello declined as he kneeled beside the old man. "I'll buy you a new one if you'll tell me where Mister Eli was headed."

"Mister Eli?"

"The man you were just speaking with."

"Oh? The Pennsylvanian?"

"Yes."

"Eli is it?"

"Did he say where he might be goin'?"

The old man thought it over a long moment. "That strike in Hornitos must be a whole lot bigger than I figured."

"Hornitos?"

"I done said it. You gonna buy me another bottle, anyways?"

Otello dropped a twenty dollar gold piece in the old man's lap. He moved to the door without replying.

The old man shook his head in wonder. He picked up the gold piece and bit it. He delighted in his good fortune.

CHAPTER TWENTY SIX

Eli rode smack into the middle of a race war. The Mexicans and whites of Hornitos, and other adjacent mining camps, were at each other's throats. Eli could hear the echo of scattered and sporadic gunfire a mile before he reached the outskirts of the mining camp. Carefully, he skirted the town from the small hills above and paused in a grove of trees. He looked down at the flash of guns and gunsmoke rising from the main street of the camp. He saw Mexican's and miners, who had emptied their guns, going at each other with bare knuckles and farm implements. He watched hand to hand combat to the death. He took a rough count and figured the Mexicans were holding their own. As the number of dead on each side mounted, Eli worried.

Eli prayed the Joshua brothers were not among the dead. He could smell they were nearby. In his minds eye, he knew they were very close.

Given just a little more time he would find them.

God forbid, some Mexican would take away the killing that rightfully belonged to him.

"Damn!" he cursed under his breath. "Goddmanit!" he cursed again. Twice more than he had ever cursed before on any day of his life.

Eli paused and wondered what to do. He decided to ride down into the middle of the fray and take his chances. He started to ride down the hill. He paused. His left ear picked up the sound of booming hoofbeats. He turned in his saddle to see a dozen Mexicans on horseback bearing down on him.

Eli looked at them for only a moment as he wondered if there were too many.

He decided there was.

He turned his horse and whipped it into a full gallop in the opposite direction.

The bullets from the Mexican revolvers zinged past Eli's ears in such volume, he feared he would be hit in the back real soon. There was no opportunity to draw and return fire. He hunched down in the saddle and tried to make himself one with the horse. His horse was as fast as advertised and that speed was saving him for now.

Eli held on to the horse for dear life as he prodded it to go even faster.

The horse responded with a burst of speed that left the Mexicans almost out of pistol range. Just before his pursuers faded out of pistol range, they fired one last volley of shots. One bullet tore through Eli's right boot and took a chunk out of his foot. Another blew a piece of his saddle away.

Eli felt the sting of the bullet but was more worried about the saddle. To his amazement and delight the horse did not break stride.

Eli looked back as he cleared a steep hilltop. The Mexicans had pulled up and turned away. Eli continued at full gallop until he could no longer see them.

When he did pull up, he looked at his right boot almost full of blood. He felt searing pain and saw a gap where the tip of the boot, and his right big toe had been. It hurt bad but he looked at it dispassionately. If he were not worried about stopping the blood flow, he would have ignored it.

He took off the boot and tied his bandanna around his foot. He looked up when he heard gunshots echoing from the other side of the hill. He took a position behind a huge oak. He drew his revolver and waited.

Eli was not surprised to see Otello mount the hill at full gallop, pursued by five Mexicans. Otello was tall in his saddle returning fire. Eli shook his head in disdain that Otello would give them such a target.

Eli had to smile, slightly, when Otello blasted one Mexican out of his saddle.

Otello rode directly at the oak tree Eli took cover behind. Eli held his fire until Otello was almost on top of him and the Mexicans were in range.

With cool precision, Eli fired five rounds. Three found their marks. Three Mexicans left their saddles dead—with three near identical wounds.

Otello dispatched the remaining Mexican. He pulled his horse up in front of Eli. "Oh! Oh, Mister Eli! Thank you! I thought I was a goner for sure!"

"What the hell are you doing here?"

Otello looked at the dark, mean look in Eli's eyes. He shifted in his saddle wondering how to answer. "I . . . I just came to help."

"And you can just go. Now!" Eli aimed his pistol at Otello.

"There's no call to treat me this way, Mister Eli. You see what's happening here. A man needs all the help he can get in this country."

"I don't. Are you going or do I shoot you where you sit?"

Otello shook his head. "You'd shoot me just like that?"

"You know me, Otello."

Otello looked at the malignant countenance of Eli's face. He tried to see behind the, now lifeless dark eyes. He smelled an aura of menace that made the hair on arms stand up. "No, sir. No, sir . . . .I don't think I do."

Eli cocked the hammer of his revolver.

Otello thought it over. He pulled back on his horse's reins. He, slowly, backed away. He gave Eli one last look. He turned his horses's head and rode down the hill.

Eli put this gun away. He mounted and rode to the top of the hill. He watched Otello until he was satisfied he was gone. He turned and rode in the opposite direction—as if he knew where he was going.

He stopped when he came to a mine shaft opening. An opening

with a freshly painted sign above it. The original name had been painted over. The new sign read:
"New Pennsylvania Mine Prop: Jules Joshua & bros."
Eli stared at the writing. He could not read it all. Stella had taught him to read enough to recognize all he needed to recognize. He touched the fresh red paint of the "J" in Jules. It came off and stained his fingers. He smiled, sardonically. He stepped back and sniffed the wind.

"The Lord has done good this day!" Eli's happy soul cried out. He took a deep breath and blew it out hard.

Eli checked the load of his guns and made sure he had additional loads.

He moved his horse close to a tree by the mine shaft opening and started to dismount. He was halfway out of the saddle, when a bullet tore into his saddlebags. The bullet sprayed hardtack and beans all over his back. He felt his horse tense beneath him. He began to balk at the sting of bullets around her. Another bullet crashed into the ground at her feet and the horse bucked Eli off.

Eli hit the ground hard. Bullets began to rain down around him. He tried to get to his feet. He grimaced in pain when he put his right foot down. He ignored the pain and came up ready to fire at the Joshua brothers.

He was disappointed to see another group of Mexicans bearing down on him.

Eli tried to run. He half-ran as bullets tore into the ground around him and ricocheted powdered rock into his face. Eli could feel the ground shake from the thunder of their horses hoofs. He made his way to only a few feet from the mine shaft opening.

As he looked at the dark hole opened in the rock, something inside him rebelled. The idea of going underground again made his chest tight.

He cursed that old fear.

He made himself enter.

The Mexicans were almost upon him. He hobbled inside and tripped. He rolled shoulder over shoulder into the darkness of the mine shaft opening. He was followed by hot lead, flying rock debris and Mexican curses one did not need to know the language to understand.

He was too busy to notice the lone figure of Otello watching from a distance. Watching and waiting for a proper moment to help his friend.

CHAPTER TWENTY SEVEN

The ricocheting bullets drove Eli ever deeper into the darkness of the mine. The damp smell of the wet seams brought back horrible memories. Memories Eli dismissed as quick as they came upon him. Eli stopped at a mine juncture and looked back at the distant opening. He could see the Mexicans dismounting, firing at him as they did.

He turned and hobbled deeper into the darkness. The mine was active and there were kerosene lanterns stationed every few feet of the main shaft. Eli knew better than to light one.

The darkness was familiar to his practiced eyes. He still retained that ability as he looked for a good place to make a stand.

Eli knew he had no hope of surviving in the main shaft. His only hope was to find a side shaft and pray they would not follow.

As the first Mexican reached the mine shaft opening, Eli grabbed a kerosene lantern and moved down the darkest side shaft he saw.

Two bullets glanced off the wall just behind him. Eli turned and saw a young Mexican standing at the entrance with a smoking revolver in each hand.

Without hesitation or emotion, Eli fired a single round that killed the young Mexican instantly.

Moments later, Eli paused as the timbers shook and the rock seemed to move. He stopped and backed against the wall to listen.

It was quiet for a long moment before the Mexicans started arguing among themselves. A few loose rocks fell around him. He did not move. He listened.

The Mexicans stopped arguing for a moment. A few seconds later, they hurled a barrage of curse words at the darkness. Then there was complete silence.

Eli did not trust the silence. He stood deep in a depression in the wall. He took shallow soft breaths as he perked his ear for the slightest sound. His foot ached but he ignored it. He wondered whether another shot might bring the roof down on his head.

He perked his ears and heard only the familiar sound of dripping water.

Then he heard the sound of the creaking leather of a new boot. Creaking leather and breathing. The sounds came from the shaft on his left.

A shaft that was lit with two widely spaced lanterns.

Eli was wondering how the Mexicans got in that way when a revolver barked and a bullet whizzed by his ear. The bullet blasted a lantern hanging above his head. Broken glass and kerosene fell on Eli and went twenty feet in every direction.

Seconds later a support timber broke.

The broken timber creaked and strained then shattered. A huge load of rock dumped itself on the mine floor between Eli and the gunfire. Rock dust and smoke obscured the little light coming from the two lit lanterns.

Eli decided to make his way up the shaft to his right. He hoped there would be a smaller shaft off at an angle so he could circle behind the shooter.

Outside, The Mexicans hurled one last volley of curses at the mine shaft opening. They shot the freshly painted sign to pieces—most of the bullets directed at Jules' name.

Then they holstered their guns and rode off.

Otello waited until they were some distance away, then moved inside the mine.

Eli made his way, hopping as fast as he could, to the safety of a large granite outcropping.

He determined this to be a good place to make his stand. He checked his gun and listened to the darkness. He grimaced when he heard the ominous creak of support timbers.

"No shots! Comprendo? One more shot in here and this whole

mountain is coming down on our heads. All our heads! *Comprendo?*" Eli yelled.

His only reply was an echo. Then he heard the sound of someone running. Someone running off to his right in the tunnel he had just abandoned. The sound was coming in his direction. He tensed and aimed his revolver in the direction of the sound.

"Start shooting, and so will I. We'll all go out together, *Amigo*!" Eli snarled as he scouted the tunnel around him.

There was no reply.

Eli thought about it. He remembered the shoot-out at the river. He remembered Jules and his brothers had disguised themselves as Mexicans. He cursed himself for not thinking of it sooner.

He hoped he was right.

He, frantically, looked around for a better place to make a stand. Immediately his eyes fell on a shaft of light fifty yards ahead. A shaft of light coming from somewhere on the outside.

Slowly, with his gun pointed ahead, Eli backed his way toward the shaft of light. He stayed close to the wall. So close the icy water soaked the back of his shirt.

Eli's heart jumped with joy when he saw the source of the light. The light streamed down the length of a glory hole. A glory hole to the outside. A glory hole with a rope ladder that led up a hundred feet to the surface.

In his joy Eli stepped too much into the light. He reached for the rope to test it. When he did, a bullet tore by his hand taking a piece off the back. The wound wasn't painful. It was the stupidity of stepping into the light Eli cursed himself for.

Eli stepped back too quick and fell to the wet mine floor.

The reverberating echo of gun's report shook loose more rock. It fell all around Eli. Eli rolled flush with the wall. He eased into the darkest outcropping.

In anger more than thinking, Eli pointed his revolver at the darkness. He fired two rounds into the tunnel. The tunnel literally shook and rocks pelted his face. His rounds ricocheted, harmlessly, some yards into the blackness before his eyes.

Then it was quiet once again.

Eli sat in the darkness and thought it over. He remembered he had promised himself never to hesitate again. He decided it was time to make a move, no matter the outcome.

Cautiously, Eli inched his way to a spot just beneath the glory hole. He positioned himself in a crevice just opposite the rope ladder. Hot blood trickled down the back of his hand. Cold blood gathered on his wounded foot. His foot ached with stiffness and he was a little dizzy. He looked at his wounded hand. It was swollen and taunt. He wondered if he could climb the rope ladder.

Then he wondered if it was the smart thing to do.

As he was wondering, a section of the tunnel behind him broke loose. When the dust cleared, that escape route was blocked off with a wall of crushed rock.

The decision was made for him.

Slowly, he eased his left shoulder out into the tunnel and looked up ahead at the darkness. He strained his ears for the slightest sound. The light from the glory hole lit the tunnel for a hundred feet and Eli couldn't see any movement. He took a deep breath, another, then hopped for the ladder. He reached it and began climbing as fast as he could.

The rope swayed and groaned under his weight. He found it hard to grip with his wounded hand and got little help from his feet. The rope was slippery and difficult to grasp so he slipped back inches with each foot he advanced. Each time he stopped, he listened for any movement, above or below.

The pain in his foot was intense, and Eli had to pause more than he wanted. He knew he was exposed and vulnerable. He knew he had only moments to make it up the rope.

Eli was almost to the top, when the gunman broke into the light below him. Eli could barely make out the gunman's face but could see the revolver the gunman aimed right at his head.

Eli froze for an instant, not out of fear, but out of surprise. "John? Big John Joshua. My God! My God!" Eli sighed.

Big John pulled the trigger of his revolver. The hammer fell but the gun remained quiet. Big John pulled the gun down and cursed it as he checked the chambers.

Eli moved over the top of the ladder and onto the ground outside. He lay flat on the ground and gathered his breath. He pulled his revolver from his belt. He eased back to the opening. He aimed over the side of the glory hole. He looked down and was surprised Big John had not moved.

Big John was such an easy target. He had moved over further into the light and stood below Eli working frantically to free-up his gun. He was almost pathetic—almost sympathetic.

Eli, calmly, fired two rounds into Big John's huge chest.

Big John was jolted by the shots. He staggered back out of the light. Moments later, he pitched forward and fell back into the light directly below Eli. Eli, calmly, methodical and without passion put another bullet into his head.

Otello heard the shots reverberating from a distance to his right. He pulled his gun, checked his load, made the sign of the cross and moved cautiously in that direction.

The echoes from the gunfire reverberated up and down the tunnel. Eli waited until they subsided, then cupped his hands and yelled down the glory hole. "Come on out into the light, Jules. I got something to give you! I know you're down there!" Eli waited for a reply. There was none. "I expect those Mexicans was after you, not me! God knows what you done to make them mad. But whatever it was I'm glad. This is a mighty good place to end it. Wouldn't you say?" Eli cackled the hoarse laughter of near madness.

Eli paused and checked his gun. He did not expect a reply. He did not need one. He knew Jules was listening somewhere in the dark. "I got you a little gift. I've been saving it for a long time. I brought it a long way. All the way 'round the Horn, Jules. It's something a very pretty Pennsylvania lady and an even prettier California lady told me to give you," Eli chortled.

Eli's words echoed without response. He delighted in the thought that Jules was somewhere in the darkness cowering—shivering with fear.

"Come on and get it. Come on you, miserable bastard! Come on!" Eli swore into the glory hole.

There was no answer for a long moment.

Now the quiet made Eli uneasy. For a moment, he had to wonder at his sanity.

"It's a long way from Pottsville, Pennsylvania, Eli!" Jules' voice echoed up the glory hole.

Eli could not restrain the joy he felt from hearing that voice. He wanted to get up and dance a jig. He made himself get control of his feelings. "It is that, Jules."

"I was thinkin' on Pennslyvannia lately."

"Don't worry, I promise to send your body back."

"That's mighty nice of you. Would you be wantin' the same courtesy?" Jules' voice seemed to move closer to the edge of the glory hole below. "Is that where you want me to send yours, Eli?"

"No. It'll be yours, Jules. This time I'm above ground. You're the one stuck in the miserable stinking bowels of the earth. Smell that thin, musty air, Jules? Feel that tightness of the rock all about you. Well that mountain's gonna' be on top of you real soon! Just like you left it on me."

"Why don't you come down here, Eli? I want to see you, boy!"

"I expect you do."

"You figure there's anyway of talkin' this out?"

"Not likely."

Neither spoke again for several long minutes.

"None of it turned out exactly like I expected, Eli."

"It turned out bad enough," Eli snapped.

"Damn it, Eli! Neither of them women would give me the money! I didn't want to kill me no woman. You shore do get yourself some feisty womenfolk," Jules said as if they were talking about the weather.

Eli felt such rage he had the urge to crawl down the ladder and do something stupid. He let it pass until he was cool enough to think clearly. He took the revolver and turned the gun handle with the notches around. He took a knife and began whittling a notch in it. The wood chips fell into the glory hole beside Big John's body. "You know what I'm doin', Jules?"

"I expect you're gettin' right with your maker 'cause you gonna meet him real soon!"

"Nope! I'm cuttin' me my third notch in this here gun butt. I expect to have six notches before this day is done!"

"You think you some kinda gunfighter, Eli? You know all you is, is a hard rock coal miner who ain't no better with a gun than nobody else."

"Well we'll see about that. I'm going to kill you for all the evil you done, done, Jules. That's all there is to it. Now do you want to die down there or come up here and see the good earth one more time?"

"I suppose you'd better come down here and kill me, Eli. Just the same cowardly way you killed Big John. Except my gun's working fine. See!" Jules jumped into the light and fired three times at the sky. The bullets missed Eli by a wide mark. They made him flinch enough to where his return fire was wide. The bullets ricocheted off the mine shaft floor harmlessly.

Jules disappeared into the cover of darkness.

Moments later, the earth rumbled and shook—then came apart with a loud roar. The tunnel's ceiling gave way and fell. It hit with such force a flume of rock dust burst out the glory hole and a hundred feet into the air. The moment the rumbling subsided, Eli pulled himself to the edge of the glory hole and peered down. The tunnel was strewn with rocks and dust. Enough rock and dust to bury an army of men.

Eli should have believed that Jules was dead.

He didn't believe it a moment.

Eli knew he would have to go down into the tunnel. He knew he would have to see Jules' lifeless body. He would have to poke a finger in Jules' lifeless eyes before he could sleep well again.

There was no movement or sound from below as Eli pondered his next move. He lay on the lip of the glory hole staring down for several moments. Finally, he slowly eased himself onto the rope ladder. Holding his revolver at the ready, he moved methodically down.

On every rung he paused and peered at the rock strewn mineshaft below. There was no movement but he didn't trust his senses.

He was halfway down the ladder when he thought he heard the rocks move. He tensed and wiped the sweat off his brow. He eased himself down another rung.

All was quiet.

He was one rung away from lowering himself into the shaft when he heard the rocks move off to his left. He moved back up one rung. He looked at the broken rocks and tried to convince himself that any normal man would be dead.

Then he remembered, Jules wasn't normal.

He lowered himself one more rung, then studied the tunnel floor.

The rock had fallen in sporadic piles. Eli figured to drop in behind the largest pile to his left.

He would use it for cover and observation. He knew it would be painful to his wounded foot, but if he didn't drop quickly, Jules would have too long to make a good shot. The fall was only six feet, but on his foot it would feel like sixty.

Eli took a deep breath and blew it out hard. He said a quick prayer. He let himself go and fell toward the tunnel floor.

It seemed that he was suspended in air for an hour before he hit the hard floor. He cried out in pain as his wounded foot landed on a jagged rock.

His cry of pain echoed up the glory hole. Then there was silence.

Eli sighed in relief. He felt better as he eased himself back against the far wall and chuckled cynically. For some reason, it all seemed a little ridiculous. Painfully, he eased himself up on the rock pile to his right. He started to look things over.

He froze as he heard the rocks move behind him. He turned over just in time to see Matthew crawl over the top of the rock

pile. He did not get his gun out before Matthew fired a round that went wild.
Eli tumbled behind a huge rock outcropping. Matthew emptied his gun. All the bullets missed.
Eli heard Matthew's gun click empty. He looked around the outcropping directly into Matthew's whiskerless face.
Matthew gave him a half-smile and meekly lowered his gun. Eli looked into Matthew's young eyes. They were frightened, fawn-like eyes. Misty eyes pleading for mercy. Eli felt no guilt as he put a bullet into each one of them.
Matthew twitched his last death throw as Eli took out his knife. He chuckled as he carved the fourth notch in the handle. "That's four notches, Jules! If you and Sly are alive come on out. I want to cut me six notches in this here gun in time to get to town for a nice dinner!" Eli said coolly.
The only sound in reply was Matthew's body rolling over into a dark corner and the endless dripping of cold water to the mine shaft floor.
Eli felt a cough forming in his throat. He fought it hard knowing it would give away his position. But the dust was thick and he could, finally, suppress it no longer. His cough echoed the length of the rock-filled shaft.
Then there was an eerie silence.
In the brief time that Eli had closed his eyes to cough, Sly Joshua had moved up behind him.
Sly had inched his way in the shadows. Now he was close enough to Eli to put the barrel of his gun next to Eli's temple.
"You ain't puttin' no more notches nowhere! It's way past time you died for real!" Sly cocked the hammer of the gun.
Eli turned to see the look of pure evil on Sly's face just as Sly pulled the trigger. Eli lashed out at the gun barrel. He rolled away just as the bullets exploded from the muzzle. The bullets blasted into the rock floor. One ricocheted into Sly's stomach. It caused him to drop his gun and fall to the floor in agony.
Eli watched him squirm in pain without delight or sadness.

"You bastard, Eli Llynne! You bastard! 'Least you can't cut no notch for me! You can't 'cause I done kilt myself!" Sly groaned.

Eli shrugged. He leveled his gun at Sly's head. He cocked the hammer as he pressed the barrel inches from Sly's face. "That ain't exactly the way it is," Eli said calmly as he put a bullet into Sly's left eye.

Sly looked at Eli with his right eye for only a second before it closed in death.

Long after the echoes from his gunfire had stopped, Eli sat with his back to the hard rock wall. He listened for any movement.

As Eli looked at the piles of rock and debris in the mine shaft, and heard no sound, he wondered if Jules might be dead. The thought that a rockslide might have cheated him of the pleasure of personally killing Jules did not sit right on Eli's inflamed mind.

All the forces that had worked on Eli's innately gentle nature to make him into a cold, methodical, almost unfeeling killing machine had done a good job. He had killed five men and yet he now felt cheated because he was not able to kill a sixth man. There was a pure bloodlust in his heart and mind. Even if he found Jules Joshua dead beneath some rocks, he would still put some bullets in his head before the bloodlust would be satisfied.

If Eli found Jules alive, he would play with him awhile. Make Jules really sweat while he considered his impending doom. Eli would string it out as long as possible. He wanted to hurt Jules a whole bunch before he would end it.

At one time Eli's soul had been a fine, stately tall redwood reaching for the glory of the heavens. It was now a gnarled and warped sapling, driving tap roots deep into the darkest part of the most foul earth.

Where he had been a reluctant killer, pondering the words of the good book, Eli was now a godless man with anger at all creation festering in his heart. Once he had loved so deeply that love had made him a weak, hesitant man. Now he was as hard and cold as the dark rock he had once mined so long ago—and he loved the feel of the gun he held in his hand.

Killing the Joshua brothers would not bring back Lydia or the Captain or restore Stella to health. No matter, the reasons for the killing were not uppermost in his mind now. Something had flipped a switch deep inside his being and brought forth his savage nature.

The territorial imperative of the beast within him had been violated most grievously. He was now out of the back of his cave—not only to make it right, but to enjoy doing so.

"Jules 'iffen you be alive come forward and let me kill you like I 'kilt your brothers! Don't be hiding back there in the darkness. The hiding is over. This is a day of reckoning!"

Eli peered into the darkness as dust, once again, caused him to start coughing. He coughed longer this time. As he coughed, he felt the presence of evil surround him. He looked up to see Jules holding a revolver in his face.

The blood was pouring from large wounds in Jules' head, dripping down into his eyes. Jules wiped it away as best he could as he snarled at Eli. "I don't know what hell you came outta' but wherever it was I'm gonna' send you back there!"

Jules tried to fire accurately but the blood in his good eye obscured his vision enough to make him miss.

Eli cocked his revolver but didn't shoot. Jules was such a pitiful looking animal. There was blood pouring from his mouth and his good eye was hanging halfway out of the socket. He was blind.

The sight made Eli hesitate.

Jules fired one more round wild. Then his gun clicked empty. Jules clicked it until his arm grew so weak he could no longer hold the gun up.

Eli, slowly, withdrew his second, fully loaded revolver. Coolly he brought the barrel up until it was on a direct line to Jules' head.

"No Eli. I'm empty. I'm unarmed. I can't see you. You can't shoot me now, Eli. It's not Christian. You're a Christian man Eli. You know what the bible says."

Eli cocked the hammer.

"Eli if you do this you'll go straight to hell. You know Lydia didn't cotton to guns. Lydia didn't like no kinda' killin' nohow," Jules pleaded.

Eli pulled off a round.

The bullet blasted away a small sized boulder to the right of Jules' face.

Jules tried to pull back but he was too weak.

Eli pulled off another round that zinged inches over Jules' head.

"Oh, God! Please don't shoot me, Eli. I'm hurtin' all over. I need help. I'm bleedin' bad from everywhere!" Jules gurgled.

Eli fired a round that whistled by Jules' left ear. He delighted in the fear on Jules' face.

"Eli all my brothers is dead ain't that enough revenge?" Jules coughed bright red blood. A few loose rocks dribbled to the mine shaft floor. "Eli there's almost ten thousand dollars in my saddlebags. That's more than I took from you. It's all your'n. You just back off and you'll not be hearin' from me again."

Eli fired a round that whistled by Jules' right ear. He almost laughed as Jules recoiled in fear.

"Eli I'm helpless I can't move. You can't shoot a helpless man!"

Eli fired a round that hit the rocks in front of Jules and blasted away rock fragments that tore small holes in Jules' face.

"Okay you bastard I'm tired of beggin'. Go ahead! Go ahead and shoot me in my person! I ain't beggin' no more. I'm glad I killed your woman. You hear that? I'm glad!" Jules sputtered just before Eli started to fire and his gun clicked empty.

Jules' ears perked up. He grinned. He turned to flee down the mine shaft.

Eli, quickly, reloaded his gun and peered into the darkness where Jules had run. He decided not to shoot. Eli cursed as he hobbled after Jules. He paused as he hit a stretch of the mine shaft where there were no kerosene lanterns and it was pitch black dark.

He felt really uneasy as he moved, slowly into the darkness. He stopped as he thought he heard movement. He turned to see a slight reflection of light from Jules' revolver—just before it cracked him in the face.

Eli fell hard to the floor.

Jules stood above him in the weak light. The patch was off his left eye. The scar from Lydia's scratches outlined a look of pure evil. Jules picked up Eli's gun and looked at it. "I ain't near as blind as I said," Jules chuckled. He studied Eli's gun. "You done cut five notches in this gun handle, Eli Llynne. You think it's a proper thing to do to whittle a man's life into ungodly wood like this? You think you're some kind of gunfighter, Eli? Well if you be a gunfighter . . . you shouldnt'a hesitated to shoot me. Eli, I thought all this trouble mighta' made you into a gunfighter but I see it ain't!"

Eli rubbed his head and tried to focus his eyes.

Jules loaded the gun and sighed hard. "You still just a dumb old coal miner who got no business messin' 'round with guns! There's gonna' be six notches in this here gun but the last one is gonna' be your'n!" Jules grinned as he leveled the gun to fire.

"I don't think so!" Otello said as he stepped into the light. He leveled his gun at Jules' head.

"You?" Jules turned to see him.

Eli was dizzy and could barely make out the fuzzy image of Jules standing above him.

Eli, frantically, moved his hand around the mine shaft floor looking for his gun. He found nothing. "No! No! He's mine! Back off, Otello!"

Otello saw Jules ready to fire. He did not listen to Eli. He pulled off a round.

Jules fired at the same time.

Their bullets missed their marks.

They fired again and again. The smoke from their guns obscuring their targets until Otello emptied his gun.

Jules withheld one bullet.

Otello's gun clicked empty. He started to reload. Jules shook his head and grinned malevolently. "Oh, my! I got me only one bullet and two men to kill. Oh, my! I wonder who?"

Otello leaped for Jules.

Jules cracked him across the face with his gun barrel.

Otello fell to the floor of the mine.

Jules stood over him and aimed the gun at his head. He cocked the hammer. He stopped. He turned the gun towards Eli. "Guess who?" Jules chuckled.

Eli's hand found the handle of a pick axe.

Jules moved in for a close shot.

Eli, slowly, closed his big hand around the pick axe handle.

Jules placed the barrel of the gun only inches from Eli's head. "Just so you know, I won't be takin' your body back to Pennslyvannia, anyways," Jules chortled. His finger pulled at the trigger.

Eli rose up. He swung the pick axe just as Jules fired. The blade of the pick axe found Jules' stomach. The force of the blow threw off his aim. The bullet went wild.

Eli's eyes were clear enough to see Jules stagger back into the darkness.

Jules coughed globs of blood. He tried to remove the pick axe from his gut. He dropped to his knees and wailed in agony.

Eli saw nothing else as the ceiling gave way and a ton of rock came crashing down around him.

CHAPTER TWENTY EIGHT

"When I was a child, I spake as a child. I understood as a child, I thought as a child; but when I became a man I put away childish things. For now we see through a glass, darkly; but then face to face; now I know in part, but then shall I know even as I am known. And now abideth faith, hope, love; and the greatest of these is love."

Eli saw his mother, Rachel, sitting by his bedside reading from the good book. It was on the eve of his sixth birthday. The day before he, eagerly, looked forward to going into the mines with his father and the other men.

"The good book says, thou shalt not kill and he that smiteth a man, so that he die, shall surely be put to death!" She smiled at him. "You understand all that I done read you, son?"

"Yes, Mama!" Eli cried out from a great darkness. A stifling enclosure where putrid, soaking sweat permeated everything. A terrifying hell where he could not get his breath. A feverish, unreal dream world where he struggled to reach consciousness.

"The book also says an eye for eye, tooth for tooth, hand for hand, foot for foot. Burning for burning, wound for wound, stripe for stripe. And I will kill you with the sword; and your wives shall be widows and your children fatherless!" Eli's father looked at Rachel sternly.

"That is an old testament admonition. It is not what Christ came for. You listen to me, son. This mean world might be full of killin' but I don't want you ever doin' any of it. Now you promise me on your immortal soul! You promise me that, son!" Rachel looked at her husband who shrugged.

"Yes, Mama. I understand. You have my word. I will never,

ever kill anyone. I promise on my immortal soul!" Eli promised as he looked as he mother's kind eyes and peaceful face.

Rachel stroked his hair with approval and affection.

Eli's father smirked and let his wife have her way.

"No, Eli. I'm empty. I'm unarmed. You can't shoot me now, Eli! It's not christian. You're a christian man Eli. You know what the bible says."

Eli cocked the hammer.

"Eli if you do this you'll go straight to hell. and you know Lydia. Lydia didn't like no kinda' killin' nohow!" Jules paused in Eli's nightmare.

"Thou shalt not kill, Eli, my son. Because times are hard, don't mean you have to sin against God. Don't ever spill your fellow man's blood."

"Yes, Mama, I promise. I promise I will never ever kill anyone. I promise on my immortal soul!" Eli repeated.

He looked at his mother with confused young eyes. She smiled back at him. It was then she held him in her arms. She embraced him in his dreams as she never had in his life.

"Eli? Eli Llynne, don't you die on me!" Stella broke into his dream. She washed at his fever with a cool damp cloth. "I've had to fight gambling men and whoring men and men with no compunctions about beating up on a woman. You are the only man I ever knew that treated me decent. So you'd better open them eyes and talk to me!"

To Eli, Stella's voice sounded like she was in the deepest shaft of a distant mine.

In the dark part of the dream, Eli had seen himself descend into a lake of fire. He had come out drenched with blood so thick it would not drain from his body. He had never felt such extremes of hot and cold.

There was great physical pain, but an even more terrible anguish in his spirit. He could not escape the dream. The dream where he killed the Joshua brothers over and over again as Rachel looked at him with displeasure. The dream where he cut a notch on a wooden gun handle, while an angry God sliced out a corresponding piece of Eli's beating heart. Sliced it out and ate it as his mother gave God her approval.

"No! No! No, I didn't kill anyone!" Eli awoke screaming.

At first Eli thought it was still a dream. Stella's face was as angelic as it was welcome. Maybe he had died and this was heaven full of God's forgiveness.

Stella reached out with a wet towel and touched his fevered brow. "Eli, are you alright?" Stella looked at him with concern in her eyes.

Eli shivered for a long moment, unsure if he was awake or dreaming. "Stella?" He reached out and touched her hand. "Stella?"

"Welcome home, Eli. Would you like something to drink?" Stella handed him a glass of water.

Eli drank hungrily.

"I was so hot! So damn hot!" Eli held the glass out for a refill. Stella refilled it twice before he was satiated.

"You had a bad dream with the fever." She felt his forehead and seemed pleased. "I believe the fever has broken."

"Dream? Yes. The Joshua brothers?"

"You spoke of them."

"My gun! Where is my gun? I've got to . . . . "

"Easy, Eli. Easy! It's over. It's all over."

Eli looked doubtful.

"They are all dead and buried thanks to you. You and Otello," Stella said looking very worried.

"Otello?"

"He was hurt bad. But he is recovering nicely."

Eli lay back on the overstuffed feather pillow. He sighed hard. "How long have I been here. The dream? The fever. How long?"

"It has been eight weeks since they pulled you and Otello out. I believe the dream has lasted only three days." Stella thought it over. "You called for Rachel and Eli. Your father, he was also named Eli?"

"Yes. Rachel? Yes. My mother. Oh, God Stella! How? How did I get here? I'm in Sonora? How?"

"The hard rock miners are good people, Eli. You should know that. They found you and Otello barely alive. They brought you both home."

"Otello? You say he's okay?"

"He's mending fine."

Eli sighed in relief. He looked at Stella. He remembered her pain. "You? You? You're, okay?"

"Yes. Thanks to a Chinese Doctor from Frisco. Doctor Chanson Woo."

"Woo?"

"The same one who attended you for the last nine weeks."

"Nine weeks?"

"It'll be two months tomorrow. How do you feel?"

"My head really hurts. I'm sore all over." Eli felt his bones and was relieved to see them all intact.

"They said a boulder hit you a glancing blown. You were very lucky,"

Stella said with a touch of melancholy in her voice. She held his hand tightly. "It's all over, my love. All over and we are both safe and well."

Eli smiled as he thought about it. He was not so sure. He sat up higher in the bed feeling weak. "Did they find the others?"

"Eli, please? It's all over," Stella looked away a moment then did not look him in the eye.

"No, Ma'am. 'Less you tell me they found his body."

Stella did not reply for a long moment. She gave Eli a hard look. "They brought out three bodies so far."

"Three? One of them is Jules' body for sure?"

"No. His three brothers. But they said there was no possibility of anyone getting out of there alive," Stella said.

Eli gritted his teeth and looked at Stella with unyielding eyes. "If they ain't found his body then he ain't dead!"

"That's preposterous. The ones they pulled out are hardly recognizable."

"My gun. He had my gun. Did they find my gun? He would be where it's at!"

"Eli? Eli Llynne! They only found you because you and Otello were in the only nook without a ton of rock on it. Now you just thank God you're alive and here. You forget about that gun and those awful Joshua brothers. They are all dead and that is God's justice plain and simple."

Eli looked at her with anger then tenderness. "God's justice, Stella?" Eli turned his face away from her.

"Yes!" she insisted.

Eli took a breath and blew it out Hard. He turned back and studied her face. It was good to see her eyes sparkling again. He had no strength for a long argument now.

Eli touched the small scar on her forehead where Jules bullet had grazed it. "You're alright? You're . . . you're alright?"

"Yes! I'm alright! Don't put me off. I know what you're thinking. "Stella's eyes showed displeasure.

"You're angry with me?"

"You just broke a terrible fever, Eli. I would like to see more thanksgiving in your heart for the blessing of life you have been given. It's over. It's all over!" Stella said firmly.

Eli sighed hard, then downed another glass of water. He studied the firm look on her face.

There was no paint on her face. Her face was clean, unblemished and smelled of the honest soap she used to scrub it. The fine texture of her alabaster skin set off her emerald eyes like fine gold sets off quality diamonds.

Stella was a handsome woman, a good woman, and a strong woman not to be trifled with.

Eli was still weak but not too weak to reach for her strong hand and hold it in his. Their eyes met with honest emotion then danced away with lingering shyness.

"You're right. Maybe the fever has left me cuckoo. I'm glad to be here. I'm so damned hungry."

"I don't believe you."

"What are you talking about?"

"You aren't thinking of food, Eli Llynne. You are hardening your heart for some more thoughts of killing."

Eli was determined to dismiss her concerns, for now. He half-laughed. "The truth is, I'll always have those thoughts, 'til I know what's what. Right now, I'm just a very hungry man."

Stella looked deep into this eyes.

Eli did not flinch.

Stella wasn't completely satisfied, but let it pass. She took her hand away and moved toward the kitchen pantry. "Well then I'll fix you your favorite, biscuits and gravy. There's a plump chicken in the yard I can fry up for you."

"Lot's and lot's of biscuits and lot's and lot's of gravy!" Eli stood up and felt woozy. He barely managed to keep his feet as he watched Stella go about fixing his meal.

Eli was hungry for food but deep inside he felt another hunger. Deep in his bones he felt that Jules Joshua was not dead. It was a feeling he could not explain and he swore to himself he would not speak of it to anyone—specially, Stella.

Today he would feed his stomach. Tomorrow, if need be, there would be time enough for more killing.

Eli sat at the kitchen table and reveled in the simple joy of just being alive. It was good to be alive. Even his soreness was a welcome feeling. For now, he would savor life and suppress any other feelings.

He watched Stella working at the stove and marveled that he had her and she was well.

The wonder of her presence was a constant delight. He had no idea why she still cared for him. He thanked God that she still did.

As the invigorating feeling of life filled his being, he felt all shyness and pretense vanish. Suddenly he had the urge to tell Stella how much he loved her. To tell her over and over without the smallest hesitation or blushing.

At that moment, he decided he would make the most of what life there was to be lived this day. He got up from the table and walked over to Stella. He put his strong hand on her shoulder.

Stella turned and looked at him with smudges of flour on her face.

"Eli Llynne if you want dinner then you go back to bed and get out of my kitchen. Shoo!" Stella laughed her rich fulfilling laughter.

"I love you."

Stella was too stunned to reply.

"I love you more than I loved Lydia or the Captain or my kin. I love you with all the strength of my being. I love you with all the will God gives me and my heart is so full of you, I sometimes think it might break up inside."

"My, goodness," Stella smiled

"I love you, Stella O'Brien. I love you and this day I set myself the task of writing you a poem expressing these feelings in written words of a poetic nature."

Stella felt his forehead. "Well, it's not the fever."

"No, ma'am. Except the fever I have inside for you," Eli took her in his arm and kissed her long and passionately.

When he let her go, Stella stepped back and almost fell down.

"Oh! My goodness gracious! I don't know what's gotten into you but I think I like it."

Eli took her into his arms once more. He kissed her hair softly. "I'm hoping you have similar feelings for me and I'm asking if you . . . you would . . . would you consider marrying half a man?" Eli asked.

"Is this the you talking or that growling stomach?"

"I expect a little of each."

"I see." Stella turned away and thought it over.

Eli turned her back to face him and looked deep into her eyes. "I'm not the whole man I was, but inside I'm all put together for you."

"What do you mean half a man? No! I wouldn't marry half-a-man, but you . . . well seems we've been through this before. You're a little out of sorts now, but you'll be well soon. When you are well, we'll just see what we'll just see!" Stella looked at him with eyes that hinted at approval.

"I thought I as dead, Stella. I thought I'd lost you."

"Yes. I thought I was dead, Eli. I thought you were dead also,"

Stella smiled.

"It gives a mighty smart flavor to life don't it?"

"Yes. Yes it does."

"We are alive and that is something to celebrate. Though I do feel a mighty ache in my bones."

"Well you get that ache out. I don't intend marrying up with a man who is old before his time."

"Yes, ma'am." Eli looked at her. He could not hide the love in his eyes. The thought of her love made him buoyant and he felt stronger than he had ever felt in his life. "I take that as a yes?"

Stella pretended to pout a long moment and enjoyed the anxiety in his eyes. "Well I suppose, since you poured out all those heartfelt sentiments, maybe it is," Stella said.

Eli took the spatula from her hand and took her into his muscular arms. They did not kiss but held each other firmly. They embraced in a hug more of comfort and understanding than of passion.

"It's good to be home, Stella."

"Welcome home. Now get out of my kitchen! Shoo!" Stella broke the hug.

Eli smiled as he moved back to the table and looked at a small bag of gold dust. He opened it and poured the shiny flakes into his big hand. He turned back to Stella and looked at her with deep affection. This time there was no shyness in his eyes.

"I am sorry I'm not a poetic man. You deserve poetry. I will say that there is nothing found in the earth by man or beast that I will ever prize as much as you," Eli shook the gold dust from his hand. "I will defend my home and you to the death, and I will do all that I can to make of myself a passable husband."

Stella looked at him with a hint of moisture in her mischievous Irish eyes. She wiped her hands on her apron. She paused and let her eyes drift over his. She smiled. She threw her arms around his neck. They kissed with a tenderness that would have turned into passion had not the gravy begun to smolder on the stove.

CHAPTER TWENTY NINE

The wedding was the main event of the social season for the good people of Sonora. Eli was pleased with it, except for the few drunks that had tried to crash it.

Otello had handled that by benevolently bestowing a quart of whiskey on them, then quickly expelling them from the premises.

The chilling shadow that had passed over Otello and Eli's friendship had passed.

Eli would never apologize for his actions towards Otello.

Otello did not expect an apology. The invitation to be Eli's best man was apology enough. Besides, Otello's thoughts had turned to New Orleans. Everyone who read his book told him that was where he should go to find his parents. Otello had hired a tutor and had begun to read himself.

Otello agreed with everyone else. Louisiana held the key to his origins. He would leave for New Orleans right after the wedding.

To the sound of gunfire and firecrackers, Eli and Stella became man and wife. The circuit riding Minster was not the most eloquent speaker and many in the audience went to sleep from drink or boredom.

Eli and Stella did not care. They were giddy with love's headiest fever. They were more than hungry to end the long night of nothing and begin the feast of everything. They kissed longer than respectable but without shame as they turned to greet the cheers and hoots of the miners.

Otello had the second kiss from Stella after the ceremony was over. In the softness of the touch of her lips he understood Eli's great love for her.

The reception was ten feet from the garden where the wedding had been held. Once all were present, Otello held up a glass half full of Irish Whiskey and proposed a toast. "We drink to Mr. and Mrs. Eli Llynne. Godspeed to them in all their endeavors. And many, many children to bring laughter to their great house!" Otello said.

Scotty limped up beside Otello.

"And blessed remembrance to good friends absent!" Scotty added.

"Hear! Hear!" Everyone cheered and drank, and reveled in the happy spirit of the moment.

Otello watched the festivities for only a few minutes, then began to ease his way home. He was almost free when Scotty stepped in his path.

"You leaving without saying a proper goodbye, Laddie?" Scotty chided.

Otello looked embarrassed. "Goodbye, Mister Scotty."

"New Orleans, aye?"

"Yes, sir."

Scotty handed Otello a piece of paper. "An old salt I used to sail with. If he's still there he might be of use to you."

Otello looked at the name and address. He was pleased he could read it.

"Ian Ferguson
113 Jackson Street
(or thereabouts)
New Orleans"

"I can read it, Mister Scotty! I can read it! Thank, you. Thank you! I'll be sure to look him up."

"Just don't believe any of his tall tales or be giving him any money you expect to get back."

Otello laughed. He paused and sighed hard. "You will say goodbye to Eli and Stella for me?"

Scotty thought it over. He nodded agreement. "You got enough travelin' money?"

"Oh, yes, sir! That claim has been mighty good to all of us," Otello stopped and looked sad. "I owe so much to the Cap'n."

"Aye! We all do. We all do."

They fell silent and the moment became stilted. They barely fought back their emotions.

"Well if you was a woman I might give you a farewell kiss. Since you ain't, I'll just shake your hand and say, Godspeed!" Scotty held out his hand.

Otello ignored the hand. He gave Scotty a fond embrace.

Scotty gave him a half-embrace in return.

"Goodbye ny friend. I'll keep in touch," Otello said as he broke the embrace.

"Aye! You do that now. You hear?" Scotty replied.

"I will. I truly will."

"Aye! Well godspeed. Did I say that? Yes. You sure you won't have just a wee one more before leaving?"

"No thanks, Scotty," Otello paused. "It's their day"

Scotty nodded agreement. He gave Otello a pat on the back and left.

Otello smiled. He took one more look across the distance at Eli and Stella surrounded by laughter and well wishing.

There was a great melancholy in his heart as he turned and walked briskly away.

CHAPTER THIRTY

The months with Stella that followed were the best of Eli's life. The claim that Captain Hopkins had put in Eli's name was producing high grade ore. On good days, it produced buckets of sizable nuggets.

Scotty had shared in the good fortune. As a result, he had sent to Scotland for his childhood sweetheart. The size of the dowry he offered had gained her parents approval and she was on her way.

Eli chuckled when he thought about all the local dance hall girls Scotty was going to disappoint.

It was a heady, happy time.

Unbroken, unshadowed happiness that was strange to Eli's soul. Tender, loving, sunlit, boundless happiness that was hard to take in such large doses.

Unfamiliar happiness that he resisted as a weakening influence. Disarming happiness that made him ready to forgive—almost to forget.

Giddy happiness that, at last, swallowed up bitterness and made him as agreeable a man as ever lived.

Not only was Eli rich in money but Stella had insisted on him being educated and refined. She had seen to it that he had two reading and writing tutors and an elocution teacher from the San Francisco Opera.

Eli had taken well to the lessons and was already working hard on composing the poem he had promised Stella. He decided, after getting three words down on paper, it was going to take a lot longer than he figured.

Everything was going well with the promise it would only get better.

The day that Eli and Stella moved into their new home, the great house on the highest hill in Sonora, Eli heard the rumors for the first time.

At first, Eli was irritated that someone would spread such rumors. He could have dismissed them easily if they had not had the ring of truth.

". . . as ornery a man as there ever was. He's got only one eye and he's lame in one leg 'cause of that mining accident up in Hornitos. Shot three Mexicans in the back because they was snoring too loud!"

The old timer had said as he sipped a shot of whiskey in Eli's favorite saloon. "Yes, siree! They tried to hang him up around Hornitos but he broke out of that jailhouse. Yes, siree!"

Eli had studied the old man's face for a long time. He had wanted to dismiss his ramblings as those of someone vying for a free drink by telling tall tales. But others had brought tales of a one-eyed man who survived a mine cave-in Hornitos.

Deep inside, Eli had always known, despite the rumors that Jules was not dead.

The stories confirmed it.

It was now a matter of what to do about it—if anything. It had been almost three months now. It had taken a great effort to, almost, purge his soul of that great darkness. Eli was not sure he wanted to go back again.

Eli sat at the kitchen table and looked at the bible on a nearby table. "When I was a child, I spake as a child. I understood as a child, I thought as a child; but when I became a man, I put away childish things." Eli sighed hard as he remembered Rachel reading those words to him. He opened the bible and was pleased he could read most of them himself.

The easy thing would have been to put away any thoughts of pursuing Jules Joshua. Everything was going well for Eli. Stella was with child and Eli eagerly awaited being a father. He was able to buy her the latest Eastern and Paris fashions and she was the toast of Sonora society.

To Eli's mind, when she was dressed in finery, Stella was the prettiest woman on earth. Offers to buy his claim would make him a rich man. If he could put thoughts of Jules out of his mind he stood to have a happy and complete life.

But the old timer's tales haunted him. As did the ache in his gut that told him it was the truth.

"*Diall! Diall!* He is truly the devil himself!" Eli picked up Stella's favorite chair and smashed it. "Jesus! Good God almighty! God knows I killed him every way I know how to kill a man! Don't this godless thing ever end!" Eli swore.

He looked at the broken chair. He did not want to upset Stella so he, frantically, tried to piece it back together. It didn't take him long to determine the chair needed extensive repair work. He cursed himself as he moved to the tool shed to get the tools to repair it.

Once inside the tool shed, he pushed away cobwebs looking for his old tool box.

Eli had been able to afford to hire handy work done. He had not been inside the tool shed in a long time. He moved boxes around until he saw the shiny metal of a gun barrel poking from the embroidered handkerchief Lydia had given him.

Eli unwrapped the embroidered handkerchief and the Celtic Crucifix fell out. Eli picked up the crucifix and looked at it then re-wrapped it in the handkerchief. He lay the handkerchief aside and, eagerly, reached for the gun. For a brief moment, he puzzled over why the handkerchief and crucifix did not mean as much to him as did the gun. Eli respected the memory of Lydia but the crucifix and handkerchief did not move him to very much sentiment.

Not nearly as much as seeing the gun did.

Eli, reverently, held the gun in his hand and delighted in the way it felt. It was more welcome and familiar than the glad hand of an old friend.

Eli shook his head as he remembered Stella telling him they had not found his gun. It hurt Eli that Stella had lied, even though he knew her lie was meant to serve a good purpose.

Eli tucked the gun in his waistband and moved back inside the house.

Once inside, he took a bottle of whiskey from a cupboard. He poured himself three fingers in a glass and drank it down. He poured another three fingers and was sipping it, when Stella came through the door.

She was dressed in a green satin dress that made her look like a fashion model. Her beauty almost took his breath away—almost made him forget his anger.

"It's from Paris, Eli! Isn't it gorgeous?"

"That it is. It 'shore enough is."

"Not "shore". "Sure!" It sure enough is. My, God we pay that teacher a fortune. Aren't you listening to her?"

"I 'shore am," Eli said coldly.

Stella did not like the coldness in his voice. She froze when she saw the gun tucked into his waistband. "You've been in the tool shed?"

"I believe . . . as I can recall . . . this is the first lie that has passed between us."

"It's not lying to protect what is yours from harm."

"Yes it is. But that don't mean I don't understand why you did what you did."

"What do you intend doing with that damn gun, Eli?"

"I intend to find Jules Joshua and kill him dead."

"You'll do no such thing!"

"I'm sorry, Stella but that is what I intend full well to do!"

"Don't talk about sorry. That's over Eli Llynne! I won't stand for any such talk in this house! I heard those rumors. I know he might be alive. So what if he is? There's five notches cut on that gun. That's more than enough killing for one man's lifetime!"

Eli looked unconvinced. He pulled down the whiskey. He poured three more fingers. He shook his head, slowly and eyed her, malevolently.

Stella looked at him angrily. She took a knife from a drawer and handed it to Eli.

"If you really care for me and this life we have here, then you cut Jules Joshua's notch into that revolver gun handle. If you don't we'll never have any kind of life together. If you don't really believe he's dead . . . whether he is or not, then there ain't no use of us going on with this marriage!" Stella insisted.

Eli took the knife and withdrew the revolver from his waistband. He laid the gun on the table.

He looked at her auburn-haired beauty. He marveled at the fiery spirit in her simmering green eyes.

She smelled of early spring jasmine and honeysuckle. There was an aura of stardust in her countenance. He loved her more than he had loved Lydia or the Captain or himself. He started to carve a "sixth notch" into the gun's handle.

He stopped.

"It's over, Eli. The road has ended. If you love me you'll believe, as I do, that Jules Joshua is dead and buried under that mountain in Hornitos. Please tell me, for the sake of our future . . . our love . . . that you truly believe that the carving of a notch on that gun ends this matter once and for all!" Stella insisted as she looked deep into Eli's eyes—Eli's soul.

Eli let the knife slice into the wood. He cut half a notch. He looked up at her and paused. "Cutting a notch in this here gun would be the same as lying outright. Lying ain't a healthy thing to do, Stella."

"Healthy? You think it's healthy to think of, to dream of, to lust after killing all the time?"

"It ain't exactly like that."

"Oh? What is it like?"

"It's like a fire in the coal mines."

"Oh, Jesus! Am I going to have to sit still for some mealy mouthed homely?"

"My father died in a fire in the coal mines. You know, once a fire gets started in a coal mine you can put out some of it . . . maybe even most of it . . . but you never get all of it. Maybe that's where hell is because it burns forever."

"What the hell does that have to do with us?"

"I got a mining fire in my gut, Stella. I done put out some of it, but I ain't put out all of it," Eli said calmly.

"Damnit, Eli! This is our life you're talking about here! Who knows where Jules Joshua is? For God's sake, who cares?" Stella fumed. She stopped and let her hands fall to their waist. She gave him her best Leprechaun look. "I'm with child, Eli!"

"Yes. And I thank you, kindly, for that."

"You thank me? That's it? You thank me and go on about your sorry business?"

Eli looked contrite only a moment before he looked at her hard. "You listen to me, Stella. This ain't no ordinary man. As long as he's alive there is no way of tellin' when he might come for me and mine. That's the long and short of it!"

"You aren't ever going to be satisfied are you, Eli?"

"Not 'til I see his dead body with it's head blown off. Not 'til I poke my finger in his dead eye."

"That's your final word on it?'"

"I'm sorry."

"No you aren't! You're not sorry. You're just a mean vengeful person who don't know when to quit!"

"All I got to do is see his dead body! When I see that, then I rest easy."

"Go! Go, Eli Llynne! Go get that sixth notch in that damn gun handle! Hell! Get another gun and cut a dozen more!" Stella stopped and gave Eli the most hateful look he had ever seen. "But don't expect me to be here when you get done with your nasty business!"

Eli looked at her with fondness. "It ain't exactly like that."

"The hell it ain't! You ignorant coal miner! I should have known better!"

"You tryin' to shame me, Stella?"

"Yes, I am! You can have a wife and family or you can just walk out that door and go chase your ghosts. You got a hard choice to be making here, Mister!" Stella drew close and shouted in his face.

Eli pulled back some. He nodded agreement. "It's as hard a one as I ever made."

"The miners in Hornitos said they don't know how no mortal man could have survived that cave-in. But you did. Now instead of thanking God Almighty, you're sitting there thinking of looking to make sure Jules Joshua is dead."

"He ain't no normal, mortal man, Stella."

"Who cares! To my mind he's dead, Eli! Dead! Dead! Dead!"

Eli drove the knife into the table. He started to sip the whiskey. He threw it out.

Stella let her sweet breath touch his face. She stroked his hair gently. "If you love me, please give it up!"

Eli touched the small scar from the bullet that had grazed Stella's head. She did not flinch. He wanted to pull her to him and kiss her. He wanted to hold her close.

She backed away. "That was yesterday, Eli. I'm well now. So are you . . . .if you wish to be," Stella insisted.

"God Almighty knows I wish it was possible!" Eli grimaced.

"You hard headed miner! What do I have to do to get through to you?"

"It ain't exactly like that."

"Oh, shut up!" Stella started to storm out of the room. She paused. She turned and looked back at him. For a moment, a look of understanding passed her face.

"I will see to it you are well taken care of, Stella. Scotty will stand in for me."

"Oh? In all respects? Should I redo the bedroom in highland stripes?"

"There's no call to talk that kinda' talk, Stella."

"Go to hell, Eli Llynne!"

Eli smiled sadly. "I expect so," he said as he let his finger run up and down the gun's barrel.

"That's it? No more discussion? You will do this thing against my will?" Stella grumped.

Eli studied her compelling look for a long moment before he

nodded agreement. As he did, the sparkling Emerald Green of her Irish eyes turned to a mean shade of burnt amber hatred.

In that instant, all the bright things that had passed between them dimmed into a hovering darkness.

And Eli knew he had lost her forever.

"Don't nod your head. Say it! Say it aloud, Eli Llynne!"

"Say it?"

"That you do this freely and with malice toward your wife and your unborn child. Say it!" Stella's face quivered with rage.

Eli thought it over. His gut twisted and his mind was hot for a long moment. He gathered all his inner strength and cooled down. Finally, he stood up and looked at her with eyes drained of feeling. "I have to go to Hornitos and do some prospecting. Will you be here when I get back?"

"Hell no!"

Eli put on his hat. He turned and took one last, long look at her. He reached out to touch her.

Stella backed away glaring at him.

"I'd be obliged if we could make this a friendly parting."

"I don't think so."

"I see. I'm sorry. Goodbye, Stella."

"Goodbye, you son-of-a-bitch!"

Eli flinched at her words and the anger in her eyes. He looked down at the revolver with the missing notch.

He hesitated only a moment before he picked it up and stuck it in his waistband.

When he looked up, Stella was gone.

Eli grimaced and pushed aside the hurt he felt inside. He gathered a few belongings and made his way outside where he saddled and mounted his fastest horse.

Once in the saddle, he paused and did not sit easy. The woman had confused his purpose and he despised the weakness he felt inside.

Eli almost dismounted.

Then his thumb felt the handle of his gun absent the one notch he wanted most of all.

With a hard sigh of renewed resolve, Eli nudged the horse into a full gallop and did not look back—as he rode hard into the moonless night toward the darkness of the unseen horizon.

THE END